COFFEE WITH CHICORY

and

OTHER STORIES OF
CULTURAL CROSSROADS

Arshud Mahmood

Copyright © 2010 by Arshud Mahmood

Published by Arshud Mahmood

All rights reserved. No part of this publication may be reproduced, stored in a retrieval system or transmitted, in any form, or by any means, electronic, mechanical, recorded, photocopied, or otherwise, without the prior permission of the copyright owner, except by a reviewer who may quote brief passages in a review.

Library of Congress Control Number: 2010936529

ISBN: 0615401139
ISBN-13: 9780615401133

Printed by CreateSpace in the United States of America

To order additional copies, please visit www.Amazon.com, www.CreateSpace.com/3481473, or www.ArshudMahmood.com

The carved, hardwood door frame bordering the cover design is from a tribal compound in Southern Afghanistan that was damaged during the war following the Soviet invasion. The door frame was salvaged, transported, and sold as an antique by refugees coming into Pakistan, and now forms the entryway to my brother Farrukh Mahmood's house. The door leafs are inlaid wood fashioned by artisans in Lahore. The image on the cover is from a photograph taken by my son, Omar Mendoza Mahmood.

**For Zayn
my grandson**

as he discovers his own cultural crossroads

Contents

I

1. Mango Walla 3
2. Princess Durdana 9
3. Sugar Cane 19
4. Gurkha 27
5. Master Clubfoot 43
6. Taliban at the Door 55
7. Baba-ji 69
8. Soccer Match 89
9. A Day with Guests 101
10. Hanna Lake 109
11. Blood Money 125
12. The Migraine Tonic 133
13. The Driver Class 145

II

14. Coffee with Chicory 157
15. Kodiak 175
16. Six-Way Thrusters 183
17. The Fishing Life 191
18. Forty at Sea 211
19. Francoise Sagan is Dead 223
20. A Different kind of Dentist 235
21. The Visible Moon 241

III

22. The Moorish Arabesque 255
23. Flyboy 279

I

Mango Walla

Each vendor who came through the alley had his own style; one pushed a cart, another carried a basket on his head, while a third one had his load flung over his shoulders. Those who sold staples – vegetables, kerosene oil, or milk – did their work without much flair. They announced their wares in a threatening voice, as if ordering you to buy. You could not expect to bargain with them much, if at all. They knew their customers approached them only when they truly needed something, after all, you don't enquire about firewood or flour unless you are ready to cook. If they saw no one approaching them, they kept walking at a brisk pace. Obviously, another vendor selling the same thing had just gone through the neighborhood, and no amount of hawking was going to convince people to buy another bottle of kerosene or another pound of potatoes.

The sellers of luxuries – ice cream, glass bangles, cotton candy, or balloons – had a very different approach. Their voices were lyrical; they lingered, and repeated their calls, as if trying to create a desire before attempting a sale. They often held a sample of their merchandise in their hand, and tried to offer it to people who made eye contact. One vendor offered glass bangles in

COFFEE WITH CHICORY

various colors and sizes, some with specks of glistening golden paint. His sales skill and personal attention were unmatched. If a woman peering from behind a doorway so much as motioned with one finger, he would stop, unload his basket on the front steps, and start unwrapping stacks of glittering samples. If the customer extended her arm through a half-open doorway, the vendor would try to see the size of her hand and wrist, and then offer to have her try on a few bangles. He would hold a stack of four or six bangles, and help the woman slip them over the hand and down to the wrist, without seeing her face. For the rule in bangle merchandising was that if the customer tried them on herself, and a couple of the bangles broke, then she was going to pay for them. However, if she let the vendor put it on her wrist, and a bangle broke, then he covered the loss.

Most women, after choosing the color and the design, would let the vendor hold their hand, and slowly manipulate the tight fitting bangles on to the wrist. To look good, the bangles had to be a snug fit on the wrist, and for some of the young, unmarried girls, the only man who could publicly hold their hand was the bangle vendor. He was careful to keep his gaze low, and that way he could speak with the customer, but without looking at her. Later on she might come out into the street, when could be seen, but not spoken to.

After the preliminary selection of color and design, the vendor would gently hold the customer's fingers. Holding on to the wrist with one hand, he would stretch the fingers, manipulate the bones, and gently massage the customer's hand until it was supple enough to allow the delicate and brittle bangles to slip over the bone structure. His work was precise, but also dangerous, as a broken bangle could easily cut through the skin, earning the customer a couple of free bangles. It was much later, when I was older, that I began to appreciate the allure of the sonorous jingle and jangle of the delicate glass bangles around a woman's wrist, and fully understand the sensuality of the bangle vendor's trade.

The mango vendor's merchandise fell between a luxury and a necessity. It was true that one could live without mangoes, but each variety reached its peak of ripeness and flavor for only a week or two. Too early, they are sour, too late, they are over-ripe and tasteless. The peak of sweetness, flavor, and texture was very short. Even if it was a luxury, there was some urgency attached. This was still the 1940's, and commercial refrigeration or cold storage was not available for storing fruits. Mango wasn't a luxury into which you could delve any time you wanted. And, after all, it was food, and one's health was important.

I grew up with an intense liking for mangoes, which lingers to this day. Mango, or *'aam'* as it's called in Urdu or Hindi, was something I could never resist. Seeing me relish the mango slices, my mother would often laugh and tell a story. I heard it dozens of times while growing up. The story happened when I was three or four years old.

COFFEE WITH CHICORY

One particular mango vendor who came through our neighborhood developed a special sales technique aimed personally at me. He would linger near our house, and repeat his call of *Mangoes, sweet mangoes* until I appeared on the doorstep. He would put his basket down, cut up a mango, and start handing me the slices one by one. Apparently he was sure that our family had the means to pay for his merchandise. As I was finishing up my mango, he would knock on the door. My mother would come out to see me sitting on the front steps sucking on the mango seed, with the juice running down to my elbows. Invariably, a sale was made.

My mother's problem then was how to keep the rest of the mangoes hidden until my father returned from work, and we all had had our dinner. Hoping that I would soon forget, she would hide them from view, and avoid any mention of their name. My parents could converse in fluent English and decided that in my presence, they would use the English word "mango," rather than the Hindi or Urdu word *'aam.'* It took me a few days, but I caught on to it, and one day in a particularly bad mood, I threw a tantrum, shouting, "I want mango *aam*", "I want mango *aam*," trying to cover the fruit in every language.

Growing up I heard my mother relate this incident dozens of times. Each time it would make people laugh, but used to upset me very much. As a teenager if I were being difficult or rude, particularly in front of visitors, she would start telling the story, making everyone laugh. Sometimes all she had to say was 'mango *aam*,' and that was enough to utterly deflate me. I would shut up and go sit in a corner to mope. I was well into my twenties before I accepted that it was a funny story, and could laugh with others upon hearing my mother say, 'mango *aam*'.

Princess Durdana

I AM AWAKE early in the morning, about four years old, lying in my bed listening to the sounds around me. From my window I can hear the birds chirping. They seem very noisy today. I can hear the servant in the kitchen fanning the hard coal stove. The coals must be red hot by now. I hear him chopping something, and know that he is going to make an omelet. After a while I hear the sound of china teacups and saucers, which means my dad is coming to the kitchen for his breakfast. I get out of bed, and walk out to the kitchen. My dad is already there, looking at the newspaper, and my mother is pouring tea for him. I go and stand near her. She hugs me. My dad notices me, "How is the little prince?" He picks me up in the air, and puts me down on a chair next to him. My parents always speak Urdu when I am around, although I have overheard them speak to each other differently, in Punjabi, which sounds funny to my ears. They want me to learn Urdu well because that is how all the people who live near us speak. My mom and dad don't want the neighborhood kids to make fun of me when I go outside to play.

My dad puts down the outer page of the newspaper, and starts looking at the inside while drinking his tea.

COFFEE WITH CHICORY

I pick up the first page and look at a picture with some writing under it. I run my finger along the writing, and pretend to read: "The king has decided to sit down in his big chair today." My parents laugh. Then I pretend to read some more, put down the newspaper and start eating toast and omelet.

"Should he be going to school?" my mother asks. "Seems like he wants to read."

"He's still too young. The school won't take him until he is at least five," my dad replies. "He'll have plenty of time to learn to read and write." I know how to hold the newspaper upright by looking at the pictures. Breakfast is over, and my dad leaves for the hospital where he works as a doctor. I play in my room for a while, and then the servant comes and tells me, "Roshan is here, waiting for you."

I laugh, "Where?"

"Outside."

I hurry to put my sandals on and run outside. He's right. She's out there. I wait everyday for her to come. But I get confused and think that she is not coming. And then she shows up. Today she has brought a small paper boat for me.

"How is the little prince," she asks, "Are you ready for a sea adventure?"

It's very exciting. I nod and laugh.

I hold her hand as we walk out of the house. I like holding her hand. In her other hand she is holding the small boat made by folding a paper.

"What kind of ship is this?" I ask.

She looks at me, smiles, and says, "This is a pirate ship."

We walk along a narrow walkway through the hedge and across the lawn to reach the fountain behind the hospital. Roshan is taller than me, and already goes to school. I think she is 9 or 10 years old. She always knows in which direction we should walk.

"Are you ready to go to sea?"

I nod. I have seen a river, but never the sea. I think it's much bigger.

She puts the boat in the shallow pond around the fountain. We both put our hands in the water and make waves. The boat floats away from us, and starts going around the fountain. Roshan flicks her left hand, and sprays water on my face. "Don't," I scream. I try to push her into the water, but she grabs my arms tight, and starts laughing, "Don't," I scream again. She gently lets go, and says, "Behave. Now where is the boat?"

I look for the boat. It is on the other side of the fountain, and is having difficulty staying upright; the water from the fountain is creating waves in the small pool. The boat is getting dangerously close to the fountain. Water starts to spray on the boat. Roshan and I try to help the little paper boat get out of the stormy fountain spray. A small gust of air comes and pushes the boat further in toward the fountain. The paper gets wet, the boat starts to sink, and then it disappears underwater.

COFFEE WITH CHICORY

I am sad about all the pirates that were in the boat. But Roshan starts to laugh.

"We'll make a new one tomorrow, with new pirates."

She holds my hand; we walk and come to a flowerbed in the hospital garden and see a gardener working. He has a small scoop in his hand to dig up the dirt between the flowers.

"Can we have one flower for the little doctor," she asks him. Everyone calls me 'little doctor'. Everyone who lives around our house works for the small hospital where my dad is the only doctor. We live near Delhi in a small town called Ghaziabad. Once a month when my dad gets his salary we ride the train for half an hour to get to Delhi. My mom goes shopping and I get to eat ice cream. I have heard some people talk about a great war that has just ended. I also know that India is ruled by a king who lives in England.

The gardener looks up. His face is sweaty. His hands are rough, and dark, and covered with dirt. He nods, and goes back to digging in the planter. Roshan reaches into the flowerbed, and picks a yellow flower. It has a row of yellow petals in a circle around a dark center. She hands the flower to me.

She looks at the gardener. He is facing away from us, bent down, squatting on the ground, digging up the flowerbed, and not paying any attention to us. She hold up a finger to her lips and looks at me. Then she quickly reaches into the flowerbed, takes a red flower, and puts it in her hair. She holds my hand, and we start to walk away very fast. I try to look back but she shakes my arm. It seems dangerous, and very exciting. I am not allowed to do things like this on my own.

On the way we stop and look at a man who is sprinkling sugar on an anthill, and speaking under his breath, perhaps saying a prayer. The ants all swarm to the sugar. We stand and watch him for a while.

"What are you doing, sir," Roshan asks him.

He looks at us, keeps whispering prayers, and does not answer. Roshan stands behind him and makes faces. I also make faces. Then we walk away.

We leave the hospital garden and walk back toward the houses. We reach Roshan's house first. It is smaller than our house. There is no one home, but the door is open, and we go in. A newspaper is lying on a chair. I pick it up. I want to show her that I can read it. I look at the picture, run my finger over the writing.

"Today, the king has decided to sit down on his big chair".

She laughs, "That is not what it says here, silly". She looks at the paper, "It says the viceroy is visiting the king in England".

She goes to the other room, returns with an old primer in her hand and shows me a picture. "What is this," she asks?

"A cat,"

She shows me the letters for a cat. "Now read it," she says.

COFFEE WITH CHICORY

The primer is full of pictures, and words. We read for a while and then she walks me back to my house. I think I am hungry now.

The next day, Roshan comes again. We go out to the flower garden. She puts one flower in her hair and gives one to me. We go by the fountain and float a new boat. We check the anthills. We go to her house. She takes out the primer, and shows me how to read some more. I go to her house every day and after some time I can read little stories in the primer. Some of the stories are only three lines long.

One day at breakfast my father is sitting and reading the newspaper. My mother is sitting next to him, working with her knitting needles. They are having tea. My dad puts down the first page of newspaper, and starts to read the inside page with his second cup of tea. I pick up the first page, look at the picture, and say, "The king is meeting with Mr. Churchill."

"Yes, yes," my mother says. "Now finish your porridge."

I look at a second picture: "The viceroy is inspecting the policemen in Calcutta."

My dad puts down the paper he is reading. "What did he say," he asks my mother.

"I don't know," she says. "He just makes things up."

"Read it again," my dad says to me.

"The viceroy is inspecting the policemen in Calcutta."

He takes the paper from my hand and looks at the picture. "I'll be..." He shows me another picture.

Princess Durdana

"The king of Nepal at his court in Kat... Kat... Katmudu."

My father laughs, "Katmandu."

My mother has stopped her knitting, and is looking at us. She is smiling. "Is he right," she asks?

"He is close enough. Have you been teaching him?"

"No. I don't have the time."

"The servant then?"

"Couldn't be, the servant does not know how to read."

"Who taught you how to read?" he asks me.

"No one."

"No one?"

"No one. Well, except Roshan." I say.

"Who is Roshan," my father asks.

"The dispenser's daughter. I think her father works at the hospital pharmacy."

"Ram Lal's daughter? I know he is quite a scholar."

"Maybe his daughter is one too," my mother says, "Perhaps we should get him some children's books."

Several days go by. One morning, I am playing in the front veranda. The postman comes by the house with a packet that has a small book for me. It has a colorful cover, *Princess Durdana and the Evil Magician.* I sit down and try to read. I can read it, very slowly. Princess Durdana lives in a rich kingdom with her father, who is the king. One day an evil magician puts a spell on the king. The princess goes on a quest to remove the spell. I read the book each day and learn bout her adventures during her quest. The spell is finally broken and the magician is defeated. One day, when the story is almost finished, the postman brings another book, *Princess Durdana and the Enchanted Treasure*. This time I finish the book before the next one arrives, *Princess Durdana and the Gallant Prince,* and I have to wait for several days. Each day I ask my mother for a new book, "I don't know," she says, "It must be on its way."

One day I overhear my mother tell my aunt, "I think he is in love with Princess Durdana." They look at me and then they both laugh. I don't know what they are talking about. I am about five years old. I ask my mother, "Did the postman bring the new book?"

After she has had her laugh, my mother turns to me. "No, the book did not come. Perhaps tomorrow." I am beginning to get upset with this postman. I think I'll ask my father to have a talk with him. Whenever my father has a talk with someone, things happen. Or maybe we should change the postman and get a new postman. "Don't worry," my mother says. "Your princess will be here tomorrow." What is she talking about? She is not just my princess. She has a whole kingdom. She is the princess for the whole kingdom.

The next day I am playing in my room when the servant comes and tells me, *Princess Durdana* has arrived.

"Where, where?" I go out running, and see that Roshan is standing there. "Where is she, where is she?" I ask her.

"Who, what are you talking about?"

Then I see the postman approaching. He is holding the new book about Princess Durdana. I laugh and grab the book from his hand.

"Let us go and look at the flowers," Roshan says.

I don't say anything. I am sitting down reading the book. Princess Durdana is asking the king about going on a hunt with her friends.

"I'll see you tomorrow," Roshan says. I don't say anything.

"Bye," she says.

I wave my hand without looking up.

Sugar Cane

I AM ALMOST seven, and we recently moved from Delhi to Lahore. Sometimes I see a lot of people in the streets marching and shouting. My dad tells me, "Indians want the British to leave." In Lahore there are new sounds, new smells and a new language, all very different from Delhi. I hear a vendor hawking in a loud voice, and he seems to be saying, "Sugary Canes…. Sugary Canes…." – what in the world is he saying? I cannot understand what he is selling. I go out and stand on the top step of our front porch, and see him pushing a cart piled high, but I don't recognize his product. Last week I inadvertently stopped the tobacco vendor, got scolded, and now have to be more careful.

The vendor stops two houses away, repeats his call, and a couple of kids run up to him. The situation appears to be safe so I decide to be brave, walk down the steps into the street and ask,

"What are you selling?"

The vendor smiles, but his two young customers turn around, look at me, and start laughing. I am confused. The vendor holds up his hand for me to wait, gives the boys some change and a paper sack, and they run away, giggling, looking back.

COFFEE WITH CHICORY

"Where are you from?" the vendor asks me with a smile.

"We have just moved here from Delhi."

"That explains it. But you are in Punjab now, and everyone here talks in Punjabi, while you are speaking Urdu." This explains nothing to me about what he is selling.

"I visited Delhi once." he says, "What glory. Do you know the Mogul emperors had their court in Delhi?"

He seems more interested in chatting than selling. I vaguely remember something my father told me about the Moguls when we visited the Red Fort in Delhi. Obviously, those two boys who laughed at me knew nothing about the glory of the Mogul court. Anyway, I don't care what language I speak, I want to buy some snack, so I hand him the money, and he gives me a small paper sack with what appear to be chunks of wood.

I walk back toward our house, pick one chunk out of the sack, and bite into it. Sweet, sugary juice starts running over my fingers and chin, dripping on my shirt and over to my shoes. I stop at the front steps, unsure of how to eat this snack. Mundu, our new servant, is coming out of the house, and sees the quizzical look on my face. He grew up in Lahore and speaks Punjabi.

"So you found some sugar cane, go ahead, it is very refreshing," he says. He takes one piece from the sack in my hand, "Here, this is how you eat it." He bites into the piece of sugar cane, slurps, while simultaneously sucking up the juice, "Sssssss….." thus avoiding any drips. I try to copy him, and make a loud slurping sound. Some of the juice still trickles down to my elbow. I try again, louder, "Shshshshshsh……" much better. It seems fun. It is delicious, and guaranteed to annoy any adult within hearing range. No wonder this fruit never made it to the Mogul court.

We may have moved to a city full of peasants, but it sure seems like a fun place. The local language, Punjabi, is now freely being spoken in our house. Prior to coming here, while in Delhi, rules were different. "Don't speak in Punjabi like an ignorant person," my mother would command, "how will you talk to the other kids when you go to school?" When I was within earshot, my parents would avoid speaking in the Punjabi language to set a good example for me, so it was rare or accidental if I heard anyone speak in my mother tongue. I began associating speaking in Punjabi with lack of education, and considered Urdu, the language spoken in Delhi, a mark of learned and civilized behavior.

Upon returning to our native Punjab, our family's Punjabi-ness has surfaced with a vengeance. There is a constant stream of visitors to our house, apparently all of them related to us, and all fluent in what is a new language for me. An aunt who came yesterday asked me, "Are you proud to be a Punjabi." I turned to my mother and asked her, "Are we proud?" – and they both laughed.

Another week goes by during which I discover more vendors and their wares, and run out of the house every time I hear a hawker to buy the next snack. One evening I overhear my dad speaking to my mother, "The school year begins next week, I think I should enroll him." I am unconcerned, as I have not heard my name yet, and then my mother replies, "Definitely, at least that will keep him away from the vendors." School again – well, even after our move, some things have not changed. I remember school from last year, and it did not seem to be an interesting place. There were many kids, but we were not allowed to play, and everyone from teachers to students seemed under stress. But why do I have to go to school? We are living in our own native province, speaking Punjabi freely in the house, so who are we trying to impress now?

It is Monday and I am awakened rudely at an unusually early hour, force-fed something that I suspect to be to be nutritious since it does not taste good. I am then stuffed into clothes that don't appear to be appropriate for playing. I accompany my dad to the new school and on the way doze off at least once. We reach the school, and go through enrollment. So far I have not felt any stress, perhaps it begins later. One of the school clerks asks me, "Is it true that you attended school in Delhi?" I nod, pleased; we are definitely in a civilized place now, and I am tempted to ask him if he has heard of the Mogul court, but he is busy writing something in a big ledger.

The classes are to begin the next day. We are done with enrollment and I accompany my dad to a stationery store to buy school supplies and primers for writing and arithmetic. We also purchase a satchel that I can sling over my shoulder; I try it on, but it keeps slipping, so I put it over my head, and hang it with the strap across my chest as I have seen the postman carry his heavy bag of letters.

We get home, and the day seems to have gone quite well. I sit with my satchel, and examine the new-bought supplies. I have two lead pencils, a pencil sharpener, a slate tablet for writing, rather heavy, as it is a slab of natural slate-stone, two crayon-like stylus pencils made of a soft stone for writing on the natural slate, a small rag of a towel for wiping the slate, one notebook, two primers, one for reading, which is full of pictures and simple words. I am pleased to see the familiar letters and words, and linger over the book. I open the second primer, but it has no pictures, and appears to be a jumble of numbers. I quickly close it. It might be arithmetic.

I go over all my scholastic possessions, taking them out of the satchel and putting them back in several times. The satchel is made of light brown canvas, with brown leather trim and a leather carrying-strap. I sharpen the two pencils, and try to write with one but the lead breaks, and I have to sharpen it three times before I get the hang of how hard to press down on the lead, so one pencil is shorter now. I am a little alarmed, so I pack the satchel another time and put it near my bed.

"How is he going to go to school?" my mother asks.

"It is quite close, he can walk to it," my dad replies.

"But there is a busy road to be crossed."

"Well then, Mundu can walk with him." Mundu only speaks in Punjabi, so he and I always have this strange, bilingual dialogue, where I keep asking him in Urdu, and he always replies in Punjabi. Sometimes I have an uneasy feeling that we do not fully understand each other, but so far nothing disastrous has happened.

The next day I'm rushed through my morning unceremoniously – waking, washing up, changing, eating, and then it's time to leave. I have my satchel slung across my chest and over my shoulder, and we start walking. The busy street is full of bicycles, horse carriages, ox carts and occasional motor vehicles. Crossing it is quite exciting, as there is no crosswalk, and the traffic never stops; the pedestrians dodge, the vehicles swerve, and they are able to maneuver around each other. The presence of pedestrians does not cause any great disruption in the flow of traffic. The various wheeled transports on the road, hand carts, ox carts, horse carriages, bicycles, motor-cycles, and cars, all have such varying speeds that there's plenty of dodging around and swerving going on even without the pedestrians. Buses are the only thing that make me nervous, and I let them go by rather than hurry across their path. They seem to be lumbering along, and not able to maneuver very well. "All bounce and go, and no consideration for anybody," as I heard someone say.

After crossing the busy street we are walking along a tree-lined street that has very little traffic, and we are able to walk on the pavement itself. Mundu keeps pointing things out.

"There is the hospital where Doctor Sahib works."

I know he is talking about my father, as everyone calls him doctor sahib. Some days I am too tired or bored to walk, so Mundu finds a rock or a piece of wood that we kick as we go along, keeping track of it until we reach school. He makes kicking the same rock again and again such fun that I don't mind going to school each day. This Punjab may be very far from the Mogul court, and a little rough around the edges, but it seems to be joyous, and fun, just like its sugar cane.

Gurkha

"August has started, and he'll be 7 in a couple of weeks." I hear my mother telling my father. My dad does not say anything, so my mother continues, "I am going to ask some of the neighbors to come to his birthday, so let me know if you want to invite anyone special." The year is 1947, and we live in Lahore.

Birthday? Does that mean presents? I walk out to our front verandah and look through the trellis. I see my friend Vikas playing with the scooter he got for his birthday. Seeing the scooter, I am sure birthday means presents. I walk over to his house. It is not much of a walk, as our houses are connected, and all I have to do is go down the front steps from our verandah, walk along our house, and climb up the steps to Vikas' house.

We both climb on to the scooter, but with two of us on board it doesn't go very fast. We take turns riding it back and forth. I like it when I ride it alone, very fast, almost to the edge of the verandah and then stop it at the last minute. Sometime I run into the wall and fall down, laughing. Vikas also laughs and falls down on top of me. We get very tired, and his mother gives us milk and cookies. After the snack when we are alone, Vikas says

COFFEE WITH CHICORY

"Look, look."

"What?"

"Look down here, stupid, in this pocket."

It is a box of matches. My eyes open wide – what now, there are so many possibilities. He goes to his father's room and returns with two cigarettes. "Let us go to the drawing room," he says.

My heart is pounding; I walk along a wall, like a cat, only invisible. We get to the living room, hide behind the long sofa, near the thick drapes, and stick a cigarette each in our mouths. I am not sure what is next. Vikas hands me the matchbox.

"Light it up."

I don't know what he is talking about, "What?"

We are both whispering, which makes it hard to understand. I open the box, and all the matchsticks fall down, I must have been holding it upside down.

"What are you doing?" Vikas is getting angry. It takes us a while to gather all the matchsticks, but they wont fit back in the little box. We leave some on the carpet. Vikas lights a match, I start blowing into the cigarette stuck in my mouth, hoping to produce some smoke, but nothing happens. Instead of lighting our cigarettes, we just sit and watch the burning matchstick. It gets shorter and shorter, and then his fingers get too hot.

"Ouch," he drops the burning match to the floor. Both of us get up behind the sofa and stomp down wildly.

His mother walks into the living room, "What is going on here?" She sees us with cigarettes in our mouths, grabs the cigarettes, and gives one hard smack each, "You naughty kids."

She sees the matchsticks scattered on the floor, picks them up and puts them in the box. How does she manage to fit all of them in that little box? She tells me to go back to my house. No, Manu cannot come and play with me. I think she wants to talk to him some more after I leave. I get home and sit alone in the back room, very quiet.

I hear someone coming in through the back door into our courtyard. It is my uncle. I run to him and he picks me up.

"How is my little one," he laughs, lifts me high above his head, until I can touch the light bulb hanging in the middle of the room.

"You two are going to break that light one day," my mother sounds angry, but she is smiling, and happy to see her younger brother.

They sit down for tea, and he tells my mother, "I saw the riot on my way over here. Today it was behind the vegetable market. The policemen were ready, and broke it up in a hurry."

My mother looks serious. I eagerly hang around. My uncle finally finishes the tea and wipes his forehead with the back of his hand, which means he is ready to take me for a walk. I bring my sandals so he can help

COFFEE WITH CHICORY

me with the clasp on the left one. He gets up, but my mother looks concerned, "Is it safe?"

"Yes, yes, we won't go very far. I just came through the main *bazaar*. It is all peaceful around here."

I look at my mother and nod, "Yes, it is all peace and full."

She smiles and gives me a hug. I hold my uncle's hand and we walk out. The sidewalk is busy. As we get to the main intersection I hold his hand tightly. We go by the row of shoe stores and over the little footbridge to get to the candy store. It is closed. I feel like crying. My uncle looks around and spots a pushcart vendor selling cotton candy. This is even better. I yell, "Pink, pink", because I like pink cotton candy. I get busy eating and we head back. I am eager to get home and look in the mirror. Whenever I eat cotton candy I get a pink mustache above my lip. I don't like the white cotton candy. Once it gave me a white mustache and Vikas made fun of me, "Old man, old man."

My cotton candy is finished but my hand is still sticky. As we get to the main intersection we stop. There is a crowd gathered around the intersection, and there are some policemen. One policeman stops us, and talks to my Uncle. I cannot understand what he is saying. My uncle tells the policeman, "No, no, we live by the hospital, two blocks to the right, not left." He tells the policeman my father's name. He is a doctor at the railroad hospital. The policeman waves, "Go ahead, but don't stop in the intersection." We start walking, and then I look at the intersection, there is a man lying on the street. His mouth and his eyes are open, but he is not breathing. His legs are crooked, and one arm is bent under him. His head has a cut above his left ear. The head is broken, open on one side, and something has spilled out. It looks soft and gooey, and fleshy, but not bloody. My uncle tugs at my hand and pulls me away from the dead man. I keep pointing at the man's head but don't say anything. "It is his brain," my uncle says. I look back one last time as we head back home.

We walk very fast.

"Who is he, who is that man?" I want to know.

"He is a Gurkha."

"What is a Gurkha?"

"Gurkhas come from Nepal or Tibet or some place like that," he says. "Anyway, they are different from us."

We keep walking. The man looks just like other men, so what does my uncle mean by 'different', I am puzzled. Maybe he means the Gurkha's brain is different. We get home, and my uncle goes to the back courtyard. I know he goes there to smoke. I forget to look at my pink mustache in the mirror, and run directly to my mother.

"I saw a brain today," she looks puzzled, "Truly, I did. It was a Gurkha brain." She goes to the back courtyard, and I follow her. My uncle puts the cigarette out. My mother is shaking her finger at him, "No more walks." My uncle does not say anything.

COFFEE WITH CHICORY

My father comes home late. I go to tell him about the Gurkha brain, but he is busy talking to my mother.

"Five dead men," I think he said, and "Train station". He sees me and stops talking. He hugs me and my mother takes me to my bedroom.

A few days later my uncle comes to visit us again. He sits down with my mother; they have tea, and talk about the riots. He tells my mother, "Tonight there will be a curfew, and no one will be allowed outside after dark."

Outside, the sun is very hot. My mother tells me, "It is hot weather. It is too hot to go out". My friend Vikas comes over, we play in the shade in our front verandah, and ride his scooter back and forth very fast until sweat starts running down our faces. My mother gives us lemonade. I like my lemonade very sweet, so she adds more sugar in my glass. Manu likes his lemonade sour, so she squeezes a lemon into his glass.

My dad comes home in the evening. Doctors have to work all day. I eat dinner with him, and by the time we finish dinner it is dark outside. After dinner my father likes to listen to the news on the radio.

"There is no good news on the radio," my mother tells him and he turns the radio off. "It is very warm in the house," she says, "Can we go out for a little walk?"

"Yes," he says.

"Is it safe?"

"Yes, it is safe. There is a curfew at night."

I also go out with them. We come out of the house and walk by the hedge along the side yard. During the day the hedge is green, but looks black in the dark. I smell something very nice. As we walk, the nice fragrance becomes strong. My mother reaches over and plucks a small white flower from the hedge.

"Queen of the night," she says, and holds the flower up to smell it, then gives it to me. I also hold the flower up to my nose, sniff, and say, "Queen of the night."

My father says, "The plant is called night-blooming jasmine. The blossoms are closed during the day but open up on warm nights."

"Well, I like the name queen of the night," my mother says.

"Yes, dad, queen of the night."

As we walk and I sniff the small white blossom in my hand, the night does not seem hot any more.

The hedge ends, we keep walking, and the fragrance becomes very faint. Up ahead I see a man standing under the streetlight. He says something very loud, and two other men come out from behind a wall. All three of them are coming toward us and their shadows are getting longer. They stop near us. They are policemen and are holding rifles. I hold my father's hand tightly. They say something about the curfew, and about being out at night.

"I am a doctor," my father says, "I have a curfew pass." He lets go of my hand. I grab my mother's leg, and she puts her hand on my shoulder. My father looks through his pockets, takes out a paper, gives it to one of the policemen who looks at it with his flashlight, and motions us to move on. We continue our walk.

We walk up to the corner of the main bazaar. There are no people in the bazaar, and we turn around. On our way back we see a dog coming toward us. It is a big dog, and as he comes close to us he starts barking. I hold my dad's arm with both hands and cling to his leg. The dog starts growling. We all stop, and I start crying.

"Where is your walking stick today," my mother asks?

I look at my dad; he does not have the walking stick with him. "Dad, please show it to him." My dad looks at me; tears are streaming down my face. "The curfew pass, dad, please show it to the dog."

My mother laughs. My dad steps very fast toward the dog, says "Shoo," and the dog runs away into the bushes. My mother is still laughing. I look around. It is too dark to see anything. There is nothing funny. We walk back home. I try to walk fast all the way. When I grow up I will have my own curfew pass.

The next day Vikas comes over to play with me. We start playing, and then his mother shows up. My mother sits down with her and they have tea. Vikas' mother is crying. I cannot understand what they are talking about. After tea, they get up to leave. She hugs me before leaving, and asks Vikas to hug me also. Vikas and I look at each other. We think it is funny for us to hug, and we want to laugh, but we look at our mothers who both look sad. His mother takes Vikas' hand and they leave.

My uncle comes to see us in the afternoon. My mother has the tea ready, but he does not want to stay. He is telling her about some houses that are on fire. He is also telling her about some people who are dead. That night my father comes home late so we do not go out for a walk. He is telling my mother about some people he saw on the train station. Somebody had hurt these people. I drink some milk and go to bed.

I wake up the next morning and hear my mother's voice. She is shouting and sounds angry. I get out of bed and find her standing at the front door out in the verandah. She is looking toward Vikas' house, where many men are going in and out. Two men run out of Vikas' house carrying a big suitcase. One man runs out holding a mirror, some others are carrying away pots and pans. My mother is scolding them. All of them. She calls one of them, "Son of an owl." Another one she calls, "Bastard." I am not allowed to say those words. I think she is saying some other bad words also. Two men come out of Manu's house carrying a big suitcase, and come to our front door, "Lady, here is your share, just be quiet." My mother tries to hit one of them but they both run away, carrying the suitcase. Soon all the men are gone. My mother comes and sits down. She looks sad.

"I want to go and play with Vikas," I tell her.

COFFEE WITH CHICORY

She has tears in her eyes, "Vikas is gone," and she picks me up in her lap. "Vikas is gone with his mom and dad."

"What about her little sister?"

"She too, they are all gone."

"Where, mom?"

"We don't know. They left in the middle of the night, before the looters got to their house. I hope they are in a safe place."

"Mom, why did they leave?"

"Vikas and his family are Hindu." "What is Hindu?"

"They are different from us."

Different? I don't remember anything different about Manu. His dad is just like my dad; he is also a doctor in the same hospital. His mom is also just like my mom. They both give us lemonade, and milk and cookies. I go to my room and play alone. I am puzzled. They must have become Hindu last night, perhaps in the middle of the night, just before leaving. I would have wanted to see what Vikas looked like.

My uncle comes late in the afternoon. There is no tea today. He and my mother just talk. He does not leave in the evening, but stays at our house. Late in the evening the sky is red and we can see smoke.

"It is a fire," my uncle says, "That was a Hindu neighborhood. The looters finally succeeded."

No one says anything, and there is no talking. Before going to bed I hear my mother asking my dad. "Is this happening in other cities?"

"Yes," my dad says, "Hindus and Muslims are killing each other, and looting and burning each other's neighborhoods."

She says, "I am worried about my mother and sister."

I know she is talking about my grandmother and my aunt.

Next morning as I am eating my bowl of porridge in the kitchen, I hear some noise at the front door. I run up to see my grandmother and aunt walking in. My mother is hugging both of them, and all three of them are crying.

"Thank God you are safe," she tells them.

I also go and hug them. Usually they bring toys and candy, but today they have not brought anything, not even their bags.

"We had to leave with the clothes on our backs on the last flight out of Delhi," my aunt tells my mother. Then she picks me up, "Don't worry, we will get you some candy and toys from the *bazaar*."

I am not worried. I know that they always give me candy and toys. They sit with my mother, drink tea, and talk for a long time. They are telling her about their neighborhood, and someone who got killed. I don't know what people they are talking about. I go to my room and read a storybook that has pictures in it. It is the story of a princess. Then I lie down and doze off.

I wake up and hear many voices, walk out of my room, and go to the kitchen. I see several new people sitting there. They are eating, and talking excitedly.

"Come here and meet your aunt and uncle," my mother says, "they just came across the border."

I keep standing in the doorway. I have never seen these people before. The man my mother says is my uncle has a bandage on his head.

"Come and say hello to your cousins. Take them to your room and play."

I notice the boy and the girl sitting next to a lady. I go stand next to them and try to hold their hands. They look scared, and cling to their mother. The boy does not want to play, he wants to eat some more. The girl keeps looking down at the floor. I also sit down and eat a sandwich. "We walked all night." The lady is telling my mother, "The next caravan was attacked and everyone was killed."

By the time I finish eating, the boy and the girl have slumped down next to their mother. Both asleep on the floor.

That night I sleep in my parents' room. In the morning I wake up and go to my room. There are several mattresses on the floor, and some more new people I have never seen before are sleeping on them. I turn around to leave, then I notice the boy and the girl.

They are playing with my fire engine. This is my favorite fire engine. I go up to them and snatch it away.

"Mommy, mommy, save me," the girl shouts, runs away and hides behind her mother. The boy starts crying. People in the room stare at me. I don't know what to do. I try to give the fire engine back to the boy, but he won't take it, and keeps crying. I put the fire engine on the floor next to him. I walk out to the front veranda, and see that there are four cots there, and men are sleeping on them. All four men have bandages on their arms and legs. Then I notice that one of them is not asleep. He is staring at the ceiling. He looks very pale. Another one looks asleep because his eyes are closed, but he is moaning. I don't like being in the verandah, and go back into the house. I am getting hungry, so I go the kitchen. I find my mother there. She is talking to three ladies who are having tea. I recognize my grandmother and give her a hug. She kisses my forehead and sings something to me. It does not sound like a lullaby, and I don't understand the words. It must be a prayer, and after saying it she blows on my face. My mother gives me breakfast.

I go to our courtyard in the back of the house. Our cook has set up a large stove out in the open, and two large pots are on the stove.

"Come here, little sahib," he calls me, "I am cooking for everyone in the house."

COFFEE WITH CHICORY

Another servant is helping him. I sit there on a stool and watch them. There are pieces of meat and vegetables, and rice, and some dough for making bread. He gives me a piece of radish, and I put it in my mouth. It bites my tongue, and I spit it out. The cook laughs and gives me a piece of carrot. It is sweet.

In the evening everyone has dinner together. There is a bright gas lantern in the courtyard that is making a hissing sound. A large rug has been spread on the ground, and some people are sitting on the rug eating. Others are sitting on cots. I see the boy and the girl. The boy is holding my fire engine. I go and sit down next to them. "Mommy, mommy," the girl starts shouting.

"It is OK. He is your cousin," her mother says.

I don't try to take the fire engine back. I eat my dinner. After dinner I go to my parents room. My father is talking to my mother, "I am sick of attending to trains full of dead and dying."

"Yes, it must be horrible," my mother says.

"I have requested a transfer," he says.

"But where can we go?" She is concerned.

"I have asked to be assigned to a hospital as far away as possible from the Indian border," he says, "We are moving to Quetta next month, near the Afghanistan border. I heard it is a beautiful and quiet town."

"Pray to God that rioting and killing will stop now," my mother says, "there are two separate countries now."

"I hope so," my father says. He picks me up, "Happy birthday," he says.

Gurkha

My mother takes out a box form under the bed, it is a new fire engine, and has a siren on it. I start laughing, and play in their room with the new fire engine until I fall asleep.

Master Clubfoot

I AM seven years old. We have recently moved to the town of Quetta near the Afghanistan border. This is a peaceful place. There are no Hindu-Muslim riots here. A Hindu family lives down the street from us, and I sometimes play with their kid – Shyam Lal. Rows of camels and herds of sheep pass by our house several times a day, accompanied by Baloch nomads.

I have started third grade in a new school. It is early in the morning, and while getting ready for school I ask my mother, "Do we live in a village?"

"Who told you that?"

"Nobody. Our school gate says, Killi Village School."

She laughs. "We live at the edge of the city, and it is not a big city like the one we came from."

"Is my school a village?" "Ask daddy, maybe there was a village here."

My dad has already gone to the hospital where he works.

I finish my breakfast and get ready to walk to school, but the servant is still busy with his chores.

"I can walk alone today," I tell my mother.

"Just wait," she says, and goes to check on the servant. I follow her, "I'll be careful."

COFFEE WITH CHICORY

"No," she says, "The city is full of Pathans, and they are wild people."

The servant is now ready, so I pick up my satchel, and say to her, "They are not all Pathans. And they are not wild." She is having her breakfast, and pours some more tea into her cup, "How can we tell?" she says, "We don't speak their language."

The servant helps me carry my things, and we start walking toward the school. On our way to the school we have to cross a busy road. This is the main road coming into town over the pass through the mountains. Sometimes big trucks come on this street, and there are always many camels loaded with large sacks, tied one behind the other into long trains that stretch for 8 or 10 camels. We cross the road very carefully.

As we get close to the school gate, I ask the servant to turn back. I am seven years old, and don't want other kids to see him.

"When school ends," he says, "I'll be waiting near the gate."

I nod, and he leaves.

I go to my classroom. The class begins and we practice multiplication tables. One kid stands in front of the class near the teacher's table, facing the classroom and shouts in a singsong voice, "Two times two is four." All the kids repeat after him, singing at the top of our lungs.

"Two times three is six," we continue, and it takes almost an hour to reach twelve times twelve, by which time some of us are hoarse. It is great fun to shout in the classroom, but I am not sure if I remember anything. I have heard that next year, in the fourth grade, we will be able to say the tables all the way to sixteen times sixteen, and then the following year, in the fifth grade, all the way to twenty by twenty. It will probably take us two hours each day.

After the multiplication tables it is time to work on arithmetic problems. The teacher starts writing numbers on the black board. "Now add them." I write down the numbers on my slate with a slate pencil, and try to add them. The teacher asks us to put our slates away, and shows us how to add correctly. I look at the slate. I must have a different way of adding, because my answer is different. Finally, we get to the reading part, and he asks a kid to read. The kid reads haltingly and stops after reading one sentence. The teacher asks a second kid, this kid stops after the second sentence. Then he asks me, and I read the whole paragraph, keep reading till I finish the whole page. When I turn the page, the teacher says, "Stop, stop." All the kids are looking at me. It is an interesting story, and I want to continue reading.

We study all day, and after a long time the last bell rings, telling us that the school is over for the day, and I come out to the gate. The servant is not here. Why is he not waiting for me? Everyone is going home, and I am afraid to walk alone as I might get lost, but I am also afraid to be left alone at the school. I feel like crying.

COFFEE WITH CHICORY

"Ready to go home?" A voice calls me from the back, and I turn around to see that it is one of the teachers, "Want to walk with me?", he asks.

I don't know what to say.

"Your dad is a doctor, isn't he?"

I nod.

"Come on then, I am going by your house."

I start walking with him. How does he know all this? But teachers know. "Had a good day today?" "Yes, master sahib."

We start walking and I look at the way the teacher is walking. On his right foot he wears what looks like a half shoe, and as he steps on this foot, he bends down and almost falls over. But he steadies himself, and then steps on the left foot, the good foot. Now he stands straight, and takes a big step. He keeps walking this way: step on the right foot, almost fall over to the right, get steady, and step forward with the left foot. He takes another big stride, landing on the right foot, and then almost falls over, and we keep walking.

"Do you know how to add?"

"Yes, master sahib."

"Can you divide numbers?"

"Yes, master sahib."

"You can?" He looks at me.

"Only small numbers, master sahib."

He laughs, "Can you say the multiplication table for 9? Go ahead, say it."

Master Clubfoot

I start haltingly. Across the street two kids are trying to mock how the teacher walks, and one of them falls over. They start laughing, and one of them shouts, "Master Clubfoot," and they run into an alley and disappear. I feel that everyone in the street is looking at us. I don't know if people are looking at Master Clubfoot's walk, or if they are trying to listen to me struggling with the multiplication table.

We reach the gate in front of our house, and I can see the gardener working in the front yard. The servant comes out and is relieved to see me, "Oh good, you made it back. I have been so busy." The teacher lingers, and asks the servant, "Is doctor sahib at home?" "Yes, he is, please wait," and the servant goes back into the house. Chairs have already been set up in the front lawn for afternoon tea. The teacher sits down in one of them. I think it is difficult for him to stand.

My father comes out and sits down with the teacher. I go to the side yard and ride on the swing. The servant brings tea for them. They talk and have tea, and after a while, the teacher gets up, shakes hands with my father, and leaves.

That evening at dinner my father says to my mother, "His teacher was here today."
"Which teacher?"
"Master clubfoot," I blurt out.
She glares at me, "Who taught you that?"
"I heard some kids say that."

COFFEE WITH CHICORY

"Never say that again."

I eat quietly and listen to my dad. "The teacher said he reads well, and his writing is improving."

"And?"

"But he is having difficulty in arithmetic." I start having difficulty swallowing my food.

My mother puts down her fork, "He needs some tutoring, but you are always busy with your patients."

"Yes, I know," my father says, and then looks at her.

"Don't look at me," she says, "running this household with three servants is a full-time job."

"Yes, I know."

"The annual bazaar is coming up, and the ladies at the club expect me to run the raffle again. You know how important the bazaar is for the community. Last year we raised…."

"Yes, I know," my father interrupts, "I have asked the teacher to tutor him, he'll be here tomorrow."

I remember when I joined this school; my dad and I went to see the headmaster, who sent me to another teacher. This teacher asked me many questions about adding, subtracting, and dividing different numbers. He asked me to read from a storybook, and also asked me to write some words. As long as I can remember, I have been able to read, so I did not have any trouble with the storybook, but the rest of the time the teacher did not look very pleased. We went back to the headmaster's office where they were having tea.

"He reads very well, but needs work in other things," the teacher said, and left me in the headmaster's office.

"Because of the partition," my father said, "His schooling has been interrupted several times." Then they talked about the partition of India, the British Raj, and about Pakistan.

The headmaster said finally, looking at me, "We'll put him in the third grade, I think he can catch on all right."

The next day I go to the school, and we go through our usual routine, starting the morning with group practice singing multiplication tables. After that we solve arithmetic problems on our stone slates, and then some calligraphy practice on wooden tablets with reed pens. I return from school in the afternoon, change my clothes, go to the back yard, and climb up the mulberry tree for a snack. From up in the tree, I see some bricks in the vegetable garden, and decide to go build a fort. Right then I hear the servant calling, "Come down now, the master sahib is here." What? I just came home from school; my head is still spinning from the numbers I saw all day. I climb down with a sigh, and come to the front lawn. A small table with two chairs has already been set up. There is a glass of lemonade for the teacher, who is there waiting for me.

"Hurry up, young man."

Young man, who is he talking to? I look around, but there's no one else around.

COFFEE WITH CHICORY

"Sit down," he says, and I take a seat.

"What is the homework for today?"

I think there is some, and I look through my satchel. First I work on the addition and subtraction problems. Then he helps me with the multiplication and division problems.

The following day after school, I go to the side yard and start building the fort with red bricks. I see the teacher enter our front gate. "Hurry up, young man," this time I know he is talking to me, and I go look for my satchel. He limps across the lawn to his chair, and sits down. By the time we finish, there is not much time left to play. I see that my brother and sister, and the kid from next door, have all been playing.

This happens each afternoon. I begin a game – hide and seek, building a fort, chasing butterflies – and I hear "Hurry up, young man," from across our front lawn. The servant has learnt too, so the table is ready, and the lemonade is brought out. I never get to finish any game. I don't like this school, I don't like this master sahib, and I don't like the arithmetic problems. I miss playing in the afternoons.

Many days go by. One day at school, something strange and different happens. Our class teacher asks us to solve a long division problem that he has written on the blackboard. We copy the problem on to our slates, and after a couple of minutes I raise my hand.

"Yes, what do you want?" the teacher asks.

"Nothing, master sahib," I keep my hand up, "I have the answer."

"You?" He takes my slate and checks, "He is right," he says to the class. A few days later I score a perfect 100 on the long division test.

The third grade ends, I am promoted to the fourth grade, but my tutoring continues. I always have to remind myself not to say Master Clubfoot in front of my mother. I have learnt that my school is indeed a village school, although the former village has slowly become a part of the city. And most of people who live in the village area are not Pathans but Baloch, who speak a different language. There is one Baloch kid in our class, Hamid, who always scores high in every test. No kid can beat him.

After another year, my 5th grade class starts. I am older now, and walk to school alone. The master sahib still comes to our house each afternoon and I hear, "Hurry up, young man." Now we work on difficult problems. For many months there is no play in the afternoons. Finally, the fifth grade is coming to an end. In school we practice each day for the final examination. Hamid, the bright, Baloch kid, aces every practice test. I hear two kids whispering that he might stand first in the district. The teachers always nod to him after the tests.

One day, the headmaster comes to our class. "Remember kids. This examination is for the whole district. Make us proud." I think he was looking at Hamid. I am afraid of the final examination. Many other kids are also afraid.

The examination day comes, and a new teacher comes, one we've never seen before. One by one, he writes each problem on the black board. We solve the problems on our slates, he checks them, and notes down our scores. Hamid, the bright kid is sitting right in front of me. Halfway through the test I look at him, and he looks pale. During the long division portion of the examination he throws up on the floor. He looks very sick and keeps moaning. Someone helps him out of the room, and he does not return. Perhaps he is too sick to continue. A janitor comes and cleans the floor.

Once the examination is over there is a long vacation, after which I go with my dad to the school to get the results. He goes into the headmaster's office while I wait outside. He comes out looking happy.

"You did well," he pats me on the back, "you stood first in your school."

On the way home, we buy some sweets to take home. We reach home and he tells my mother, "He will get a scholarship for the next three years." She gives me a hug, and kisses me on my cheek. I have to wipe my face as I am too old to be kissed by ladies. "It was that kind master sahib." Is she talking about master clubfoot? Must be, "the kind master". I never liked calling him master clubfoot.

I don't say anything to anyone about Hamid, the kid who got sick during the test. For my sixth grade I start at a new school, and I never see Hamid again. Some people say that his family moved away. Every first of the month I am called to the front of the class, and handed fifteen rupees in cash, the full amount of my scholarship. This continues till I reach 8th grade, and each time I am handed the money I think of the kind master sahib and the kid who threw up during the long division test.

Taliban at the Door

For the last three years we have been living in Quetta, a city in the Hindu Kush Mountains near the Afghanistan border. I've just turned ten, and our family has recently moved from a sprawling suburban bungalow to a row house in the town. It's a cold October night in a new neighborhood, and an unfamiliar house. We sit down to dinner in the warm kitchen, when there's a loud knock at the door.

"Who's trying to spoil our dinner?" My mother is displeased. The servant is taking the lamb curry out from a pot on the stove, my father has already changed into his pajamas and robe, and my younger brother and sister are reaching for their favorite stools. I get up to check as a louder knock comes, and someone shouts, "Talibaaan!"

I unlatch the front door and in the dim streetlight see two boys standing at our door front, holding a large bowl. The younger one is about my age, has a ready smile on his face, and speaks first, "From the mosque," he points to a small-whitewashed building at the street corner with a rudimentary minaret. The elder one is in his teens, notices my puzzled face, and points a finger to his chest, "Talib."

COFFEE WITH CHICORY

I still have a blank look, so the younger one holds up the bowl, "For the food." I nod and turn around, leaving the door slightly ajar.

"Beggars, I think," I say upon returning to the kitchen, and I am immediately scolded by my mother. "Don't speak like that, they are religious students. Here, take this to them and ask for their blessing." Even if Taliban means religious students, I am not about to ask these two for any blessing. I hand over the plate full of rice and lamb curry to the older boy who transfers it to the bowl, which already has meat, vegetable and rice dishes, poured one on top of the other. They head back as I watch them putting pieces of lamb into their mouths, perhaps unsure of their share once they get to the mosque.

The next night it is the younger boy alone, and I ask, "What is your name?"

"Gul Hasan," he replies.

"Are you a Pathan?" I ask, though it's quite obvious from his baggy pants, long tunic-like shirt and a skullcap around which a turban could be tied, not to mention his ruddy cheeks, stout build and the accent.

"Pashtun," he corrects me.

I had said the word used by non-locals, "OK, Pashtun."

Gul Hasan comes on most nights at dinnertime and sometimes we have a chat. He is from a small village about thirty miles away. His family does not own

56

any land, so he is not needed to work in the orchards. His family wants him to get an education, but cannot afford to send him to the government-run school that requires him to pay for textbooks, school supplies, and a monthly tuition fee. An uncle brought him to the city and dropped him off at our neighborhood mosque. Here he is given a place to sleep, taught how to read the Koran, and gets to eat.

We've been in our new house about a month. Gul Hasan comes to collect the food one night and says, "Come and see me at the mosque."

I have yet to step into the mosque a block from our house. Like most families in Pakistan, we are 'cultural Muslims'. We celebrate the major festivals, and try to attend the Friday congregational prayers when we can.

Another month goes by before I enter the small white washed building. From the outside, the building appears to be a single room, with a tall column on the outside, intended as a minaret to signify a place of worship. If it was a real minaret, someone could climb up at prayer time to shout a call for prayer. Another telltale sign is the odd orientation of the building, pointing due west – toward Mecca. The city streets meanwhile are laid out in a grid at a slight skew from the prime directions and follow the topographical slopes between the two mountain ranges that skirt the valley.

Upon entering I notice that the building is divided into two unequal rooms with separate entrances. The larger of the two rooms is the prayer hall, its floor covered with mats woven with date palm fronds, and a stack of books in the right front corner. Toward the center of the front wall is a small archway for the *Imam* who would lead the prayers. The other, smaller room appears to be where all 4 or 5 of the Taliban live.

I spot Gul Hasan immediately, with a small broom in his hand dusting the prayer mats half-heartedly.

"Hey." I manage to draw his attention and he breaks into his ever-ready grin.

"Come in," he motions when I'm already inside the main room. He comes over and slaps me hard on the shoulder. I timidly punch him in the chest. "Are you done with your chores?"

"I am now." He hangs the broom on a hook in the left rear corner of the room. We walk out into the courtyard, and I throw him the soccer ball I have been holding. He stops it with his left foot, and with a naughty grin kicks it back to me hard, hitting me in the chest and breaking into laughter. Just then a bearded man comes out of the small room, and with a scowl on his face addresses Gul Hasan, "Have you done your lessons yet?"

"Yes," Gul Hasan does not sound very sure of himself and the man is unconvinced.

"Go in and repeat them," Gul Hasan looks at me helplessly, then walks into the prayer hall and picks up a book. I pick up my ball, turn around and leave.

Taliban at the Door

March is here and we are finally seeing some signs of spring. Also, this is the month during which my grandfather passed away about ten years ago. My mother is keen that we should not forget the dead, and likes to have some commemoration at his anniversary. The usual formula for families like ours is to have a reading of the entire Koran in one afternoon, followed by a dinner for friends and family. In our old house we could easily gather some relatives and acquaintances, but many of them live clear at the other end of town. They will probably all show up for the dinner in the evening, but we'll have difficulty in gathering enough people to finish the Koran in one afternoon.

And then my mother hits upon an idea, "Go to the mosque and talk to the *Imam* – the man who is in charge of the building. See if some of the Taliban can come and read the Koran." I am not too convinced that this will work, but reluctantly walk over to the *mosque* to deliver the message. To my surprise, their response is enthusiastic, and by mid afternoon, we have about ten Taliban sitting cross-legged on the Persian carpet in our living room. Each of them has a portion of the Holy Book in his hand, and is swaying back and forth and reading the Arabic text aloud.

I want to go out and play, but my mother reminds me of my duty to my grandfather, so I sit down with Gul Hasan and start reading. Neither I, nor anyone else in the room understands Arabic, but we are all reading it with reverent enthusiasm, some of us bordering on being emotional. We may not understand the meaning, but we all believe these are holy words. With a dozen people reading, and some of them very fluently, it takes us less than three hours to wrap up the entire text. The *Imam* says a short prayer to bless my grandfather's soul, mixing phrases from Arabic, Urdu, and some Pashto, but no one seems to mind. God must understand all languages.

Our two servants walk in with platters of rice, lamb and chicken, and the Taliban do complete justice to the meal. The meal is almost over when my dad returns from the clinic. That night all of the attendees enjoy sleep on a more than full stomach, and my mother is happy to have done something to bless my grandfather's soul.

A year goes by in our new house in Quetta. I have become familiar with our neighborhood, and go to the mosque a couple of times a week for the evening prayers. There are always a few religious students hanging around the mosque, reading the Koran, and doing some chores. They depend upon donations of food and cash from the neighborhood. They seem to just drift into the mosque, some staying for a few days, while others hang around for months, and then just fade away. Around religious holidays when the donations go up, their numbers swell up, and then slowly come back down when the donations dwindle. They seem to come from the poor villages in the province. Gul Hasan and a couple of others have been staying here more steadily through the year.

As happens almost every evening, tonight there is a knock on the front door and the familiar call from the street, "Talibaaan." I get up from my stool and carry the plate of food to the front door. It is Gul Hasan, holding the large bowl with both hands "I didn't see you last night." I say, handing over the plate. He puts the bowl down on our front steps. It is half full of food from the neighborhood. I recognize some potatoes, but everything else is mixed up. He starts to pour from our plate into the bowl. "Wait, wait. Taste it first. You like our food." He keeps pouring the rest of the plate into the bowl, and says, "I'm unhungry." I laugh. He says some strange words in Urdu, but I try not to make fun of him. I know even fewer words of his language, Pashto. Usually, he is in a hurry to get back to the mosque so they can all start eating, but today he lingers. I remember my half eaten dinner, and turn around to go in, "See you tomorrow."

"Wait," he says. He is struggling for words. "You a doctor?"

What is he talking about? There is confusion in his face. I think I know. He has seen me play with the other kids in the street. Some of them call me 'little doctor.'

"My father," I tell him, "He is a doctor."

His face lights up "Yes, yes."

"Are you sick?"

COFFEE WITH CHICORY

"No."

I hear my dad calling. "Well, then. Bye."

"My mother," he says, "sick."

"Where is she?"

"In village." The servant is probably coming out to look for me. "Come tomorrow morning. Talk to my father."

He nods, and I go in.

Everyone is done eating, and the servant is bringing fresh peaches out of the refrigerator.

"What took you so long?" my mother asks.

"Talking to Gul Hasan."

"Who?"

"One of the Taliban from the mosque. He came for food".

"He can talk?"

"Yes, he can talk. His mother is sick."

"OK, finish you dinner."

I hurry through my plate as my brother has already started eating the peaches.

The next day is Sunday. I am awake very early, and lying in bed, count the ceiling cracks – noticing a new one in the left corner. I hear the tinkling of English china teacups from my parent's bedroom. They are having bed tea. There is a knock on the front door. I hear the servant's footsteps across the inner courtyard, out to the front door, and then to my parents' bedroom. I hear my dad's voice, "Call him in." The servant crosses the court again, "He won't come in." I get out of bed. My dad finishes his tea, puts his robe on, and goes out, and I follow him. It is Gul Hasan, and he speaks in Pashto with my dad. I have watched my father have limited conversations with his patients about their ailments in half a dozen different local languages and dialects including Pashto.

My father comes in to the house and speaks to my mother. "I'll go and check the sick woman." "Check her? Where?" My mother has plans to go shopping I think.

"In the village."

"What village? Will they pay?"

"No, not likely." My father tells the servant to get the hot water ready in the bathroom.

"Do what you like." My mother gets back into bed.

"How about a Sunday drive?" my father asks.

"I am not going to any village," she says.

Did he say a drive? I go to my room and change.

An hour later, my dad, Gul Hasan, and I are in our new car, driving to his village. We are on the main road to the Afghan border and pass by many orchards. The mountains are getting closer. We cross two large streambeds, both dry. We get to the village, and stop along the main road. Kids come running and gather around the car.

Gul Hasan gets out. "I call uncle." Soon he returns with a rugged man wearing a turban, "My uncle."

COFFEE WITH CHICORY

The uncle's Urdu is a little more understandable, "Thank you doctor sahib," he says, "This way."

He assigns a teenager to stand by the car so the kids won't scratch the paint.

We follow Gul Hasan and his uncle on an uneven path between the homes. Some kids follow us, others stay around the car.

"You've given her some medicine?"

"Yes." The uncle hands a bottle to my father.

"Just aspirin?"

"Yes."

We get to the house. The walls are made of adobe, the same color as the earth around, just like most other houses we passed on the way.

"I'll examine the sick woman." My dad says to the uncle.

"Yes."

We follow him through the main door into the courtyard, and then across the courtyard into an inner room. The walls are painted white. There is no furniture in the room. The floor is covered with a deep red Afghan carpet woven with rough wool. We sit down. A rope has been stretched across the middle of the room like a clothesline. Three large white sheets hang from it, and we cannot see beyond the sheets into the other half of the room. My father opens his medical bag, takes out the stethoscope, and puts it around his neck. Gul Hasan and his uncle are also sitting with us. Several minutes go by. Nothing happens.

"Well?" my father says, "Where is she?"

"Here."

"Where?"

"In this room," the uncle points to the sheets hanging from the rope and dividing the room, "The other side, with my wife."

"How long has she been sick?" The uncle sticks his head around the white sheet, and asks in Pashto. I hear some whispering, and then one woman says something to the Uncle. His head appears on our side of the room. "One month," he says.

"Does she feel hot?" Again, the question is translated and sent around the curtain, there is whispering of female voices, an answer comes back, and is translated to us.

"How about her digestion?" "Digestion?"

"Can she eat OK?" The three-way dialog is translated back and forth between two languages and across two halves of the room for several minutes.

Then my father says, "I have to examine her?"

"Examine?"

"Yes".

Again, several minutes go by, but nothing happens.

"I am not here to give her a test in arithmetic. I have to examine her body."

"Her body?" the uncle is visibly alarmed.

My father is losing patience.

"With this." he holds up the stethoscope.

"Oh, the instrument," the uncle says, and pushes the end of the stethoscope under the white curtain.

COFFEE WITH CHICORY

My father sighs, moves closer to the white sheet, and holds the stethoscope up to his ears.

"On her chest," he instructs. "Breathe deeply." He listens. There is some shifting on the other side, accompanied by the sound of glass bangles, and deep breathing. "Again. Once more. Now on her back." My father listens to the stethoscope, and then puts it away, takes out a thermometer, and gives it to the uncle. "This end. Under her tongue." The thermometer disappears around the partition. After a couple of minutes my father says, "Give it back now." He reads it, shakes it, and puts it back in the antiseptic bottle. "Her pulse."

"My wife can check," the uncle says, and speaks to his wife. My father looks at his wristwatch, "Start counting; now," and after a few seconds, "Stop. How many?" The count is communicated to the uncle in a whisper in Pashto, and translated by him to us in Urdu. My father thinks for a couple of seconds, "Impossible. Her pulse cannot be 200. I'll check. Her hand." There is the sound of glass bangles again, and a hand emerges under the white drape, wrapped in a shawl. "No shawl." The shawl is pulled back, revealing a woman's fair hand with chapped skin. Her pulse is checked, and the hand withdrawn.

My father looks through the bag and takes out a syringe, "I have to give her an injection," he says, "a shot." There is the sound of some metal jewelry. This time the woman's hand as well as her arm comes out from under the sheet. It is fair, but very pale. After the shot, my father puts the syringe back and writes a prescription. "The pharmacy in the main bazaar. Go there." Then he hands a package of medicine sample to the uncle, "For today, with food." He starts closing the bag. A tray with pastries and small china bowls full of green tea is brought in. The pastries have a thick, red and green sugar glaze on them, and are very, very sweet. The tea is too hot for me to drink. My father and the uncle drink the tea and then we get up and walk back to the car.

The uncle has gone ahead, so Gul Hasan leads us back along the uneven path through the maze of houses, with the kids following us all the way back to our car parked along the main road. The uncle is already there, holding a rope tied around a goat's neck. "Doctor Sahib, please accept."

My dad laughs, "Do you see any room in the car?"

The uncle looks puzzled, and looks toward the back seat where he can see plenty of room. My dad is not about to ruin the back seat of his brand new 1954 Chevy Bell Aire with white-wall tires and two-tone paint – a pueblo tan body and a coral white roof.

"Don't worry," he says, "Your nephew is from our neighborhood," and shakes hands with the Uncle. Gul Hasan stays back, probably to look after his mother, and we drive back to the house. My mom is instructing the servant about lunch preparation.

"The shops are still open", my dad tells her.

She answers with a stare.

Baba-Ji

Returning home from school, I haul my bike up the front steps to park it in the entry hallway, then take the satchel full of books off the carrier mounted over the bike's rear wheel.

"I'm home," I announce to no one in particular, walk into my room and stuff the satchel in the desk. I think I want a snack before looking at the homework assignments.

The work is so much harder in the 8th grade compared to last year. I realize that this is the final year of middle school, and the teachers are preparing us for high school, but they don't have to kill us.

My mother is sitting in the dining room chatting with one of the ladies from the neighborhood, and catches a glimpse of me going toward the kitchen, so I greet her, but don't stop. Walking across the courtyard, I hear my mother saying, "Yes, yes, he practically came with my dowry". I know she is talking about Kasem, our live-in servant. I open the kitchen door, and see him sitting on a low stool in the corner of the kitchen.

"I need a snack, Kasem".

He holds his hand up, as if telling me to wait, and keeps sitting on the stool. I can see he is completely

COFFEE WITH CHICORY

engrossed in listening to my mother. He loves this story about how he came to live with us, and I can't expect him to do anything until my mother is done telling the story. I'll have to get my own snack.

"Did he work at your parents' house?" the visiting lady asks my mother.

"What work?" my mother says, "He was too young to work. His parents were sharecroppers on my uncle's lands, and left him at my parent's house in the city so he could learn some trade. While he lived with us he started helping out in the kitchen, and then refused to go and learn a trade in the rough workshops."

I start making a sandwich, and then turn to Kasem, "Can you help me?"

"Shhh," he holds up a finger across his lips to silence me, and points toward the dining room, as if to say, 'Just be quiet and listen'. I have not been paying attention, but now realize his favorite part of the story is coming up.

"So how did he agree to leave your parents' home and come with you to this faraway town?"

"My father re-married," my mother continues, and my step-mother treated him very badly."

I sigh and sit down next to Kasem on another stool, and we both listen. "He became very unhappy," she says, "and one day when my step-mother was scolding him about something or other, he did something drastic."

"What?" the lady asked with concern in her voice, "He didn't hit her, did he?"

"No, no," my mother sounds amused. "In fact, quite the opposite. He jumped out the third floor window into the street below."

"Oh my God."

This is the exclamation Kasem has been waiting for. His joy is now complete, so he gets up to help me, though his ears are still glued to the story.

"It was a row house, a five story walk up," my mother continues. I think she enjoys telling the story as much as he enjoys listening to it. "He is lucky," she says, "He not only survived the fall, but he also didn't get run over. We didn't have many motor vehicles in that street, but there were plenty of horse carriages, and some ran quite fast. He could have been crushed under the hoofs of a fast horse. He did break one arm and three ribs, and had to be hospitalized."

Kasem looks at me with a grin on his face, "Yes, yes, I have heard the story," I tell him, "and I'm trying to get a snack right now."

"Yes, I could have been crushed, but I didn't care. I wanted her to pay." He looks at me with a triumphant look in his eyes, "And I made her pay," he says, "I really made her pay."

"What are you blabbering", I cannot stand his idiotic glee anymore, "You jumped off the third floor window, you broke your arm, you broke three ribs, and nearly got killed. How did she have to pay?"

"Oh you don't know! So you don't know it all?"

"No, I don't know. What else is there?"

COFFEE WITH CHICORY

"You don't know about the hospital bills she paid? You obviously don't know about the three new undershirts."

"What undershirts?" I haven't heard this part before. "What about the undershirts?"

"The doctor told her to go and buy three new undershirts and sheared them with a pair of scissors. Right in front of her eyes. He then put them as padding around my ribs and put a cast around my chest. How do you think she felt then? It served her right."

I have heard stories of my step-grandmother's stinginess, and how she never threw anything away. During the five years he worked in her household, Kasem never got any new clothing, and even at festivals only got hand-me-downs. Buying three new undershirts would be painful enough for her, but then to see them sheared and sliced? He's right. He did hurt her plenty. The only way the doctor could be sure the padding was sterile was to ask for three brand new undershirts.

My mother is finishing up the story, "When he got back from the hospital, she did not want him in her house anymore, and that is how he ended up here."

Kasem is about ten years older than I am. Every morning he gets up early to get the fire going in the kitchen. My mother likes to cook on a hard coal fire.

"I don't like charcoal," she tells me. "It is not hot enough and it burns out so quick."

"Yes, *Ammi*," I nod my head in agreement. The hard coal fire from breakfast lasts well into late morning, giving her the chance to have a second and a third cup of tea before lunch.

Igniting the hard coal fire every morning is Kasem's duty. Today I am up early, so I go to the kitchen.

"It's so cold here, Kasem."

"Yes, yes, have a seat and just watch how it warms up," he says, cleaning last night's ashes out of the kitchen stove. Then he grabs two pages of an old newspaper, "This newspaper is old, right?" He asks me, since he cannot read or write. I nod, so he crumples up the newspaper, and stuffs it in the bottom of the stove. Next, he picks up an empty bucket lying next to the stove, and walks over to the small storeroom across the courtyard. A couple of minutes later he returns with a handful of kindling, and the bucket full of hard coal. The kindling we have is the best kind, split from old railroad sleepers. My dad works for the railroad, and they are always fixing the train track, taking out the old, decaying wooden sleepers that are literally falling apart but make great kindling.

I sit on the low stool rubbing my hands to keep warm as Kasem says to me, "Now watch how I make a bird's nest". He arranges the kindling on top of the crumpled newspaper in a loose trellis so hot air can rise up. Next, he carefully places lumps of coal in the stove, right on top of the kindling. The little stack of shiny pieces of hard coal is getting high, and I eagerly wait for

COFFEE WITH CHICORY

it to collapse, but nothing happens. Now we get to the part I have been waiting for.

"Remember Kasem, I get to light it."

"Yes, yes, I know," he says, and hands me the matchbox. I get off the low stool, squat down right next to the stove, light a match, bend down low, reach underneath the grate, and hold the flame up against the crumpled newspaper. The crackling starts within the paper, races up through the kindling, and reaches the lumps of coal. I watch the fire climb up from below the grate. There are many small gaps between the lumps in the stack of coal, and the smoke rises up through the openings. Now comes the hard work, so I move back. Kasem moves his stool next to the stove, and with the woven date-palm frond fan in his hands, he starts fanning below the grate, so air is pushed up through the stack of coal. The smoke rising up into the chimney becomes thicker, darker, and acrid; some of the coal lumps start to glow, and I scoot up close to the warmth.

Reaching home from school the next day I drag my bike up the front steps, dump it in the entry hallway, and holler, "Kasem, I want a French toast, fast." I don't hear any response, which is not like him. Maybe he has gone out for an errand. He knows I return from school at this time, so how can he just disappear. I don't care how sensitive he is, my mother is going to hear about this from me. I'm getting all worked up as I open the kitchen door. He is sitting right there on his low stool.

"Are you deaf, Kasem? And where is the French toast?" He does not move. I'm furious, "I'm going to tell my dad when he comes back from the hospital." He doesn't even lift his head up. Does he even know I am in the kitchen, and how urgent it is for me to have a French toast, without which I may never understand algebra? Obviously not. I go to the pantry, pick out the medium frying pan and hand it to him. He just sits there with the frying pan in his hand, looking at his sandals as if contemplating the latest footwear fashion. I shake his shoulder, "I said, French toast." He stands up, unusually erect. I never knew he was this tall. He then slowly lifts up his head. He is not looking at me, but past me. I look behind; there is nothing there, just the empty courtyard. He takes a step toward the kitchen door. I am standing in the way, and for the first time he turns his face and looks at me. I stagger back on my heels. Oh my God, what has happened to his eyes? They are glowing, as if his stare could drill a hole. I get out of the way, and have to lean on the cupboard to steady myself.

He walks out into the courtyard, and his shadow in the late afternoon sun makes him look even taller. He walks one step at a time, each time planting himself firmly on the ground. The frying pan is still in his hand. Halfway across the courtyard the pan slips out of his hand and falls on the concrete floor with a loud bang. He goes toward his room across the courtyard, while I remain frozen. He enters the room, door closes behind him, and there is a loud crash. I shout, "*Ammi,*" run out of the kitchen, hear the sound of her Singer machine, and enter her sewing room. "Look what you made me do." The embroidery in front of her has a crooked leaf. "What is the matter with you? You have to behave like a grown up now, not shout like a kid."

"It's, it's …." The words are stuck in my throat. She is looking at her embroidery, trying to figure out how much of it she will have to take apart. Her sister is visiting us, and she wants to show her this new design. "It's Kasem. Something has happened to him. Please come." I start tugging at her arm.

"OK, OK," she says, "Be patient." She gets up, puts her slippers on and follows me to Kasem's room.

I open the door. His bed is empty; he is lying on the floor, shivering, as if from a chill.

"Poor man is sick," my mother says, "Help me get him into the bed." We both try to lift him from his shoulders, but he shakes himself loose.

"No. We'll get up," he says in a low growl.

I look around to see who is speaking. This certainly is not Kasem's voice. He gets up slowly and climbs into bed.

"Blanket," he demands, again in a deep baritone, and this time I see his lips move.

My mother reaches over to the shelf, takes out a blanket, and we spread it on him, and after a few minutes he stops shivering, but still has a vacant look on his face, and his intense gaze is fixed on the ceiling.

"Perhaps we should let him rest," I say, and start to walk out, but as I am going by his bed, he reaches over and grabs my wrist hard, painfully hard, and says, "Lemonade, with sugar."

I look at my mother, "There are some lemons in the pantry. Squeeze some and make a pitcher, then take an ice cube tray from the fridge, and bring it here".

"Sugar," Kasem says in his deep bass voice.

"Yes," says my mother, "put lots of sugar and stir." Kasem lets go of my wrist. I walk out of the room, rubbing the deep marks of his grip. I do know how to make lemonade, and with lots of sugar. In fact that is the way my friends like it after soccer practice.

I pour sugar from the container sitting next to the teapot into the pitcher, slice open half a dozen lemons with the kitchen knife, and start squeezing them into the pitcher one by one, shaking each one to make sure the pulp ends up in the pitcher. Then I pour in some cold water, take a wooden ladle and stir, stir, stir – thinking about the French toast I could have been eating by now. I stop. Some of the lemonade has swirled out of the pitcher and on to the kitchen counter. I can't forget the French toast by stirring the lemonade; it is going to require other, drastic measures. I take a tray of ice cubes out of the refrigerator, and put it in the sink for it to warm up a little so I can pry the cubes out of the tray. Standing on my toes, I reach the upper shelf of the pantry. My mother thinks that none of us four brothers and sisters can reach the top shelf, but actually I am now tall enough, and know where the imported English cookies are kept – my favorites, with the impression of a tennis racket embossed on each cookie. I reach up, but before I can quite grab the carton, it falls to the floor with a thud. I freeze. These cookies are fragile, and probably all broken now. But that may actually be good. No one can tell now if a couple of them are missing. I carefully open one side of the carton, taking care to leave most of the glue intact, and slide out pieces of approximately three cookies. Or perhaps four, there is no way to tell.

"Is the lemonade ready?" I hear my mother calling from across the courtyard, and I yell back, "Yesss" – and two pieces of the cookie fly out of my mouth.

I drop the tray full of cubes into the pitcher, stir it one last time, and hurry out of the kitchen; spilling only a little in the courtyard. As I approach Kasem's room, I hear the deep baritone voice, almost as if someone is reciting an incantation. The sound of that voice sends a chill up my spine. I slow down, open the door carefully and enter the room with the pitcher of lemonade in my right hand, and a large tumbler in my left hand. There is silence in the room. Kasem is sitting up on the bed, holding out his hand without looking at me. I fill the large tumbler, hand it to him, and he empties it in one breath. He hands the glass back to me, without looking in my direction, and starts talking, as if in verse. I have heard storytellers in small villages speak in this manner, but they are very alert and attentive, make lots of eye contact with those gathered around them, and keep people amused with hand gestures and facial expressions. Here there are no hand gestures, no facial expressions, and absolutely no entertainment, the whole atmosphere is eerie.

"Go call your Aunty Rezi," my mother says without looking at me. Thank God her voice sounds normal, and her facial expression is not frozen. I look at her again. She is just being attentive. I am glad to get out, and go to my aunt's room; her door is open and she is getting up from her prayer rug. I go inside. She is often praying, meditating with string of beads between her fingers, or talking about her dreams. Yesterday after her afternoon nap, she told us that her mother who died ten years ago came to visit her. Some people say she's very religious, some say that she's in contact with the spirits, while others say that she's losing her mind due to the prolonged absence of her husband who works at a British base in Cyprus. She looks up at me, "How was school?"

"School?" I almost forgot I went to school today, and my heart sinks with the thought of algebra homework.

"Are you going out to play?" Aunty Rezi asks. Suddenly I remember why I am in her room and shake my head, "Ammi wants to see you right away." "OK," she says with a hint of concern in her voice, as if she can sense my confusion, "Where is she?" "In Kasem's room." She puts her slippers on, and walks out. I go into my room to look at the homework. About five minutes go

COFFEE WITH CHICORY

by, I am sitting down at my desk, when I hear my mother call my name. I sigh and shout, "Coming."

I approach Kasem's room with trepidation, and the feeling of awe and dread returns, as if a force field surrounds the room. I see my aunt having a conversation with Kasem. Her voice is normal, but she is also using the singsong, half-prose, half-verse style of speech. Within moments I am again taken in by the atmosphere. Why was I thinking that what is going on in this room is in any way trivial? How could I not see that there is a presence here that is somehow holy, and the conversation utterly important? "Sit here and keep your aunt company". I snap out of it again. My mother gets up and points to the low stool she has been sitting on. I gingerly take the seat; it doesn't seem I have any choice.

I am unable to understand the conversation, but there is enough interrogative intonation in her sentences that I can tell she is asking questions. Kasem is maintaining his authoritative tone; very flat, but deep throated and almost like a chant. I am surprised that he has the vocal chords for such a low tone.

I remember accompanying my mother to a saint's tomb built above a stream bank at the edge of town. There we saw a man sitting in the back of the mausoleum, wearing a robe and lots of beads, and chanting in a very low tone. Apparently he was the caretaker of the tomb. We waited till he finished his chant, then my mother chatted with him for a few minutes while I waited. I could hear their conversation, and the caretaker spoke in the same baritone, which must be his normal voice. I have known Kasem for over five years, and I know this is not his normal voice. He often does humorous imitations and mock voices, but those are always high-pitched and almost feminine.

I keep sitting, listening, and waiting for my mother to return so I can leave this room and go back to worrying about algebra. After a while my aunt leaves the stool and sits down on a pillow cushion right on the floor, near Kasem's cot. I am unsure why she is doing this. Does she want to be able to hear him better? Is she feeling so much reverence for the person he has transformed into that she feels her seat should be lower than his cot? Her facial expression is also becoming a little vacant, as if she is being absorbed into the atmosphere that is prevailing in the room. He is not even looking at her, and is gazing at the ceiling, but her gaze has not wavered from his face. I have to keep looking away and not focus on his face, for fear of being drawn into the whole atmosphere. Just sitting in the room is difficult enough.

My aunt turns to me, and asks in her normal tone of voice, "Can you please bring me a glass of water?" "Sure," I say, and gladly get up to leave. As I am walking out, Kasem raises his head, and says, "Cookies," startling me. "What?" He does not answer me, but my aunt elaborates, "Bring a plate of cookies." I nod; go to the kitchen to see that my mother has just finished making tea. She looks at me quizzically. "Auntie wants a glass of water," I explain, and open the cupboard to get a glass tumbler. My mother has managed to fit a teapot, three cups, saucers, a strainer, sugar, cream and some teaspoons, all on a small tray. "She also wants me to bring cookies in a plate," saying this before I reach for cookies on the upper shelf. My mother raises her eyebrows, "For herself?" My mother finds it hard to believe that her sister has suddenly developed a desire for cookies. "No," I don't know how to refer to Kasem.

"For Baba-Ji then?" My mother asks. 'Baba-Ji' is a title of reverence for an old man. I remember that is how everyone refers to the saint whose tomb is above the stream bank at the edge of town. Is she implying a connection between the holy man who died over 100 years ago, and the deep-throated voice that Kasem has acquired this afternoon? Does she think that Kasem's body is somehow possessed, if that is the right word, by a good spirit, perhaps the ghost of the long-dead saint buried in the mausoleum?

I take the plate of cookies and go back to Kasem's room with my mother. She puts the tray of tea and the cookies on the side table, makes three cups of tea, hands one to Aunt Rezi, one to Kasem who is sitting up in his bed, and passes the plate of cookies around. I wait for my turn to get a cookie. Kasem finishes his cup of tea. My ears are slowly becoming used to his baritone, rhythmic speech.

"We see many places," he says in a slow drawl, "A blessed house. Yes, a blessed house. Blessed things." My mother is ready with a pen and paper. Aunt Rezi sips her tea.

"Baba-Ji, what is my future," Rezi wants to know.

Kasem looks at her, doesn't blink his eyes, and speaks.

"What do you want to know?"

"When will my husband return?"

Kasem keeps looking at her, as if trying to read the answer in her face. He then lifts his face toward the ceiling, and starts reciting a Punjabi folk song. I have heard this one before.

"Oh, how the times have changed.

Oh, how we have changed.

Where are those faces now?

Faces so dear to us.

Faces we couldn't live without. Oh those faces.

Faces we no longer remember. Faces we couldn't live without.

Oh, how the times have changed. Oh, how we have changed."

My mother and I sit there staring at Kasem. His rendition of the folk song isn't half bad. Actually, in his deep baritone it sounds rather good. Aunt Rezi is still waiting for an answer. Kasem quietly looks at the ceiling, so she repeats her question, "Baba-Ji, when will my husband be home?"

COFFEE WITH CHICORY

Kasem's eyes remain focused on the ceiling, and he says, "Look into your heart. Look very closely," looking at her, he says, "Do you want him home?"

Aunt Rezi's husband has been working at the British military base in Cyprus for the last several years. We know him to be stingy and mean, and Aunt Rezi is never happy when he is around, and everyone in the family pities her. Several minutes go by, and she finally breaks the silence in the room, "Yes, I do want him home."

Kasem turns his head and looks at her, "Night of new moon, every new moon, feed one needy family, and before the 12th moon, he will be home." My mother writes it down. She does not want aunty to forget about the night of the new moon, and about feeding the needy family.

I grab the last cookie, go to my room, and sit staring at the homework. I hear my dad's car, and go out to greet him. Not seeing Kasem, he asks me, "Where is Kasem?"

"He is in his room".

"Is the dinner ready?" is his next question.

I hesitate. "Kasem is not feeling well".

"I see," my dad says with his air of confidence, and goes in to change. As a doctor, he should be able to fix whatever ails Kasem.

With the sound of my dad's car, my mother comes out, goes into their bedroom, and shuts the door behind her. I hear their voices, but cannot understand the conversation. A short while later she comes out, sees me standing in the courtyard, "Bring your algebra homework so dad can help you," and heads toward the kitchen. I stand there scratching my head and thinking since when did she start taking an interest in my homework. Approaching the kitchen door she looks back. I have not moved. "Hurry up, dinner will be ready soon," and goes into the kitchen. I pause there, wondering what kind of quick dinner are we going to get.

I get my homework, and sit down with my dad in their bedroom. The four algebra problems holding up our dinner don't not take us very long to finish. As we approach the kitchen, my mother comes out, "The dinner is on the table," she says, "and I am going to check on Rezi," as she heads toward Kasem's room. We go in. It seems she boiled some eggs and has made egg salad sandwiches, the kind we usually take for picnics. We finish the sandwiches with help from a jar of mango chutney. With my homework done, I go to my room and turn on the radio. A play is being broadcast in which a Mogul prince falls in love with one of the maids in the palace. Listening, I fall sleep.

The next morning at breakfast I don't see Kasem. My dad has already left. He'll probably get breakfast at the hospital cafeteria. Aunt Rezi gets up and makes breakfast for us brothers and sisters and we go to school. By evening Kasem is back to normal.

Over the weeks and months I hear my mother recount details to other women in the neighborhood.

COFFEE WITH CHICORY

Almost a year goes by. I come home from school and see several women in the house. Some are from the neighborhood, and others I have never seen before. Half a dozen of the women are huddled in Kasem's room, while two are in the kitchen making tea, and three or four are talking in the courtyard in hushed tones. Then I hear the deep baritone singsong voice and realize that Baba-Ji, the saint that died over one hundred years ago, is visiting again, or at least his spirit is. I am pretty much ignored. There are enough eager volunteers for making tea and fetching cookies. The session goes well into the evening. Somehow we get fed and I go to school the next day. It takes me several days to piece together the events by overhearing snippets of conversation. Many of the women asked questions, received direct answers; each was assigned a different act of continuing charity. Other women also asked questions, but did not get an answer.

After that, every one to two years we get these visitations, attracting many women, and turning our house for the evening into a crowded revival meeting. After high school I enter college in another town, and don't hear anything further. During one visit from college I find out that Kasem has left, moved back to his native village, and gotten married. A couple of years later we hear about his divorce, and then he moves to another village to live with his nephew. Nothing further is heard of him.

Baba-Ji

Our town has grown around the tomb of Baba-Ji, the long-dead saint, and his grave is no longer in the wilderness at the edge of town, but is surrounded by homes and shops. My mother continues to go to visit the grave, and speak with the caretaker. He is old, and does not hear very well. His son is taking over the caretaker's duties. My mother does not feel the satisfaction she once did. And she misses having a direct conversation with the living voice of a long-dead saint.

Soccer Match

To get to the bare-dirt empty lot, I have to walk through a narrow gap between two row houses, and then pass under the torn fence. Several boys from the neighborhood are already there, some busy playing marbles, but most are waiting and getting anxious.

"How long does it take to get a puncture fixed?"

"One bicycle shop is just around the corner, why didn't he just go there?"

"It's not just the inner rubber bladder that has a leak, the outer leather cover is also torn."

"Walie must be at the cobbler, getting the leather cover re-stitched."

"Then Rasheed is at the bicycle shop, probably waiting for the puncture patch on the rubber bladder to dry out."

Just as a couple of the boys are about to give up and leave, both Rasheed and Walie show up, bouncing the newly repaired football, and loud cheers go up. Rasheed waves his hand and we fall into line, more or less according to height. Walie stands in front, and motions to the group, and the tallest boy steps forward, with the next taller one stepping back. Going down the line, we are quickly separated into two teams.

COFFEE WITH CHICORY

Rasheed starts the shoe inspection, and only a couple of the two dozen boys are wearing proper soccer shoes with cleats. Three have hiking boots and several others have light sneakers on, enough to get by for a friendly match. But four boys have flip-flops, and two Pashtun boys have showed up bare foot. Rasheed looks at Walie, "It's going to be a bare-foot game today," and I flinch. During last Sunday's match I twisted my right big toe – though several boys have tried to tell me how I kicked the ball wrong.

"Everyone. Check the ground," Walie says in a commanding voice, and we fan out across the lot – our eyes focused on the ground. I spot a piece of glass and pick it up. Two boys find sharp pieces of metal, while others have gathered up rocks, trash, and some sharp objects of uncertain origin. "That's it, everybody shoes off." One Baloch boy is wearing light sandal with soles made of worn out automobile tires, "My sandals are very light," he says, but to no avail, and with a groan he removes them. Soon all the shoes are piled up against one side of the playground against the back wall of a fruit canning business. We split up into two teams, and Rasheed takes his team to the other end of the playground.

"Watch me," Walie calls his team to attention, reminding us how to control the football with bare feet. "Never use your toes." I feel he is talking to me, "You'll sprain your foot." He flips the ball up with his toes and it seems he can roll his foot around it while it is in the air, "See, you can feel the ball much better barefoot. "Use the top of your inner arch to kick." He taps three fingers on top of his foot, and then bounces the ball a couple of times. "This is the power spot." A couple of us try to feel the spot above our own feet – it does feel solid. He rolls the ball toward himself with the sole of his right foot, then flips it up chest high. As the ball is falling downward he kicks it with the top of his inner arch, and using the sweet spot, kick it. The ball catches the sweet spot and sails clear across to the other end of the playground. The other team is listening to a pep talk from their captain, Rasheed, who has just assigned their positions on the playground. A Pashtun boy on their team is alert enough to stop the ball from bouncing out to the busy road and kicks it back, and somewhat inadvertently, the match begins.

For the first several minutes of play, the ball doesn't leave the center of the field. Then the Pashtun boy on Rasheed's team mounts an attack single-handedly into our half of the field, dribbles past three of our players before we realize what is going on, and two of us rush toward him. He dodges around the first player easily by swerving sharply to the left and continues to get closer to our goal.

Rasheed is shouting instructions, "Get up there, help him, to the left, to the left, watch on your right." Two of his teammates are running up, and pretty soon will be able to cover their lone striker's flanks. This is our last

COFFEE WITH CHICORY

chance. Our goalie is staying close to the left goalpost, afraid that if he comes up, the ball may go around him.

"Stop him, stop him," some of our players are yelling, but who are they talking to? We have only one defender left between the attacker and our goalie, but – oh no, it is the fat kid. I don't know his name, apparently the others don't either, or they don't remember it, or they cannot pronounce it. His family has recently migrated across the border from India. He is too slow to outmaneuver the attacker, but he starts ambling in that direction. He took his hiking boots off earlier, as this is a barefoot game, otherwise he could have at least kicked the Pashtun boy in the shin. He tries to maneuver, but he is too slow, "Stop him, stop the goal kick," says our captain, Walie. The fat boy looks at Walie with a pitiful face, but Walie motions him forward. As the attacker draws his leg back to deliver the final blow to the ball, the fat kid throws himself across the attacker's legs. Our guy may be slow, but he is not lacking in sheer mass. The attacker stumbles, his foot misses the ball, and he tumbles across the fat kid with a loud curse. The ball rolls toward our goalie who has no trouble stopping it.

"Is he OK?" Walie runs toward the fat kid, who is still on the ground, clutching his side and trying to control his moans. Apparently he caught the full force of the kick in his ribs. "It can't be that bad, it was only a barefoot kick." A couple of players help the kid get up, tears are rolling down his cheeks, and he is squirming with pain, still clutching his right side,

Soccer Match

"You did well, kid, look, you stopped the goal, a goal this early? We would have lost without you," says Walie, and pats him on the back. "And just look, you did some damage." He is pointing to the Pashtun boy who is sitting on the ground rubbing his right foot. He has twisted his big toe, and won't be able to kick the ball so hard for a while. A smile breaks across the fat kid's face, as he is lead to one side of the field. He sits to watch the game, while continuing to hold his ribs.

The game picks up again, and this time our side is mounting an attack. Our three strikers are passing the ball back and forth, as they move across the field. One of them kicks the ball, and an opposing defender tries to stop it on his chest, misses, so he reaches out with his hand and stops the ball.

"Hand ball, hand ball," our teams is shouting, and the play stops.

"No, no, nobody touched it," Rasheed says. Walie has to step in. There is an argument, but it does not last long, and our team gets a free kick, but we are still far from their goal, and their goalkeeper easily stops the ball.

"Time out, time out", one of the boys on our team shouts, and the game is stopped again.

"Mom is looking for you", his younger sister yells. She is standing at the edge of the field, wearing as stern an expression as she can manage. He leaves, causing one big hole in our forward attack group. A strong lefty, he is perfect for the left forward position.

COFFEE WITH CHICORY

At home, we are not allowed to eat with our left hand, everyone knows the left hand is reserved for use in the toilet, and at school we are not allowed to write with the left.

"Don't be naughty," the teacher would say, emphasizing his meaning with a stroke of his cane. Everyone understands that the only reason any kid would hold a pencil in the left hand is to annoy an adult, and the normal behavior for everyone is to be right-handed. The enforcement continues at school and home until every kids adapts to the right hand. But there is no scrutiny on the playground, and the strongly inclined lefties thrive, making shots that the opponents never anticipate.

"Move up, move up," Walie seems to be pointing to me, and I have to stop day dreaming "Me?" I am overjoyed to be allowed to play as one of the strikers, even if it is the left forward position. I am genuinely right-handed, and Walie knows that. "Don't try to kick into the goal, just pass it back," he tells me. I am always willing to play the left forward position, just to be able to get into the limelight, and even if I am unable to mount an effective attack on my own, I can pass the ball back to the two other forwards, keeping the ball in play and allowing them to make attempts at the goal.

Rasheed's team sends two or three other lone attackers, but we are able to hold them off, and everyone is getting tired when half time is called. A couple of the boys come with me to our house to help me carry two pitcher of cold water and two glasses, one set for each team. One boy fills the glass and hands it to the next, who drains it empty. The glass is filled each time and handed to the players one by one. Some kids wipe the edge of the glass with their fingers before taking a drink, while others make a rinsing gesture with a few drops of water, but no one seems to mind sharing the glass and everyone is able to cool off.

In this hillside town with short summers and very cool fall, winter and spring, refrigerators are still considered a luxury, and ours is one of only two on the entire street. Our refrigerator was delivered last year, a gleaming white GM Frigidaire. I remember my dad had to deposit the full price at the dealer and then we had to wait for over six months for delivery, as the refrigerator would only be shipped after the money had been received in the States. I used to accompany my dad on his weekly trips to the appliance store to check when our refrigerator would arrive.

Before we got our machine, life was different. All of us brothers and sisters loved Jell-O, so before going to sleep on particularly cold winter nights we would mix Jell-O crystals in boiling hot water in a mold. My mother would add fresh fruit to make it nutritious. Our servant would then cover the mold and leave it out in the courtyard. In the frosty mornings in the warm kitchen, wearing our jackets and mittens, all four of us would be sitting, eating spoonfuls of Jell-O for breakfast, and giggling with delight.

COFFEE WITH CHICORY

Half time has ended, and the game resumes.

"Don't just try to score on your own, try to help each other, pass the ball to your teammates," Walie tells us. We are beginning to play like a team, and are able to neutralize the three Pashtun boys from the opposing team who mount lone intrepid attacks. Our pass play is working, and we are exchanging passes as well has verbal signals. One kick from our midfield players gets through, and two of our forwards are moving the ball toward the goal.

"Get him, stop him, no not that one, on the other side, behind you," Rasheed directs his defenders, but our strikers are able to evade them. We are mounting an attack from the right side of the field, I am running up along the left side guarding our flank, and finally one stray pass comes my way. I'm tempted, but a kick from my left foot could go anywhere, so I deflect the ball back to one of the other two forwards. After a while our center striker is about to take a clean shot at their goal, one of their defenders comes and interferes with his hand, and then quickly thrusts his chest forward, but we're not fooled.

"Foul, foul," several of our players shout, "Penalty, Penalty."

Our striker is furious, and goes up to the opposing player, "What are you doing using your hands, I was about to take a clean shot." The opposing team is looking at their player; he has to make a credible pretense.

"I did not touch the ball, I stopped it on my chest, are you blind?"

Our player does not calm down, "Liar, everyone saw what you did, and your sister is a whore." We all know that the defender does not have a sister, but the insult is still valid, and he defends his family's honor with a reference to our player's mother and her reproductive organs. Everyone does have a mother, and the only appropriate response is a punch to the jaw. The defender responds with an elbow to the ribs and grabs our player's arm, twisting it behind his back. But our guy comes free, wraps his arms around the defenders' waist, wrestles him down, and now both are on the ground, kicking, punching, and shouting obscenities about the female members of each other's immediate family.

The boys on the playground have five or six different mother tongues, and although the ordinary, day-to-day communication is in the common vernacular, Urdu, during a fistfight everyone reverts to the mother tongue, displaying the cultural diversity at a fundamental level. The Punjabi obscenities mostly make references to sexual acts that have already been committed by the opponent's female relatives in the past, generally with unspecified partners, while the Sindhi speakers accuse their antagonists of convoluted incestuous relationships. The Pashtuns are the only ones who express their intentions to commit sexual acts upon male members of their opponents' family, enhancing the belief that they are descended from Alexander the Great's Greek army. The Brahwhis are the closest thing to the aborigines, being related to the Dravidians, the pre-Aryan inhabitants of the Indian sub-continent, and they add references to acts performed between male animals and the opponent's female relatives. There is no Baloch kid playing with us today. Their language is derived from Persian, and their cursing sounds almost poetic. Most of the kids have only a passing knowledge of each other's language, but all are fully conversant in multilingual obscenities.

Then there are the boys whose families have recently immigrated from India due to the partition, with Urdu as their mother tongue. People refer to them as 'refugees,' or sometimes as *'Hindustanis,'* after the name by which they refer to the country they left behind – not India, but *Hindustan.* They are very articulate, and most of us cannot differentiate between their taunts and their obscenities, which leaves us speechless. In some such cases, the only honorable response is a fist to their mid section.

Although each team initially encourages the fight, the two captains soon step in and separate the two boys, one of whom has a bleeding lip, and the other a torn, bloodstained shirt. After a joint interrogation of the two kids, and unsolicited testimony from everyone else on the field, Rasheed reluctantly concedes a penalty kick to our team. We select our strong full back, who is able to blast a kick through their goal, and we are finally on the scoreboard. With our half-time break, interruptions, arguments, and time outs, the game has been on for over two hours, and it is getting close to lunch. Some more boys are being called home, but we are able to continue with substitutes. The Pashtun boys are tireless, and now as everyone else is exhausted, their solo forays are getting closer and closer to our goal. Another one of them breaks through.

"Stop him, get in his way, you over there."

Walie is getting hoarse, but our defenders are too tired, and a kick by the Pashtun boy sails through our makeshift goals, evening out the score. The game continues for another ten minutes or so, but we have lost several players by now, and the rest are too tired to cover the field, so the game is called off, a draw, like many other soccer matches, and equally satisfying.

A Day with Guests

School is over for the day, and my friend Ali and I are walking over to his house on the eastern side of Quetta. We are both in sixth grade, where we met at the beginning of the school year. We cross the city park adjacent to our school, and start walking along the road leading toward the eastern foothills. The road climbs up gradually. We walk between stores through a business district, and then enter streets lined with row houses. There is very little vehicular traffic, but many pedestrians are walking on both sides of the road with facial features that resemble Mongols, or Tibetans – short noses, round faces and oriental eyes, just like my friend. There are no Mongols or Tibetans living in our town of Quetta, which means we're entering the Hazara Colony, which is something of an ethnic ghetto. Hazaras are not native to this area, and have migrated from Afghanistan during the last few decades. In this neighborhood I only hear what sounds like a version of the Persian language that the Hazaras brought with them from Afghanistan.

We walk by tough-looking teenage boys standing on a street corner, chatting. A couple of them are looking us over, and Ali can sense my anxiety. He waves to one of them, who greets him by name, and the others turn away.

"So you also believe that Hazara are descended from Genghis Khan's armies?" Ali asks me. I stammer, and he laughs, "Just relax, you're with me, no one will bother you."

Soon we are at his doorstep, and I realize I am stepping into a Hazara household for the first time. We walk into the sitting room, and he disappears behind the door leading into the house.

It is a simple room with a Persian carpet that stretches to the four corners. There are several large, reclining pillows along the walls. The only furniture in the room is a small corner table. Hanging on one wall are two large framed prints, a still life of a bowl of fresh fruit, and a scenic landscape of a meadow, with a mountain and a waterfall in the background. I remove my shoes and sit down on the carpet. Everything in the room appears to have been selected and displayed in a simple yet pleasing and aesthetic manner.

The door opens and Ali enters carrying a tray, "I hope you like almond cookies." On the tray is a plate full of cookies, two apples, a teapot and two small bowls. He puts down the tray on the corner table, and pours the tea into the bowls.

"Watch out, it's hot."

I bite into a cookie, "This is delicious, where do you get these?" "Oh, we have a Hazara bakery down the street."

A Day with Guests

It must be a very local bakery, because I have never tasted such cookies. The tea already has milk and sugar in it, and it is very sweet. We sit down, and chat about the other kids in school, about our favorite teacher, what movies we saw last, and about the Hazaras.

"How long has your family lived here?" I ask.

"Well, my grandfather came here from Afghanistan in the 1930's".

"Why did they move?" He looks at me and realizes I really don't know, "There was a revolution, the king was assassinated, and many people left."

This reinforces my view of neighboring Afghanistan as a country in frequent turmoil, and I change the subject. The apples are eaten last, and throughout the afternoon we are surrounded by the order and calm that prevails in the house. It's getting late now, and time for me to head back home.

Ali walks back with me part of the way, I think just to accompany me through the Hazara colony, but we don't see any unruly teenagers, and as we approach the business district he turns back as I continue toward my house, recalling and savoring the aesthetics and the order I sensed in his house.

As I approach our house, I'm reminded that in our freewheeling Punjabi household, order is something that has to be imposed with a strong will, and is ephemeral. As I enter the house I hear my kid brother's voice, "How come I am always the last one to find out these things?" Apparently, we are expecting visitors; so he is not allowed into the street for fear that he'll get his hands and clothes dirty playing marbles. I can see his right pocket bulging with marbles, and the way he keeps glancing at the closed front door; his buddies must be waiting for him outside. He moans and complains for a while, but then resigns himself and sits down.

With the news about the guests our house shifts into preparations for a military campaign. The first order of business is to put the drawing room back in order so the guests can be seated upon arrival, then the rest of the house will be tackled. The servant is being called from three different directions.

"Where are the matching pillow cushions for this sofa?"

"Here, in my bedroom," comes the answer from my sister.

"Why is the dining table wobbly, what happened to its leg?" One of the legs on our dining table is a little short, and a wooden peg has been fitted under it to keep it from rocking. But this peg is always being borrowed for use as a game piece in one board game or another, because everyone agrees that it is a lucky piece. Even on the rare days when we can find the entire set of monopoly, or snakes and ladders, or Ludo, whoever starts losing simply goes and removes this piece from the dining table leg, hoping for a change in fortunes.

"Here, take this table away," calls my uncle, who came to visit several months ago but never left, and now seems to have taken up residence at our house. It appears he had taken one of the end tables from the drawing room into his bedroom for use as a nightstand to place the glass of milk he drinks every night before sleeping.

"Where is the second end table?"

These must be really important visitors, for most guests we can get by with only one end table. One of my cousins goes and finds the table on the front lawn, where it was used as a footstool by someone who took a nap in the sun yesterday afternoon.

We are running in all directions, and slowly everything is coming together. The good tablecloths have been placed on the tables. The framed pictures above the fireplace are now oriented to catch the best light. The hat stand mirror in the hallway gets back its crocheted cover, which was used as a book wrap during the Koran reading two weeks ago. All mirrors in our house are kept covered with sheer fabrics or open-patterned crocheted curtains; I forget whether it is to ward off the evil eye or to guard against ghosts, or perhaps it is bad luck to accidentally see your own image.

Everything comes together just as the cars are entering the driveway. Two of my dad's doctor colleagues from the hospital, and one gazetted officer from the railroad arrive with their wives. This means the tea

COFFEE WITH CHICORY

will be served British style, in an English china teapot with a tea cozy, and sugar and cream served on the side, to taste. The pastries, including chicken patties, are from the best bakery in town – no local Indian, or rather Pakistani sweets tonight. Our new country with a new name was formed only three years ago and many people are still not comfortable referring to themselves with the new nationality. Our history textbook begins with the War of Roses and ends with Lord Mountbatten, the British Viceroy. India is a country the British liberated from the Moguls, and transformed into a civilized place, the books tell us.

The tea and refreshments for the guests will not be carried on a tray, but rolled in on a serving trolley, and the glasses of lemonade will be covered with small round covers made of crochet with beads hanging from the edges. Also, there will be lots of leftovers for everyone. Most of the conversation at the table will be in English, using its British colonial version.

My mother sits down with the ladies on one side of the drawing room to plan the next charity bazaar, "Yes, definitely, we should include an auction in the program," says Mrs. Malik. The other ladies nod, and my mother says, "We have to change the food vendor, last year's *samosas* brought so many complaints." The men are congregated on the other side of the large drawing room, and Mr. Malik, the railroad executive, is full of official news, unofficially, "Doc, do you know that General Kabeer is being relieved?" My father shakes his head, "I didn't know, so who is replacing him?"

There are no children with the guests, so after making the obligatory appearance and paying our respects, we go to another room and get into a hot game of snakes and ladders. We are all keeping an eye on the situation, so that as soon the guests are done with eating and there is a smoking break, the lucky game piece can be borrowed again from the dining table.

It is late evening when the gathering breaks up. The guests leave, and soon I am stuffed full of chicken patties. I am reminded of the time last month when my dad's second cousin came to visit us from their native village, wearing modest clothing, arriving on foot after walking from the railroad station. The preparations to receive him barely caused a perturbation in the household routine, and things were so relaxed that dinner had already started when my mother noticed the wobbly dining table. I was sent to look for the missing wooden peg which was fitted to the table leg as our guest watched, hanging on to his dinner plate. The absence of the matching pillow cushion was simply camouflaged by rearranging the other pillows.

Our family's social circle is very broad, and our parents are at ease when interacting with everyone from aristocracy to poor rural relatives. Our family's breadth of social adjustment also means that the house never achieves a static décor, and the appearance is adjusted to every occasion, leading to a feeling of chaos and disorder. There are some prized possessions in the house – the dining table for which the table top was carved out of a single large trunk of rosewood, the mahogany chest of drawers and the teak furniture set, all are like islands in a sea of chaos. I realize how different our living style is from the Hazara household, where esthetics are a part of the décor, and the circle of acquaintances is narrow enough that so static an order can be preserved.

Hanna Lake

"DID YOU say Hanna Lake?" I want to be sure I am hearing him right. It is noisy inside the cafe. "Yes, Hanna Lake," Zalmay repeats.

We are one block from the main entrance to the only college in town. The town is on the crossroads that lead to the rivers and plains of India to the south, the deserts of Iran to the west, and the mountains of Afghanistan to the north. The cafes and teashops frequented by the young change with the fashions, and this one happens to be the 'in' place of the moment. The college students hang out here early in the morning, between classes, and after the school is over; and both of us have logged plenty of hours.

"And how do you propose that we get up there?" I have to ask, as neither of us has a car.

"I have a plan," Zalmay looks more cocky than his usual blustery self, "I always have a plan."

"Well, let me hear it. And by the way, I refuse to ride a bike for sixteen miles on a gravel road." I take a sip of tea, "all uphill, mind you."

I look around at the other customers, who are all college students. This café used to be an unnamed tea-shop where horse carriage drivers and pushcart vendors would stop by for a snack. As more and more college students came, the usual customers were driven away. The Iranian restaurant owner seamlessly adopted a new business model, changed the furniture to look like a college café, and named the place 'College Restaurant'. The walls still have photographs of the religious shrines and prints of imaginary, impossibly romantic wilderness scenes with shafts of light, all remnants of the working class teashop days. Added to them are the movie posters from Bombay and Hollywood. A big change is in music. Gone are the woeful Pashto ballads and the Persian poems praising the minor saints, replaced entirely by movie songs and sound tracks from Bombay and Hollywood.

"You are so negative," Zalmay looks offended, but the glint in his eye gets brighter, and a smile breaks out from the corner of his mouth.

"Go ahead, spill it out," I say to him.

He can't hold it in any longer, and bursts into laughter, "Come outside, I'll show you something."

"I am still drinking my tea. Tell it to me right here."

"I have borrowed my brother's jeep."

This is preposterous. Zalmay's older brother, the Pashtun homeland revolutionary, would never, ever lend his jeep to a wasteful, decadent, college kid. "You are pulling my leg. He actually lent the jeep to you?"

This is 1955, and though the British left India eight years ago in 1947, Zalmay's family never got off the government's watch list. During the British colonial rule his father was a staunch nationalist and a follower of Gandhi, though he modified the non-violence doctrine a bit to suit the Pashtun martial spirit, "Being non-violent does not mean being weak." After the British left, the new government maintained the same surveillance list that had been used in colonial times. Zalmay's father is now old and in poor health, but his older brother has caused sufficient stir with his pursuit of the Pashtun homeland agenda. His family's big hope is that the younger son, Zalmay, will grow up to be normal and not another revolutionary.

The waiter picks up the empty pot of tea from our table. I raise my hand to indicate we had enough.

"I didn't say he lent it to me," Zalmay says, "I said I had borrowed it." "So you simply liberated it, like the Pashtunistan your brother is trying to…"

"Shhh". He puts a finger on his lips. Why is he worried? The music is loud enough; no one can hear our conversation. He leans forward, and writes on my napkin, 'Table on your right, lambskin cap, informer'. Being on the crossroads, the town is rumored to have many informers and agent provocateurs, all reporting to different governments – Pakistan, Afghanistan, Iran, India, and perhaps even Britain or America.

"My brother is out of town on business." I know this is a ruse, the brother is probably somewhere in the local mountains with other revolutionaries, or across the border in Kandahar, meeting with his Afghan handlers.

COFFEE WITH CHICORY

Zalmay continues, "Mother asked me to check on the peach orchards, near Hanna Lake."

We get up, go to the counter and pay for the tea and chicken patties. The waiter cannot remember if he brought us two, or three pots of tea, so the manager charges us for two and a half. We walk out of the restaurant to the tune of a song from a yet-unreleased Indian movie. The parking spaces in front of the teashop are occupied by Raleigh bicycles, Vespa scooters and Tiger Cub motorbikes. We walk into the side street, and there it is. Genuine World War II surplus Willys Jeep, parked there in all its 4-wheel drive glory, and with its original, faded wartime paint job. Zalmay's attempt to clean, wash and wax has highlighted the scratches and faded spots.

"That is sharp, Zalmay."

"Isn't it?" His face is glowing with pride.

We get in, and the jeep starts with a low rumble. I notice the man with the lambskin cap coming out of the restaurant and walking toward a motorbike. Zalmay engages the first gear, and we're off.

There are only two busy streets in town, so we first cruise down one, and then the other, trying our best to be seen by as many people as possible, hopefully including some girls. To help others notice us, we have rolled back the cloth top, and folded the windshield down on the hood. Finally, after doing our best at being seen, we head out on the road to Hanna Lake. At the edge of town we can see the municipal check post ahead.

"You think they will stop us?" I ask.

"No reason to. We're not carrying anything taxable." A drooping chain is stretched across the pavement. We stop. A guard in a rumpled uniform lazily comes out of the guardhouse.

"Where are you heading?"

"To the lake."

"What do you have in here?"

"Nothing."

The guard looks in the back, reaches down, brings out a bundle wrapped in a towel, and unwraps it. He is holding a brick-sized slab of cured, salted lamb, favored by travelers crossing the mountains on foot, or by some hunters. "It is *Landhi*," Zalmay says.

"I know what it is." The guard breaks a piece and chews on it, nodding in appreciation, as if to acknowledge that it is of good quality. Zalmay shifts uneasily in the driver's seat, "Can we go now?"

The guard stops chewing, "Wait. What is under here?" He reaches down behind the back seat, brings out a cardboard box, and opens it. Shiny new bullets spill out. "What is the meaning of this?" He says loudly, and reaches down again. This time he bends down, uses both hands and brings out a hunting rifle, its shiny barrel protruding from a large towel. He holds the rifle up. Zalmay stammers, "For rabbits."

COFFEE WITH CHICORY

"Very large rabbits," says another man coming out of the guard post, clad in a crisp army uniform, with an officer's insignia on his shoulder. He looks at both of us one by one with piercing eyes, walks around the vehicle, and comes up to the driver's window. "Who are you anyway?"

"Sir". My name is Zalmay," He says slowly and firmly. "I am a college student. My friend and I are driving up to the lake, and that is the truth."

The officer is not listening to us. He is looking at a small notebook that he took out of his hip pocket. "Never mind the truth," he says, and looks up. "This vehicle in on our watch list. You think I don't know you. You are that troublemaker's brother." Zalmay's knuckles turn white around the steering wheel, and the vein on his forehead starts to bulge. The officer leans forward, rolls one end of his mustache, and says, "And that old traitor's son."

Zalmay's fist flies off the steering wheel, landing on the officer's jaw.. I have always admired my friend's quick reflexes; only right now I wish they were a little slower. Hanna Lake seems very far right now.

The officer staggers back spitting blood, and reaches into his pocket for a handkerchief. From the corner of my eye I catch a glimpse of the guard in the rumpled uniform who had been standing behind the officer leaning on the rifle. He springs into action and swings the rifle butt toward Zalmay's head. Zalmay notices the twitch in my face and ducks, once again demonstrating his rapid reactions. The rifle butt sails across empty air, missing my friend and landing on my right temple. The barren, rocky hills around us swerve, and darkness descends around me.

I have a throbbing pain in my head, as I open my eyes, but I still cannot see anything. It is pitch dark and it is probably night time. The concrete floor under me is hard. I slowly reach my hand up to my temple, and the pain shoots up to the top of my head, and a muffled sigh escapes my lips. Someone else is also near me. "Are you finally awake?" I hear a whisper. Recollection returns to my head, slowly, painfully, and annoyingly. It is Zalmay's voice. I am too upset to speak with him, but say, "Yea."

"I would help you, but they tied me up to this post." Painfully I get up, fumbling around till I find him. Crouching on the floor, his hands are tied behind him. As I run my hands over his shoulder and down this back to look for the post, he gives out a muffled groan, "I think the bastards dislocated my shoulder."

Gingerly, I reach over and locate the binding; a thick jute rope. I find the end of the knot, and start pulling on the fibers. Gradually the rope start coming apart. After several minutes his hands are free and he sits in the corner rubbing his wrists.

"I wonder what time it is?" He asks. I feel my wrist but my radium dial watch is not there. "They took everything," Zalmay whispers, "Our watches, wallets,

COFFEE WITH CHICORY

everything." I check my back pocket; it is empty. He gets up and quietly starts to feel around, checking the room methodically. The effort of undoing the jute rope has made the throbbing in my head worse, so I sit down and lean back on a wall. I can hear him breathing and brushing his hand across the surfaces. A coarse, grainy hiss along the brick wall, and then a smooth, muffled fabric tone. "Gunny sacks," Zalmay says, "A whole stack of them. Seems like we are in a warehouse."

"What is in them?" my curiosity rises above my pain.

"Don't know, but they smell funny." He sniffs some more and tries to feel the texture, "Opium, I think." He stands up and runs his hand trying to count. "There must be fifty sacks here. These guys are mixed up with a smuggling ring."

He moves past the stack of burlap bags, reaching a locked door. "It is locked. But wait," he says, "The latch is on the outside but the bolts are on this side, and they are not very tight."

For the next hour we are crouched beside the locked door, turning and undoing the nuts one thread at a time. My fingers are raw and my head throbs, but I must not stop. Zalmay can only work with his left hand, as his right shoulder is too painful. Finally, all the bolts are loose but one, and we can hear the latch with the lock dangling on the other side of the door.

"Are you ready?" Zalmay makes a final check, lets go of the last bolt, and the latch, the bolts, and the padlock all fall to the ground with a dull thud. It must be bare ground outside. We slowly open the door, keeping the squeak to the bare minimum. A breath of fresh, cool night air hits us, reviving my spirits but momentarily causing a shooting pain in my head. I look up and see a sky full of stars. Our eyes have adjusted to the pitch dark of the interior so well that the starlight and the impending dawn are enough for us to make out some forms. We are surrounded by low, rocky hills on three sides. We start walking toward the open side, being careful not to trip over cobbles and boulders. After about half an hour we reach a dirt track. Guessing from the direction of the dawn coming up on the horizon, we head out away from town.

We have been walking for about an hour as the sun comes up and we can finally see the shapes of the mountains around us. "I know where we are," Zalmay says, "This is about a mile from the lake, on the opposite side from the highway."

"How could they leave us unguarded?"

"It is such an isolated area, ten miles out of town on a dirt road."

"Yes, and the building is completely camouflaged by the rocks?"

"I don't know if you noticed, the back wall of the warehouse is the hill itself."

"We better get out of the open, someone is likely to come back and check on us."

With increasing daylight we are able to leave the dirt track and take a short cut toward the lake, walking over cobbles and around boulders. It is a steep climb for about half a mile and but we approach the apex our path flattens out. I walk around a large, rocky promontory, and see the large bowl shaped lake basin in front of me, about a thousand feet below us. A few more steps and I can see the water. As in most years, the lake is only one half full, and looks rather murky. I remember seeing anywhere close to full only once in the last ten years. On one side of the bowl shaped area we see the concrete arch dam, ready to receive more water, that is if we ever get more rainfall. To the left of the dam is a small plateau with a restaurant overlooking the lake. That was the original destination for yesterday's excursion.

"They must be getting ready for the mid-morning visitors," I point to the smoke is rising from the chimney at the back of the restaurant.

"If we show up at the restaurant it is possible one of the guards will notice us," Zalmay is standing on a small boulder behind me, looking over my shoulder. He steps down and stands next to me, "We should wait till some visitors show up." We find the shady side of the promontory, nearly hidden from view, but still able to see the parking area next to the restaurant.

It must be past ten o'clock when two vans appear in the parking area and discharge their passengers. We cannot quite make out the composition of the passengers, but there must be a couple of dozen people milling around. Soon a couple of cars and two motorcycles join them. Two waiters are bringing out tables and chairs, and people begin sitting around them.

Zalmay and I climb down, staying hidden from the view of the visitors, and manage to descend to the lookout area behind the restaurant building. As we turn the corner around the building, we pause, trying to see if we recognize anyone. "I see my cousin Khalil," Zalmay says, and then I recognize two guys from our college. "This is a football team."

"Yes," Zalmay agrees, walks out into the open area, and I follow him. No one notices us. We go and find Khalil, who is sitting around one of the tables drinking tea.

"I thought I saw you two on the way over here. Weren't you on the motorbike behind us?"

"Far behind," Zalmay says, and we sit down. Khalil says to the waiter, "Two more teas here. And where are the sandwiches we ordered?"

Two cups of tea and a chicken sandwich make me feel well enough to look around. As in most years, the lake is barely half full, and the banks are beginning to get covered with brush and weeds. Some of daring guys are in the water, trying to swim. There have been years when the lake goes completely dry, with only a marsh left in its place, and a tangled mangrove vine starts to flourish in the marsh. In the wet years the water covers up the vegetation growth, but the in some places the tangled vegetation can be seen waving, like an underwater garden.

COFFEE WITH CHICORY

Some of the daring young men have climbed up on the concrete dam and are diving at the deepest point into the lake. The day is getting warm, and the water must be refreshing. Those who dive in come up looking rejuvenated from the cool water, and flush with the excitement. One of the boys on the dam shouts, "Khalil, are you scared?" Khalil laughs, finishes his cup of tea, and gets up. "Where are you going?" Zalmay asks. "Just to cool off a little." He starts climbing the concrete dam. "Go, get some, Khalil", shout one of the boys sitting on another table.

Zalmay taps my shoulder, points toward the parking lot, and sinks low in his chair. A jeep has just driven in and two uniformed men are getting out of it. The vehicle has the insignia of the Customs and Revenue Department. I also slide low and get into a conversation with the boy sitting next to me about the upcoming football tournament. The two men stand near the vehicle and look around., but soon their attention is diverted toward the lake.

A boy has just come up from a dive, holds up his hand and says, "I bet you can't go that deep." Several other boys are cheering.

"What are they talking about?" I ask.
"Look at that kid that just came up from the dive."
"Yeah, I see him, what about him?"
"See what he is holding?"
"He is holding a towel."
"No, in his other hand."

"What? It looks like a piece of cardboard."

"It is a leaf from the mangrove vine."

"So what does that mean?"

"Means he dived really deep, at least 20 feet. They are daring Khalil to go that deep."

Khalil is already in the air, swooping down, entering the water with barely a ripple. He is a natural diver and disappears underwater, resurfacing about twenty feet away, holding a leaf in his hand. There's a loud cheer, followed by applause. The other diver does not stay put very long. He gets up, dives again, and comes up with two leaves. Khalil has joined us in the mean time and is finishing his sandwich with another cup of tea. He laughs and sips his tea. The other diver joins his friends on one of the other tables. There is a lot of laughter around his table. One of his friends gets up holding the two leaves, "Another proof that the Mengel Tribe is superior to the Kakar Tribe," There is loud applause on his table, and laughter from several others. Zalmay is a Kakar, and I spot a Mengel boy sitting at the other diver's table, but I thought their intertribal rivalry ended long time ago. Zalmay shakes his head, "He shouldn't say that. The young generation has been trying to smooth things over." Khalil looks upset and starts to get up, "How can things heal when they keep rubbing salt in our wounds?"

"Let it go, Khalil," Zalmay says, but Khalil waves him off, "I have to put this punk Mengel in his place." He puts the towel down, takes another sip of the tea, and walks off toward the dam.

COFFEE WITH CHICORY

"What if I bring up a branch, will you punks shut up and let me have tea with my friends?" No one has ever brought up a branch.

Zalmay knows a lot about native plans and turns to me, "Did he say a branch?"

"Yes."

"Stop him, please," Zalmay whispers to the guy sitting to his right. There is alarm in his voice.

"What is it?" I ask. Zalmay points to the dam where the two uniformed men are talking to some of the boys. "I don't want to raise my voice," Zalmay says, "That vine is too strong. If he wants a branch, he has to use a knife." The guy on the right gets up and shouts to Khalil, but it is too late. He is already in the air, traverses another graceful arc, and disappears underwater. Almost a full minute goes by, and nothing happens. There are no ripples, no sign of movement below the water. People are standing, straining to look at the lake. Another minute ticks away, and everybody looks concerned, even the Mengels. One boy from their table gets up and shouts to two divers who are standing on the dam waiting for their turn, "Get down there. See what is taking him so long." One boy jumps in, and a couple of others start swimming in from the shore.

All eyes are focused at the spot where Khalil came up before. Almost five minutes have passed since he disappeared under water. The lake is murky, and we can't see below the surface. Ten minutes later a limp form floats up about a hundred feet away. It is Khalil.

His right hand is gripping a branch from the vine. His face is lifeless. Two swimmers drag him to the shore and pull him out of the water.

One of the uniformed men runs down and tries to resuscitate him, but it is too late. All the visitors to the lake crowd around Khalil's body. Swimmers have come out of the water. The body is being taken back to town.

Zalmay and I are able to able to catch a ride back to town unnoticed by the uniformed men who become busy with the diving emergency. With help from my father we report the smugglers to the special branch of police tasked with investigating the illicit drugs. Disciplinary action is taken against the perpetrators, Zalmay's name cleared, and his jeep returned. We become busy with our college curriculums again. For a long time afterward Zalmay wonders if there is something he could have done to save his cousin's life.

Blood Money

"So is it true what they say about this tea?" Irfan asks in his usual innocent, childlike way.

"Shhh, keep your voice down," I have to admonish him to be discreet.

Kalim just laughs, it is his sixteenth birthday, and the three of us are celebrating it with tea and pastries at our favorite haunt, the Iranian Standard Teahouse. We have been here for over two hours, and we know it is getting late, but just like any other day, we hate to part company and go home. Earlier we attended a large birthday party at Kalim's house, but we had to have our own private gathering, as we did last month when Irfan turned 16, and three months ago when I reached the same age.

"Who knows what the truth is," I have to explain to the somewhat naïve member of our trio, Irfan, "But that is what everyone says, that at this teahouse, every pot of tea is cooked with one or two poppy flowers."

"Well then, how come I don't have any petals in my teacup?"

"No silly, petals are not included, the milky nectar comes from the bulb-like part above the stem. And that's used to make opium."

COFFEE WITH CHICORY

Irfan's eyes are getting wider, "Is that why we are here every day?"

Kalim laughs and slaps Irfan on the back, "You are here because you would be lost without us."

"And you like to listen to my stories," I say. We all laugh as I pour more tea for everyone.

There seem to be two pre-requisites for a teahouse to succeed in this border town, Quetta, nestled in the western Hindu Kush Mountains. The first is to include the word Iranian in its name – our favorite, and the busiest, is the Iranian Standard, but the second and third most popular spots are the Deluxe Iranian and the Original Iranian. I don't know if anyone from Iran is actually involved in the ownership or operation of these restaurants. The second pre-requisite is to start a rumor that something intriguing, and preferably prohibited, is being included in the tea. Now, opium poppies are not a prohibited item, in fact they look just like the ordinary poppies that are growing in many gardens and front yards. When dried, the flower bulbs are rumored to produce a mildly euphoric, soothing feeling, and if that brings some of the customers back to the cafes and teahouses, who is to argue with the rumor.

My two friends Kalim and Irfan are inseparable, and have known each other since childhood. Kalim's father is the head of a Pashtun clan, and has great influence over its members who are scattered along the western portion of the border between Afghanistan and Pakistan. His family owns land in both countries, and fresh fruits are always being brought to their house from their orchards. Irfan's family is non-local, like us, but they have lived in town for decades. He was born in this region and is fluent in the local dialects. His family owns several businesses and stores in town, and is considered one of the pre-eminent trading families. Many years ago my father became the family doctor to both Kalim and Irfan's families, and I hit it off with both of them.

Our family does not own any land, a business or any great wealth. However, I do have access to our family car, a brand new 1954 Chevy I am able to borrow easily. So perhaps I'm included in our outings simply to provide transportation. But by the time we finish our third pot of tea and all the pastries and every one of the macaroons, we are close friends. But it's very late, and we leave.

I drive, and we first drop Kalim at the gate of his family compound, which resembles an urban fortress with 10-foot high walls, and two formidable-looking guards by the front gate, with their Kalashnikovs slung over their shoulders.

As we drive off, Irfan has a quiet, troubled look on his face.

"What's the matter?"

"Nothing." I know he can be moody sometimes. I go around the big traffic circle near the fruit market, and turn right to go toward his house.

COFFEE WITH CHICORY

"No, no," Irfan says, "go left."

I comply, and give him a quizzical look.

"Yes, straight ahead, and drop me behind St. Joseph's."

"You mean the girls high school?" I want to be sure, and he nods. Now I am beginning to get interested in his destination.

"Go ahead and say it. What is going on?"

He shakes his head, "Do you know about Kalim's twin sister?" he asks.

"I know he has a twin sister, but I can't swear that I know what she looks like." In tribal fashion Kalim's family keeps a strictly segregated household, with separate male and female quarters for anyone past puberty. Whenever we visit his house, as we did for his birthday celebration this morning, we are ushered in to the male section of the building, and never see his sister, mother, or any other female in the family. Irfan has been acquainted with the family since childhood when he used to play with Kalim and his sister.

Irfan explains to me that his childhood acquaintance with Kalim's sister has continued over the years, and has developed into love and romance during the last year. They have been meeting each other in an old garden behind the girl's-only school she attends. I know the garden; it is old, not maintained, and has heavy shrubbery with tall hedges that run like a maze.

"Are you crazy, Irfan? You know their culture, if someone found out their family will take it as a huge stain on their honor."

"All we do is talk, I swear." he has a wide-eyed look on his face.

"You are so naïve." We circle around the school compound to the back, where there is an old abandoned garden with many fruit trees and rows of rose bushes. As we stop, I catch a glimpse of a girl's colorful scarf behind a hedge. Without saying another word, he gets off.

"Be careful, Irfan."

I drive off.

Our high school finals are coming up, so our routines diverge. The attitudes about education are very different in our three families. Kalim knows that his place on the tribal council is secure, and even if he does not ascend to the top, he is going to inherit enough fertile land. His father wants him to go to school merely to embellish his leadership position, so if he goes into politics, he should be able to address the citizenry using elegant phrases. Irfan is heading toward a partnership in his family's business empire, and wants a few years of school merely to help his father negotiate contracts that are becoming ever more complex. Neither of them believes that what they learn in school has any relevance to their lives.

I, however, am supposed to have a career and earn a living though a profession. "Son," my father who is a physician has told me, "What you will inherit from me is a good mind, a sound body, and an education, no money or property." With the matriculation finals approaching, my routine includes going to two tutors each day, and hitting the books every night, with no time to visit teahouses. In British style, the final exams can include questions on anything we learnt during the last two years, so I have been holed up in my room reviewing stacks of notebooks and books.

For three weeks I haven't seen my friends. We have planned to get together one last time before the finals begin, at a party that Kalim's father is throwing for some visiting tribesmen. It's getting late in the evening and I'm still in my room cursing Euclid and Archimedes while cramming for the geometry finals. Finally, it is time to go to Kalim's house, so I borrow the car keys and drive off.

As I approach Kalim's family compound I can see the large colorful canopy strung between the trees in their front garden, decorated with stings of red and green lights. I squeeze my car between a Land Rover and a Jeep, and go inside the covered area where the men are gathered. Kalim is talking to a couple of his cousins. Irfan is standing next to them and spots me, "Where have you been holed up?"

I shrug my shoulders, "With Euclid and Newton."

"With who?" Irfan says with mock surprise.

My attention is drawn to the group of Pashtun young men standing with Kalim. Their friendly conversation has suddenly turned to loud, excited voices and shouts.

"You are a liar," Kalim says to one of them.

"Why would I lie? Your sister is like a sister to me also. I can't be quiet while your family is dishonored."

Kalim's face is turning red, "And you say she has been seeing some man."

"Yes, I swear upon my tribe's honor."

"And you say you know this guy?' Kalim says, "Well then, tell me who it is and I'll take care of it personally."

The young man turns around and points to where Irfan and I are standing. "What do you mean? Who?" Kalim is furious with rage. Several other people are listening in and it is becoming a big embarrassing scene in the middle of a festive party. The young man walks over and points to Irfan, "This one."

Kalim is shocked. He looks around as if taking in all the stares. He flies into a rage, "Is that true Irfan?"

Irfan turns pale. He does not answer, but is staring at the ground. Kalim's face is red, and tears are flowing down his cheeks, "And you were my best friend."

The meal is about to start, and platters of food are being brought into the canopy area by servants. Two servants carrying a roasted lamb enter the canopy area. They are carrying a large tray with the roast and two large carving knives. Kalim reaches over, grabs one and runs toward Irfan. Before anyone can react, he thrusts the knife into Irfan's chest. Blood spurts out. Irfan stumbles, tries to grab my sleeve, but collapses to the ground. I look at Kalim. He is in a daze, and steps back

COFFEE WITH CHICORY

with a horrified look on his face. Then turns around and runs away.

Faces of both friends still flash through my head. Irfan was rushed to the hospital but died on the way. Kalim ran out of the family compound, but was caught a couple of blocks away, and taken into police custody. I keep thinking that perhaps I could have, even should have, foreseen this and tried to prevent it.

The regret never leaves me during the month-long finals and the year-long police investigation, trial and court appeals. Kalim is tried as an adult and is sentenced to death. In accordance with tribal law Irfan's family is offered blood money so Kalim's life can be spared. There are appeals from the townspeople for mercy, but Irfan's parents are adamant. They cannot forget their son's murder. They refuse to accept any money or to pardon their son's killer.

I move to another city to attend college as Kalim is hanged in the central jail. The following year I come home for summer vacation and learn that Irfan's family has closed their business, sold their property, and moved away – no one knows where.

The Migraine Tonic

I REMEMBER my paternal grandfather's deep booming voice as a force field around him. He was dark-skinned for a Punjabi, and used his skin tone and the gregarious voice as part of an affect that made him stand out at all times.

"Fetch my slippers," he would roar across the sprawling courtyard, "See how brave my grandchildren are; they are fearless" – all this while he holds up his hand with a one rupee note between his thumb and forefinger. At least among us boys and girls he could invoke fear, pride and greed all at the same time. Several of us would scurry about the courtyard, and the lucky one would race to him with the slippers to claim the title of bravery and the one rupee bill. After all, the money was sufficient for one *kulfi* popsicle and a paper kite.

'Elder Grandpa', as we referred to him, to differentiate from some of the other grandpas that were part of the extended family, had been a paralegal scribe at the superior court dealing with land and property ownership disputes. In the agrarian feudal society of colonial Punjab, land disputes between clans and families lead to bitter lawsuits. He would proudly tell of his participation in famous litigation cases involving family feuds and murders.

At dinner parties he would hold court, "I worked with the English barrister Mr. Hardy on the famous Kamonki land dispute." Most of the guests had already heard the story, but the dinner was over, and the desert had not been brought out yet. Those who smoked were taking turns with the water pipe 'hookah', which had been filled with fresh ambers and grandpa's scented tobacco reserved for parties. The tobacco was grown especially for him in a nearby field, and cured by burial in the ground with herbal ingredients that imparted the scents and flavors.

"There had already been two murders in the family by the time Barrister Hardy and I got involved in the lawsuit, and one of the cousins was to be hanged the following week."

One of the guests remembered having read something about the case in the papers, and asked, "Wasn't there a search for a missing gun?"

"Yes, yes, the gun was later found at the bottom of the canal right under the GT Road bridge. I sat up till midnight for days on end, interviewing witnesses and preparing the briefs."

There were several interruptions as other guests spiced up the story, but Grandpa had the last word, "At the eleventh hour Mr. Hardy argued the case in front of Justice Munroe, and we won the case hands down. In the written decision the court made a special mention of the excellent briefs, and that was all my work." Everyone nodded in approval and hurried off to the desert table. Grandpa and a couple of other seniors kept their seats while portions were served to them.

In addition to legal matters Grandpa had a command of just about every other subject, and was very willing to match up opinions. His avocation and love, however, were herbs, and particularly medicinal herbs. He had secret recipes for half a dozen herbal remedies to cure specific ailments. Although he was very proud of his legal accomplishments, he was most joyful when preparing the herbal remedies.

His masterpiece was the headache cure, known to be particularly effective for migraines. It was very popular with older men, and rumors were that it was also an aphrodisiac. This 'headache' medicine gradually became known as The Migraine Tonic. Each spring mounds of raw ingredients would start arriving in our courtyard as his trusty suppliers dropped off piles of leaves, roots, and tree bark. For the next several days the courtyard was filled with vats in which the ingredients were boiled, stirred, and allowed to simmer till they turned to paste.

Memories differ about where Grandpa obtained the recipes and formulas for his herbal medications. He had never had any formal education, apprenticeship, or training in herbal medicine. In his early career as a young paralegal scribe, or *'munshi wakeel'*, he used to be away for a week or two at a time visiting remote villages to gather evidence and record the statements of witnesses.

"I remember when he spent a week in a village of snake charmers," one of my uncles told me many years later, "and returned holding a small basket with a snake coiled up inside. Your grandma made him release it in the fields one *'koh'* (about 1¼ miles) from our house. That was one hobby he was not going to take up while living with her."

On one of his trips he met a sanyasi yogi who lived as a hermit outside the village in a jungle, and the village residents took their sick to him for treatment. A rich landowner wanted to build a road through the area where the yogi lived to reach the central market town. Grandpa was called in by the villagers, and helped them prepare a petition that put an end to the road building. The villagers were very thankful, and Grandpa got to stay with the yogi for a week learning his methods of herb collection and processing.

I was about twelve years old when I started asking 'Elder Grandpa' about the 'sanyasi' yogi, "Who is this yogi, Grandpa, that knows all about the herbs?" I must have asked for the third or fourth time when he replied.

"You have been a good boy lately. I am going to travel to see the yogi next month, why don't you come with me."

I am excited and afraid at the same time. There is an air of mystery and intrigue about hermits who live by themselves and manage to survive in the wild. I have to get permission from my dad, but he thinks if I really want to go, it would be OK. We're on summer break from school, so a couple of days of absence from home would not matter.

I followed grandpa's lead in packing three pairs of clothes, including one for sleeping, one pair of sandals, and my toothbrush, toothpaste and comb. I selected light summer bedding consisting of two sheets, one thick, woven cotton '*durrie*' as a mattress, and a light pillow. I spread the *durrie* on the floor, placed the sheets and the pillow on it, and rolled it all into a bedroll, and tied it with a piece of sturdy hemp rope, remembering to put a loop in the rope that could be slung over the shoulder. My clothes, sandals and the toiletries went into a canvas shoulder bag, including some nuts and dry fruit.

Next morning we leave home and I trudge on behind grandpa, walking through the maze of alleys toward the main road. As we turn the third corner, I spot two boys from school, and hold my bedroll up to hide my face. They have already seen me, and with quizzical looks on their faces, start walking behind me.

"Where are you going," one of them whispers.

"To the GT Road, to get on a bus," I reply, also whispering.

"Why"? They keep following us.

"I am going on a trip with grandpa."

COFFEE WITH CHICORY

"To go where?" I keep quiet and hurry on, and they stay at my heels. When I don't say anything, one of them says, "That is not true."

"You are lying." The other one hisses. With the two boys trying their best to rattle me, I have to keep hurrying up to catch up with grandpa walking at a good stride.

"Tell us which bus you are going to get on, let us see if you know."

They're right. I don't know which bus to get on, but am afraid to question grandpa. "Well, my grandpa knows, and I'll get on the same bus that he does". This dialogue continues on through the next two alleys until we come across a street performer with two monkeys who is setting up his act, and the two boys stop to watch the show.

I also want to watch the monkeys, but we don't linger, and soon enter a wider alley that is a transition between the residential area and the main bazaar. Artisans sitting in storefronts on both sides of the street are making items for the merchants in the main *bazaar*, an embroiderer and a seamstress who get their work through a big tailoring shop, and a shoe-maker who lets the big shoe store on the main road deal with the customers and bring him the orders. As we turn the next corner we are thrust into the hustle and bustle of commerce. Sidewalks are full of people, and stores are stocked with shoes, kitchen utensils, trays full of sweetmeats, and bolts of colorful fabric. The foot traffic includes porters carrying supplies for the stores. I'm apprehensive about colliding with anyone carrying a big bundle on his head and tipping him over.

We scurry through the *bazaar* as the street widens somewhat, but is also more crowded. The sidewalks are overflowing, and many pedestrians are walking on the pavement, which also has vehicular traffic. In addition to some cars, there are occasional city buses, the scooter rickshaws and the horse drawn chariot-style two-wheel '*tonga*' carriages, all competing for the pavement with the bicyclists and the street vendors. Threading our way through all this we manage to make it out to the intersection of the bazaar with the main highway, or as it is popularly known, the 'Turn'. I never quite figured out whether the name referred to the sharp corner of the bazaar, or the gentle curve in the main highway, but in either case it is a serious undertaking to make it across the 'Turn'.

Once at the 'Turn', we find our way to the area where the buses come in from the downtown bus depot on their way east, and make their last stop at this corner at the edge of town. There is a large sweetmeat shop doing brisk business, and right next to it is a juice stall. Because of the bundle I have been carrying, I am thirsty. Grandpa senses it, or perhaps he is also thirsty, "Do you want some juice?" he turns to me, "New sugarcane has come out, and the oranges are still around."

New sugar cane of the season is my favorite snack, but its juice is sickeningly sweet, and the tangy orange

COFFEE WITH CHICORY

flavor freshens it up a bit. Ordering does not involve walking over to the juice stand, since a number of runners are going around the bus stop, with calls of, "Sugar cane, sugar cane-orange, cold juice, sugar cane". One of them finds us, and takes our order back to the juice stand. I see two guys sitting on a low wooden platform behind the fruit stand, peeling and slicing the oranges and feeding them into the juice press. Whole stalks of sugar cane are being fed into a roller press, along with chunks of ice so the juice comes out ice cold, and the effect is that of a runny smoothie in which I can taste the juice mix and feel small chunks of ice on my tongue.

Our bus arrives. The conductor asks us, "Where to?" Upon hearing that our destination is toward the end of his route, he yells to his assistant who is climbing up from the back of the bus, to store our luggage toward the front of the storage area on the roof. We get inside, and the bus gets underway. I have to hang on to one of the metal bars that run along the backrest of every seat. The front half of the bus has two rows of bench seats facing forward, with a narrow walkway in the middle. Grandpa and I find seats next to each other, and the bus travels a few miles before the bus conductor comes to grandpa to collect our fare. After settling in I turn around to take a look at the interior of the bus. A couple of rows behind us I notice two tough-looking muscular guys staring in our direction. Grandpa nudges me and says, "Don't look back". I look at him with a quizzical face. He gestures for me to keep looking to the front, and whispers, "Those two guys work for the feudal landowner whose road project I had stopped". I recall the story, which I thought took place a long time ago. Grandpa whispers again, "They tried to open the road project again a couple of years ago. I'll tell you more some other time".

I am careful not to look in the direction of the two thugs, but I am curious about the partition between the front and rear halves of the bus. The front half has two rows bench seats facing forward, while the rear half of the bus has one long bench seat that wraps around an open area in the middle. A couple of stops later the function of the rear half becomes clear when the rural passenger start boarding the bus. All passengers are allowed to bring along some belongings, and most of the people who boarded at the city stops brought along a suitcase, a bedroll, or a shoulder bag or two. However, on the very first stop near a village the young couple that boards the bus has two chickens with their legs tied together. Boarding from the rear part of the bus they simply place the two chickens on the floor and take their seats.

At the next stop one customer says he would board only if his goat could also ride with him, and pretty soon the rear half of the bus resembles a petting zoo. The only friction arises between the goat owner and another passenger who is carrying a bundle of fresh produce, and the two have difficulty keeping their belongings separate for long.

"Why don't you hold your goat back?"

"I am trying, I am trying, but you keep shoving your sorry-looking vegetables in her face."

"You are indeed illiterate. These are very expensive medicinal herbs."

"They look like weeds to me, and I am sure you can pick them on any roadside, so you might as well let the goat eat it."

"I am taking these for a sick friend, and if your goat ate another leaf you will owe me money."

The bus conductor has to intervene in their dialogue that is getting ever more heated, and warns them that if they do not calm down he'll stop the bus and expel both of them. Fortunately, the goat owner gets off at the next stop and the bus returns to its previous quiet and languor.

The rhythmic vibrations of the leaf spring suspension, the hum of the engine and the sound of the air rushing by the partially open window are making me drowsy. I close my eyes, and just when about to doze off, I am startled by a severe pain, as if someone has punched me in the nose. I open my eyes annoyed, only to realize that as the bus was coming to a stop, I fell forward and hit the metal bar behind the seat in front of me smack on the bridge of my nose, causing sharp pain and embarrassment. My eyes are watery and I rub my nose, hoping nobody saw me. The passenger on the next seat next leans toward me and whispers, "Don't worry, you will be fine soon. I have been in this bus since this morning and have already dozed off and hit my nose three times." I cannot control a glance at his nose and have to hide my smile upon noticing that his nose is quite swollen and red. Poor guy.

We reach our destination late in the afternoon and get off. A man sitting by a tea stall spots *grandpa and comes toward us with a wide grin.*

"How are you *Munshi Ji?*"

"Fine, fine. You look well, Bintu."

Apparently he is our guide, waiting to take us to the village where grandpa has to transact his legal business. The guide has already hired a *'tonga'* horse-carriage that is waiting for us.

"All the witnesses will be coming to see you tomorrow so you can take down their statements. We will be riding by the murder site on our way, and day after tomorrow I will take you on a tour of the disputed land." He gets it all off his chest and then waits for questions.

"Tell me exactly what was the victim's involvement in this dispute, was he the landowner?"

"No, no, he was a distant relative who happened to be visiting the owner, and offered to mediate, but things got out of hand and he insulted the other party."

Grandpa thinks for a while, as if making mental notes, and then asks, "So it happened during the mediation meeting?"

COFFEE WITH CHICORY

"No," our guide says, "Everyone left calmly that day, but the following morning this relative was walking along the canal bank on his way to the bus stop, and someone stabbed him."

"OK, I understand it. Point the location out to me as we go by."

It takes Grandpa two days to complete his legal investigation and take down all the statements, and then it is time to go see the yogi. We walk out of the village and follow a trail through the surrounding farms and on into the forest. After about three hours of walking, we come to a shallow, but very wide stream. We take our shoes off and hike up our pants. Grandpa slings the shoulder bag high up under his arm, grabs my hand and we enter the water that feels cool on my hot sweaty feet. The sensation of soft mushy earth under my feet is strange, but soon we are walking on small pebbles and then across one of the sand bars full of sharp sand particles. The stream is getting deeper as we go further across, and soon it is above my knees, but the current is quite gentle. I look back and see that we have come quite a ways from the bank, while the other side is still far away. I pray that it does not get any deeper. As we cross the last sand bar and step into the water again, it suddenly become deep and I slip, and as his own legs are disappearing underwater, he manages to hold me up and we are soon across the stream. We dry our feet and legs for a few minutes, then roll down our pants, put our shoes on, and we are underway again.

The Migraine Tonic

This time we take a diagonal trek across the wooded area. The grade is rising, and our trail is now going uphill. After some climbing the trail begins to level off again, some distance away we can see a small clearing with a hut in the center. The hut looks sturdy with sides made of wooden poles and a thatched roof on top. At first I can't see an entrance, and think we are at the rear of the structure, but then I realize that one of the sidewalls is a baffle and the actual door to the hut is hidden behind it. The arrangement provides a visual camouflage and also keeps strong winds from barging in through the front door. If there are any windows in the structure they are well shuttered or closed. The clearing around the hut is not very large, and the ground is bare, and then I spot a woodshed in one corner of the clearing that is stacked with chopped wood.

Grandpa sits down on a boulder under a tree, takes off the backpack and starts taking his shoes off.

"You go and check if the Yogi is in his hut," he tells me. "These new boots are killing me," as he peels his socks off.

I put down my backpack next to the boulder and make my way toward the hut that is about thirty steps in front of me. It's late afternoon, and the lengthening shadows of trees are casting alternating layers of dark and light patterns on the ground in front of me. I notice that there is a thin wisp of smoke rising in the back of the clearing.

The shape of the hut becomes distinct as I get close to its wooded surroundings. The camouflage is so effective because a large, mostly dead tree acts as column in holding up the entire right side of the hut. I approach the hut toward what looks like it might be a door panel, and I think I hear a moan. I push on the door and as it opens with a creaking sound the moaning gets louder. It takes a few moments for my eyes to adjust and I see that an old man is lying on the floor, bleeding. I yell, "Grandpa," and run out. Grandpa enters the hut, takes one look and tells me, "Go fetch my bag." I run out, grab his bag and run back in. "He looks bad," Grandpa says, and gets busy trying to help the yogi. Over the next hour the yogi is in an out of consciousness, but before taking his final breath he is able to give Grandpa enough information to identify his attackers, who turn out to be the two men we saw on the bus. Grandpa arranges for the final rites and burial with the help of the villagers, and we return to the City. It takes three years, but the killers are finally brought to trial and hanged.

Years go by, I leave home to go to college and then to America, and my only visit to the yogi becomes hazy with time. When I hear that grandpa passed away I decide to sit and write down what I remember about his interest in herbs and concoctions, now wishing that I had spent more time learning about his hobby, which was also his passion, perhaps even more than the legal career that took most of his hours.

The Driver Class

I HAVE come to Pakistan after several years, and General Kabeer has been acting as my informal guide in Lahore. He retired from active military service about a decade ago, so strictly speaking, he is no longer a general, but still likes to be addressed as one. For the last couple of days he has had me in tow as a visiting curiosity, while I sample the sights and sounds of the city. We are driving along the main drag, The Mall, which I recall from my childhood as a broad and leafy thoroughfare. But gone are the stately horse carriages and the large sedans that used to lazily lumber down the road. The street is now choked with traffic. Today's small cars are weaving in and out, crossing paths with the motorized rickshaws spewing bluish-grey smoke.

The dashboard in our car starts beeping. I look over to the general's side, "You are not wearing your seat belt, Kabeer."

He keeps looking ahead, "I never do. Look at the traffic, it is crawling." The annoying beep persists. He looks toward me. "The seat belt will wrinkle my starched shirt. I wear the seat belt when I go on the motorway and drive at a high speed." We keep moving along. As we approach a traffic circle a car passes us as it weaves across our path from right to left. "Has to be a woman," the general exclaims.

"How can you be sure?"

"I am sure. You want to bet, let me show you."

He speeds up and starts to zigzag through the traffic, trying to catch up with the offender.

"That's OK, I accept your conjecture."

"Conjecture, I'll show you, let me catch up." This was not the calm and jolly person I started out with. We catch up to the offending car, and a man is driving it. I look at Manny.

"What?" he says.

"It is not a woman."

"So what. It is someone from the driver class, equally careless."

As we drive along, the general keeps providing comments about woman drivers, teenage drivers, drivers that have probably bought their licenses along with their cars, and of course, about the driver class. He is getting increasingly annoyed.

"Why don't you hire a chauffeur?"

"I couldn't possibly."

"Why not?"

"Do you see my new Toyota Camry? It is impeccable. The chauffeurs sweat and perspire. My car will be ruined."

I don't see Kabeer for a few days, and then I hear that he has hired a driver. I go over to his house one

The Driver Class

morning. The general is in his garden trimming around the chrysanthemums he is planning to enter in the spring flower show at Lawrence Gardens. He puts the clippers down and removes his gloves.

"I understand you have a chauffeur. Where is he?"

"Oh, Alam. He must be loafing somewhere. You know how the driver class behaves."

As if on cue, the general's Toyota pulls into the circular driveway that wraps around the front garden. A chauffer in uniform gets out and greets us.

"Where have you been, Alam?" The general can still draw on his parade ground voice, at least to talk to his driver.

"*Sahib,* I was picking up your clothes from the drycleaners." Alam opens the trunk and takes out a stack of clothes wrapped in clear plastic, with the cleaners labels hanging from the cuffs of general's shirts and jackets.

We leave to go to his club. The general and I are seated in the back, and Alam is at the wheel. Many other small Japanese and Korean cars are also driven by chauffers, some in uniform. The sheer difficulty of driving in this traffic, the availability of easy credit, and the acquisition of cars by people who never learned to drive, has created thousands of jobs for hired drivers, and according to the general, given rise to the driver class.

I run my hand on the soft leather on the door panel and say, "Your car still smells new." The general leans over, "I had to show him how to use an underarm deodorant."

We enter the grounds of the Royal Palm Country Club and exit the car in front of the clubhouse building. General Manny signs up for a good tee time at the golf course, while I go and see the new workout area in the gym. Alam drives the car to the parking lot.

As we see the golf course, examine the gym and enjoy the refreshments at the bar, Alam stays hidden, perhaps somewhere with the rest of the chauffeurs. After about an hour we leave the club and Alam drives us to a downtown restaurant for a lunch appointment with some business associates. The general doesn't think my suggestion to include his driver with us for lunch is entirely serious. I give Alam some money to eat at a sidewalk stall a couple of blocks away.

Having served in the army the general is capable of opening doors for companies that do business with the government, some of which even grant him a partnership in return for his lobbying efforts.

"Everything is completely above board", he assures me, "All we want is a shot at the contract."

His business partners nod while slicing through lamb chops.

A couple of days later I reach his house to find him pacing in the driveway.

"Alam has not showed up for work, we have to go pick him up."

The Driver Class

"Where does he live?"

"I don't quite know. We'll take the gardener along, he's Alam's cousin."

Twenty five minutes after leaving the house we turn into an alley. Soon the pavement ends. We are driving through shacks and adobe houses, deep into an urban slum. The vague diesel smell that pervades the city now turns into an organic odor of rotting trash. An open sewer runs along the alley. We come to a stop, the gardener knocks; a young woman opens the door slightly, and immediately shuts it. A couple of minutes later Alam appears. He looks a little pale, apologizes for being late, and gets behind the wheel.

We proceed to a busy shopping area, with absolutely no place to park. Alam drops us in front of a leather accessories shop. The leather belts, wallets and briefcases are exquisitely stitched. I survey the store, caressing briefcases and shaving bags, and finally pick out a couple of items. As we come out, we can see the Toyota parked a block away, tucked into the entrance of a side alley. The general waves. I wave, but there is no movement. We walk over with the shopping bags. Alam is slumped over the steering wheel.

"The bugger is asleep."

Manny shakes his shoulder. Alam is unconscious. The two of us with the help of some passersby transfer the motionless chauffer to the rear seat, and the general drives the car with its annoying dashboard beep to the nearest hospital.

COFFEE WITH CHICORY

Alam is taken inside, and Manny accompanies him, as I wait in the hallway. About an hour later the general comes out.

"They think it's a stroke."

"A stroke? How old is he?"

"I think 28. And that's the doctor's dilemma. So he wants to do a CT scan."

I become busy with a couple of things and do not see the General for about a week. One day we meet at the club again as I'm finishing up my workout, and he offers me a ride downtown. Alam is at the wheel. I'm puzzled. I had helped carry him into the hospital.

"He just woke up. The doctor thinks it was some sort of a temporary mini-stroke that leaves no lasting damage. A TIA."

"A what?"

"Transient Ischemic Attack. A brief stroke."

The following week the general arranges an outing to look at one of his estates, and Alam is supposed to pick me up in the morning. An hour past the appointment time I call Kabeer.

"Your driver is lost again."

"I am sorry, but the chap is sick again. This time it's serious, can you come over." I take a cab over to his place, and find him pacing the verandah in front of the house. We ride in his car to the hospital.

"The poor chap is motionless. He was admitted to the hospital again last night, into the neurological ward."

"So what is it this time?"

"Don't know. They are running some tests today."

I wait in the hallway as the general goes in to see the doctor and the patient. The MRI has been evaluated. The doctor's opinion is that it is a fungus in the brain, but it was detected early, so it is treatable. Alam's cousin is also waiting at the hospital. The general gives him the medical prescription and some money, "Remember, this medicine cannot be exposed to light. So before paying, make sure the tinfoil is still covering the bottle." The cousin nods. "And check with both the pharmacies."

Later that night we get together for dinner at a mutual acquaintance's house.

"How is your driver doing"?

"The shot was given to him on time. The doctor thinks this is a curable disease, and the growth of fungus can be reversed."

The conversation shifts to the political and sectarian protests being reported in the news. The next day, General Kabeer is late for his golf game, Alam improved a little bit at first, but is getting worse now. In fact, the doctor has stopped the shots. He now thinks that it may not be a fungus, but actually some tuberculosis that he contracted through the nose, which is attacking his brain. Another MRI has shown that it's spreading.

The next two days, the general is nowhere to be seen. I call him up,

COFFEE WITH CHICORY

"Any word on Alam?"

"The poor guy has slipped into a coma. Now the doctor is completely baffled. Everyone told me this is the best neurosurgeon in town, but he's proving to be a quack."

Later in the week I call Kabeer's house to find out that the general is out, gone to attend Alam's funeral. I see him the following day, and find him in a depressed mood. As we drive, he does not scream at any driver, and makes no comments about woman drivers, the social upstarts, or about the driver class.

"I wish I had taken him to a different doctor. This quack should have told me that he didn't know what was going on, so I wouldn't have to face his wife and children. Now I find out at that he was also supporting his old parents back in their village".

II

Coffee with Chicory

I GET into Tom Brossett's car as he adjusts the driver's seat to fit his tall, relaxed frame behind the steering wheel. The calm yet slightly amused expression on his face never changes, as though everything around him is all a game: work, office, clients, traffic, life itself. He runs the left hand through his slightly wavy dark hair and starts driving. We leave New Orleans and head down into the Mississippi Delta, intending to board a workboat at the port city of Larose.

I flew in from Los Angeles the day before, and met Tom at the office earlier today. He eases the car onto the highway heading south, and then turns to me.

"So you just graduated from school?"

"No, I completed my Ph. D. about five years ago."

"Out west somewhere?"

"Yes, Cal Berkeley." Tom is a gracious southerner, and too polite to roll his eyes, but I can feel what he's thinking: great, another hippie from Berkeley. Probably all Tom knows about the Berkeley campus is the free speech movement, the protests against the Vietnam War, and the social dropouts, and nothing about the nine Nobel laureates on the faculty, or the high ranking of the graduate school.

COFFEE WITH CHICORY

We have been driving for a couple of hours. There is a bayou, or canal, running alongside the road. There is an odd mix of rural and industrial traffic around us, and as much of it in the bayou as on the road. Small recreational boats are competing for space with workboats large enough to be called ships, some of them nearly filling the bayou from bank to bank. We are driving through the southern part of the Mississippi Delta, and looking at the bayou along the road in this flat landscape I'm unable to tell which direction the water is flowing.

Tom says, "We're so close to sea level here that the flow direction in this bayou reverses every time the tide changes." I look at him, not quite understanding the hydraulics behind his statement. "Just wait," he says, "you'll get to experience it yourself when we go out in our boat."

Going through a residential neighborhood the road runs in front of the homes, but the main transportation artery appears to be the bayou along the back. Based on the types of items stored in front of the houses, the unpaved road appears to be more of a backyard. Several of the front yards have pickup trucks undergoing repair work. One pickup truck has a tree stump supporting the rear axle, and a blue plastic tarp under it with various car parts strewn about. A couple of truck hoods are open, and appear to have been open for an extended period. One homeowner has managed to drag his boat into the front yard, and is busy painting it.

Tom notices me staring at the front yards, "You never knew the front yard can be used as a repair garage."

I shake my head, acknowledging the gap in my cultural knowledge. "So you did your undergraduate also at Cal." I'm amused at his continuing southern politeness and his patience at asking indirect questions. "Well, I was born in India, grew up in Pakistan, and after my undergraduate in civil engineering came to Berkeley for a Ph. D."

"So where were you working for the last 5 years?"

"In Southern California, consulting on the design of housing tracts and industrial facilitates."

That was sufficient background for him for the time being.

Just before reaching the port of Larose, Tom pulls into a parking lot paved with broken shells that pass for gravel in southern Louisiana. "This guy has great Poboy sandwiches," he says, and gets out of the car. Shells crunch under our feet as we walk across the parking lot and enter a shack made out of corrugated irons sheets and odd pieces of lumber. The place is well stocked with fishing supplies and groceries, and includes a deli counter. A couple of customers are waiting, and the owner is busy working on a sandwich board. "What will it be?" he says without looking up.

"Poboy," Tom says, and then looks at me, "You want one, right?" I look around for a menu sign that might tell me what a Poboy is, but no help.

COFFEE WITH CHICORY

"What's in it?" "Everything," the owner says, again without looking up.

"Including pork?" I ask.

"Everything." I think for a moment, "Do you have roast beef?"

"We got roast beef."

"I'll have that." The owner lifts his head up for the first time to look at the dummy who is turning down his renowned creation. Tom just stands there, smiling. He knows how good the Poboys are.

The owner wraps the sandwiches tightly in wax paper and puts them in a paper sack. Tom adds two sodas to the bag, pays for everything, and we continue our drive. After a few more miles we reach Larose harbor, and Tom pulls into the dock area. I stay in the car as he goes to check with the dispatchers' office, and returns a couple of minutes later, "The next crew boat leaves in one hour," he says, "we better eat." We sit down on treated lumber beams on the side of the dock and open the wax paper wraps to expose the baguette-like bread. The delicious, pungent aroma emanating from Tom's package contrasts with the total absence of flavor from mine. He takes his first bite, exposing the contents. Half a dozen creatures from the land, air and sea have given up their lives for this masterpiece. Each bite he takes exposes a different color and flavor of meat, sauce and dressing. I sigh, and take a bite of the available-anywhere roast beef with its bland sauce.

"You want a bite?" Tom manages to speak through all those ingredients. My aversion to pork is probably more cultural than religious, but it is real. "No, thanks, I can't." He nods, as if to say, suit yourself. Or perhaps he never heard my answer, and is swaying his head while enjoying his sandwich. If I ever decide to eat pork, it will be in a poboy sandwich from this shack in Larose. But not today.

Sitting on the dock, eating my sandwich, I think about the work ahead. But what is the work ahead? I know we are waiting for a boat, but what specifically are we heading into? I have reached all the way to this dock with only a vague idea of the nature of our mission, and now, as we are about to cross over from land into water, I sense the inevitability of the task ahead, and become focused enough about what I am about to get into. This has been true of many of the transitions in my life – I coast along almost to the point of no return and then finally grasp the details of what I am facing. In some instances when I reach this point and realize what I'm about to get into, I walk away toward a completely different direction. At other times I've accepted what is ahead, and plunged forward with feet first. Even when I've appeared to be unwavering and constant, I have been going along with only a vague understanding, and then been faced with some surprises, more pleasant and enjoyable than what I was expecting, while others rather nasty, or at least unpleasant to the point that I couldn't wait to get out of the situation.

Here, sitting on this dock in Larose, there is no thought of backing out. This is work. This is the field of endeavor I have chosen, plus I have a family and a mortgage. However, there is a significant gap in my understanding of what exactly is up ahead.

"Tom, as I told you I have been working in southern California checking the ground for construction of housing developments and industrial facilities, but what are we going to be doing out at sea?" Tom looks at me, trying to decide where to start. I continue, "Well, I know we are doing this for an oil company, but what exactly?"

"Same thing you've been doing before," Tom says. "We'll be checking the ground for construction of industrial facilities." He points toward the ocean. "The ground just happens to be under a couple of hundred feet of water. And the industrial facilities are offshore platforms and pipelines." I'm not very clear on how we will be accomplishing that, but decide to wait and see it with my own eyes.

The crew boat is ready on time. We board, drop our duffel bags and settle down on one of the two bench seats. Two other passengers in work clothes sit across the aisle; both are roughnecks on their way to a jack up rig. The first stop is at our workboat. As we step out of the crew boat and climb aboard the larger workboat, Tom says to me,

"I am the lead engineer; so I'll be in the engineer's cabin."

"And where is my cabin?"

"You will be in the crew quarters." I nod. That doesn't sound too bad. After greeting the captain on the bridge we go down to the lower deck and enter a small room with six bunks wedged in along three walls. There is a single light bulb hanging from the middle of the ceiling. Once person is asleep, and the other occupant is smoking in his bunk. He looks at us, and nods.

Four men are sitting in the center of the room using an overturned crate as a table, and a poker game is going on. Wagers are being made using matchsticks. I look around for a place to put my shoulder bag, but all the bunks appear to be taken. "You can take that," Tom says, pointing to a bunk full of bags and small suitcases. I stand there, waiting to see if anyone will remove his bag. The poker game continues. Tom reaches over, grabs one of the duffel bags. "Whose is it?" No one says anything, so he drops it to the floor. Next he grabs a small suitcase as if he is going to hurl it across the room. Suddenly, one of the poker players turns around, "It's mine," and grabs it from Tom. The others also speak up and the bunk is cleared.

The bed sheet on my bunk is a dusty grey. "Has the bedding been changed already?" Tom asks.

"Yesterday," someone says.

He turns to me, "Well, next week you'll have clean bedding again."

COFFEE WITH CHICORY

Again? I haven't had any clean bedding yet. I straighten the sheet; run my hand over the bed to sweep away anything I can, and put my shoulder bag on it. I notice the other bunks have pillows.

"Is there another pillow?" I start looking through the bunks to see if someone has taken two. One of the poker players stands up, "Here it is," and hands me a pillow he's been using as a seat cushion on an overturned crate. The other three players are sitting on joint stools. I hold the pillow gingerly from its edge; it has a spiral pattern of wrinkles, probably from the wooden crate, I tell myself. I shake the pillow, run my hand over the bed sheet, and sit down on the bunk to contemplate the state of affairs. After all, this is a valuable learning opportunity; I must be patient. I lie down and think some more. The poker game keeps going on about three feet away from by bunk. Finally I doze off.

Someone is shaking my shoulder. "Time to get up, partner." I open my eyes. What is going on? Where am I? A man with grizzled stubble on his cheeks is bending down. "Hi, I'm James." I look around. I am still in my bunk on this boat in the Gulf of Mexico. I look back at him. James, if that is his name, has a rugged and weather-beaten but kind face, and is wearing blue overalls. Later I learn that he is the head driller. My wristwatch shows almost 11:00. Is it nighttime?

"Let's get a bite to eat," he says. I follow him to the galley. It is dark outside on the boat deck. Yes, it is

11:00 PM. We enter the galley where a full meal is being served: steak, potatoes and a side of vegetables. Rolls and corn bread are already on the table. On a side table are pies, cookies and coffee. I pour a cup of coffee, take a sip, and spit it right out.

"What is wrong with this coffee?" The cook's helper looks at my expression and laughs. James is also smiling, "You're in Cajun country." I fail to get the significance. The cook's helper brings over a can of coffee, shows it to me and point to the label, which says, 'Coffee with Chicory'. What in the world is that? The helper hands me an open can of condensed milk, "Put in some of this." I dissolve a spoonful of sweetened, condensed milk into my coffee. Oh yes, the flavor is a little subdued now, and not all that bad.

Two young men are already eating. James looks at one of them, "Hey Robert." Robert looks up. His eyes are set well apart, and he has a strong jaw and low forehead. His arms are muscular, a dragon tattoo on each bicep, and a packet of cigarettes rolled up in the sleeve of his t-shirt. "Go and get little William," James tells him. Robert nods, springs up and leaves the galley. James turns to the other young man, "Joe, did you check the drilling mud?" Joe is eating a large piece of apple pie with two slices of cheese on top. He holds up his left hand while he finishes swallowing, and then says sheepishly, "No, James, but I'll do it tonight." "Yes, you better," James says, and Joe again plunges into the apple pie. He has a wiry frame with sunken cheeks and hollow eyes. His forearms have wavy tattoos that seem to follow his veins, and he doesn't make eye contact with anyone in the room.

A couple of minutes later Robert returns with a strapping six-footer who can't be much over 18. This must be little William. He rubs his eyes, and sits down. I remember him as one of the poker players. "Sit down and eat up," James tells him, "and better cut down on your poker". William nods, and stuffs his mouth with pieces of steak. His baby face with an eager, innocent look belongs to a teenager more than to a roughneck working offshore.

By the time we finish our dinner it is almost midnight. We walk out to the deck, where the day crew is still working. Tom Brossett is already on the deck to oversee the crew change. James goes over and stands next to the driller who is handling the control levers for the rig. The rig keeps turning, while the two drillers chat about the depth of water, the number of sediment samples taken, the performance of rig's diesel engine, and direction of the wave chop that is swaying our workboat on its anchors. Robert goes up to the roughneck handling the two large pipe wrenches, and they swap places in a smooth move that is a combination of ballet and wrestling.

Joe walks back to the pipe rack to give a hand to the roughneck who is trying to chain the neck of a 30-foot pipe joint using a lasso knot, and gives an extra twist to the chain. They nod to each other, Joe grabs hold of the free end of the pipe, and maneuvers it around as the pipe gets hoisted up the drill tower. The day-shift guy slips out from under the chain, takes off his hard hat and wipes his forehead. A chilly breeze is coming off the ocean's surface, but the rough neck is drenched in sweat from the incessant holding, chaining, lifting and hoisting of the 30-foot long steel pipe joints.

Little William stands hesitantly with his tall lanky figure silhouetted against the bright floodlight shining down from the drill tower. He is trying to focus, and finally speaks up, "James, am I going to be the mud man tonight?" James turns around without taking his hands off the rig controls, and gives William a stern look, "Get to work William. Yes, you are the mud man." William disappears behind the tall stack of barite pallets. I take half a dozen steps to the right to get a better view of what is going on behind the ten foot high stack, and see the fourth member of the day crew, all covered in white chalky barite powder as he tries to wrestle a 100-pound sack into the steel tank. He lifts the bag up from the pallet and puts it across his left shoulder like a sack of potatoes. He then walks over to the edge of the steel tank, bends forward, and, slices open the heavy paper of the sack using a straight knife. Barite chunks pour out of the sack into the tank, falling on the surface of the white, viscous drilling mud. The agitator arm in the tank turns around and blends the powder into the liquid, making it heavier. He spots William, and points his finger toward the other stack of pallets. The writing on the paper sacks tells me these bags contain the bentonite gel powder. William repeats the sack-hoisting move with the 60-pound bag and slices it open, thickening the mud. As the white flour-like fine powder flows out, some of it gets airborne, anointing William in a ghostly look. The other roughneck who is already covered with white powder laughs loudly, slaps William on the back, and walks out to the open deck, ending his shift.

I look back to see Tom walking toward me, "Oh there you are," he says, "So now you understand what is going on?" I look at him helplessly. He senses the hesitation in my face and laughs. "All right, come here. You recognize the drill rig in front of us?"

"Yes, it's a truck-mounted rig, and seems like someone just drove it on to the boat."

"That is exactly what we did. In fact, you can still see its wheels and tires, it's just that we have lifted the truck on to blocks, and then welded it in place so it doesn't get blown off the deck".

Tom looks toward the rig and calls out, "James, what is the water depth here?" James reaches out into the left hip pocket on the back of his blue coveralls, and pulls out a small, mud-smeared spiral notebook, "220 feet". He puts the notebook back, then reaches down into the right hip pocket, pulls out a round can of chewing tobacco, and puts a wad into his mouth, resulting in a bulge in his left cheek. "And how do you know that?" James looks at him to check if Tom has lost his senses. Tom is pointing toward me. James gives a chuckle and says in a forced, mock manner, "See this wireline?" he is pointing to a steel wire rope, "I attached a weight to it and dropped it down this well," he says, pointing to a hole in the deck of the boat, "When the wireline went slack, I had already reeled out 220 feet." James then looks at me, as if to say, 'You got that, dummy?'

"Thanks, James," is all I can say.

"You head out to the lab," Tom says, pointing to the wooden shack by the bulkhead, "You are the soil tech tonight, and the next sample is about to come up."

I started work at midnight, and at three in the morning I am still in the lab, and now very sleepy. I come out of the lab, walk across the open deck, and out to the port gunwale. In spite of the noisy rig working on the other side of the deck, there is an eerie stillness. I lean over the side to see the dark hue of the water surface against the boat. The boat is loaded down with the rig, the drill pipe and the pallets of drilling mud, so the waterline is only about six feet below the side of the boat. I see no separation at the horizon and the darkness from the sky to the ocean is seamless. I lift my head up to see the stars, so abundant in the absence of city lights that I am unsure where Polaris is. I hear footsteps behind me and turn around. In the dark I can see the strapping form of little William, "Next sample is ready." It's time for me to get back to work, "I'm coming." I go back to the lab, test the core samples brought up from the seabed, and do the calculations. Finally we take a break at 6:00 AM. The rig is put on low idle, and we go down to the galley.

Breakfast is ready. The cook's helper is in charge. The cook is in the kitchen during the two meals when dinner is served – noon and midnight. His assistant handles the breakfast at 6:00 AM, and lunch at 6:00 PM. Eggs, bacon, omelets are being made to order, along with white toast, and coffee with chicory. I put a spoonful of condensed, sweetened milk in a large mug of coffee. After serving James, the cook looks at me. "I'll have two eggs over easy, toast, and no bacon, please." "For toast, you help yourself," the cook's helper says, and turns around to make the eggs. Little William is the last one who comes in, and picks up several slices of bread, "I'll have eggs and bacon," he says, hesitates for a moment, then asks, "You got a piece of steak?" The assistant cook nods. The other roughneck, Robert, says, "This ain't your uncles' farm William." James smiles and says, "Let him alone, Robert. You eat what you please, William."

We finish our breakfast, go back out to the work deck, and work till noon when the day crew takes over. After working a 12-hour shift I don't care what caused the wrinkles on my pillow. The time from noon till midnight seems barely enough to take a shower, have lunch, get some sleep, eat again, and get ready for work.

It takes us three days and nights, but we finally have all the samples and it is time to leave this location. The deck area around the drill rig now begins to build into a frenzied crescendo. James is pulling up the pipe joints hanging in 200 feet of water to the seabed, and on into the 300 feet of ocean sediments penetrated below the seabed. The pulleys on the drill mast groan, churn and pull up one piece of 30-foot pipe after another in response to the rapid manipulation of rig's levers and controls by James' fingers, hands and wrists, as if he were a master puppeteer putting on an open-air performance using giant puppets with 30-foot long legs dangling from a tall tower.

"Hey-ya Robert." is what I hear each time James gives a signal that another heavy piece of steel is about to swing across the deck. And each time, one of the roughnecks manages to grab the end of the dangling pipe by hugging it and then hanging on to it as both he and the pipe drag across the wet deck in a muddy wrestling match. Once the swinging stops two roughnecks maneuvers the 30-foot long pipe towards the pipe rack where it is laid flat in a stack, building a heap of pipes that gets ever higher. James keeps his eyes focused at the pulleys and wirelines at the top of the drill tower, while his hands are on the drill rig's control levers. The roughnecks are keeping their gaze fixed on the deck and their hands and arms wrapped around the heavy pieces of steel pipe that rise out of the ocean water one by one, ascend to the top of the drill tower, and then come swinging across the deck, requiring the roughnecks to catch and wrestle them into the pipe deck.

COFFEE WITH CHICORY

Little William, the mud man over the last three days, has already drained out and hosed down the large steel vat used for mixing the drilling mud, and is now frantically trying to secure the loose bags of barite and bentonite gel on to the wooden pallets scattered about on the rear deck. After putting the last bag on the pallet, he covers the neatly arranged piles of bags with a large plastic tarp, and ties a nylon rope to prevent the entire assembly from washing overboard during the voyage to our next assignment.

As the drill crew's activities begin to ebb, the sailors are called to order by the boat captain's crackling announcement on the PA system, "All hands on deck." It is understood by everyone on board that the boat captain's announcements are only meant for the boat's own crew, the full-fledged and qualified deck hands with their Able-Bodied Seaman certifications, and the odd novice trainees that are always along to mop the deck. They hope to someday join the boat crew on an equal footing as the AB Seamen. The cook and his assistant are always working, cooking either for the drillers, or for the sailors. While the drilling crew, the drillers and the roughnecks, work on 12-hours on, 12-hours off shifts, the boat's crew of sailors and seamen works on 4-hours on, 4-hours off watches.

During the sampling the drilling crew has been active on the center deck, and as the sampling work ends, the drillers and roughnecks drift off into the showers, the bunks and into the crew cabins for smoking, sleeping and playing poker. After having been responsible for all the noise and fury they quietly melt away into the shadows and crevices of the boat, and the sailors and seamen start coming out of hibernation. Over the last three days as the drillers have been working day and night, the boat's crew has been keeping a very low profile, usually limited to one man up on the bridge as a lookout to keep watch, and to monitor the marine bands on the ship's radio.

Before the boat gets underway, the first task for the sailors is to hoist the anchors up on to the rear deck. The boat has been moored at four points for maximum stability. In 200 feet of water depth it means that our four anchors are scattered in all directions about 800 to a thousand feet away, and by now have burrowed well into the ocean floor, each anchor's position being marked by only an orange buoy. The captain must have called in the small support boat some time ago, as it is already picking up the first downwind anchor, heading in toward us. The diesel engines that run the anchor winch motors are groaning under the strain of pulling in the heavy wire rope we employ for the anchors. The screechy grind of the starboard winch to the aft of the center deck tells me that it is lifting up a 5,000-pound anchor directly out of the water, on the way to stowage on a large metal rack mounted at the rear of the boat. While the drill crew's manhandling of the rig was a display of muscle power and stamina, the seamen are now performing an athletic ballet, displaying their skill by dodging the pulleys, winches and chains.

The last anchor is barely on board as we get underway. By now the drilling crew is completely out of sight, and the boat's sailors seem to be in two or three places at the same time, and each one performing many functions in various locations on the boat. I am never quite sure how many sailors are on board. The captain is the only one who stays put on the bridge, barking orders, sometimes using his lungs, and at other times the boat's PA system.

The frenzy of diesel engines, ball peen hammers, air wrenches, and samplers around the drill rig has been replaced by a comparable frenzy of electric winches, marine propellers, rudder pulleys and chain hoists that are scattered all over the boat. This new activity continues for the next day and a half during which time the boat transports us to the next sampling location.

Every couple of days our workboat pulls up its anchors, steams for a day or two, and then anchors up at a new sampling location for two to three days. After about two weeks a small crew boat brings in fresh crew replacements, and I get off the workboat and back to my desk in the office, and get busy with engineering calculations.

Kodiak

GARY DRIVES right up to the stream bank, stops the pickup truck and jumps out. With his medium height and a muscular body, he thrusts himself forward toward the stream bank, while his straight blond hair, always in need of a haircut, swirls about. His face is flush with excitement, evident through several days of growth on his cheeks. The water in the rapid mountain stream is swirling around the rocks in frothy eddies and glassy whirlpools, and I can hear the cascading sound inside the pickup truck.

I step out, and Tony Yew follows me. All three of us have been jammed in the front seat of the pickup truck during our bouncy ride on the gravel road. Tony is a hair over 5 feet tall, with a round face so smooth I have difficulty detecting the presence of any hair growth. He wears round glasses, and straight black hair falls about his face like a mop. Hands thrust in his pockets, he walks with what would be considered swagger if he were taller, and when stationary, stands with his feet wide apart as if trying to balance himself. There is always a detached and amused look on his face.

Gary peers into the water, "Salmon should be migrating up about now." Having grown up in the arid highlands of the western Hindu Kush range in Pakistan, I know very little of the salmon, and nothing about its migration. I recall ordering a salmon dinner in a restaurant once, and thought the fish was too oily.

"Migrating?" I ask Gary.

"Yes, come up here, I'll show you." Standing at the edge of the stream, he points to the left side where the water is flowing through a bed of cobbles in a cascade.

"Look, do you see that?"

"See what?"

"There, to the left, do you see the pink shadow?"

I try to focus my eyes past the glare on the water surface, and gradually I am able to ignore the dancing water. Suddenly, my eyes are focused on the pink flesh slithering along the gravelly streambed, around the large cobbles, "But it is swimming upstream."

"Yes," Gary says, "Back to where it was born, to spawn." He stands on the bank, looking down. I see another fish follow the same uphill route, then another, and then some more after that. Gary shakes his head, "These fish don't have much time. The Coho runs will be over very soon."

I look around for Tim. He is standing a good ten feet back from the stream bank, looking slightly amused, and taking in the scenery. We are in a narrow valley, just wide enough for the small stream and the gravel road on which we drove up. The other bank of the stream hugs a steep hillside with a sporadic growth of brush and small trees. I am delighted to be standing on firm ground after having spent a month on the wobbly deck of a small ship. Our ship landed here on the Kodiak Island in Alaska a couple of hours ago, and I can understand Tim's desire to simply stand in one place and feel stationary ground under his feet.

Gary has been working as our lab technician, and I knew nothing about his interest in fish. "So you like to fish?" I ask him.

He pauses, "Well, no", he says, "But I have a bachelors degree in biology, with specialization in Ichthyology."

"Special what," Tim asks.

"The science of fish."

"So what are you doing testing sea-bottom soil samples."

"Well, at least I am out on the ocean," Gary laughs, "Tell you the truth, couldn't find a job, and didn't particularly want to sell insurance."

"There," I spot another salmon, and then another. There seems to be a whole school coming up single file around a large boulder. I look back but Gary is no longer there. "Where did he go?" I ask Tim who hasn't budged and has the same bemused grin on his face. He points upstream, and I see Gary about a hundred feet upstream near two large blackberry bushes. He has waded in almost knee-deep into the stream. I bend down and touch the water, it's ice cold. I see Gary reach down and pick something up out of the water. "Look," he shouts, "Look here, see what I got." I squint against the bright sun. Whatever he's holding, is wiggling. Gary bends down again and when he gets up, his hands are empty. "Was he holding a fish in his hand?" I ask Tim. He nods, and I'm beginning to think it's not a grin. The corners of his mouth are permanently sculpted upward on his face.

I walk up toward Gary. Again he reaches down, but this time I can see the wriggling fish, and he holds it up for me to touch. I gingerly reach over and touch with one finger. Gary laughs and thrusts the fish in my hands. I immediately return it to him, and he bends down to submerge the fish in water, still supporting it with his hands underwater. After a few seconds, the fish seems to regain its senses, and swims away. Gary walks out of the cold stream. He's shivering but his face is beaming under the bright sunlight. He must have studied something about fish; he seems so overly enthusiastic. The only fish I had ever held in my hands before was deep-fried with a thick batter, and had tamarind chutney over it.

We sit down on boulders near the stream, and watch the parade of fish swim upstream through the eddies and the whirlpools and over cobbles in shallow cascading water. An hour goes by, Tim looks at his watch and says, "We better head back." We get up, leaving the stream, the salmon, and the desolate valley, and head toward town.

Our boat, the Motor Vessel Caldrill I, came into port to restock on food, fuel, and other supplies, and plans to sail away tonight. We get in the pickup truck, and head back to town. It's almost five. Tim looks at his watch again, scratches his chin, and says, "We're not sailing till eight." I turn around and look at him, "What are you driving at?" "We should stop and get a bite to eat. We are going to be stuck on that boat for the text two weeks." Gary and I look at each other. No one is going to disagree with Tony. He is the client; an employee of the oil company that has hired the ship to investigate the sea floor under several hundred feet of water on the Kodiak shelf.

We stop near what looks like the heart of downtown Kodiak, and spot a restaurant high up on one side of the street. It takes us a little while to find parking along the scarce curb space. The street is narrow, and runs across a steep hillside. We get out of the pickup, and climb up a steep sidewalk to get to the restaurant. As we enter, we are rewarded with a view of downtown laid out below the windows, and the ocean beyond, stretching out to the horizon. We pause to take in the view. The restaurant is set up like a coffee shop, with a counter on one side. Two waitresses are working, and one of them motions us toward an empty table. I reach for the seat near the window to get a full view of the ocean. As we sit down and the full glare of the sun hits me I realize why no one was sitting at this table. I use one hand to shade my eyes, read the menu, and order a sandwich and soda. After a while my eyes adjust and I can see out the window.

COFFEE WITH CHICORY

The view of the ocean is fine, in fact better than fine, quite spectacular, but what catches my attention is something visible from a side window. It is a large boat, wedged in between the restaurant and the building next door.

"What is that Gary?"

"What?" he asks.

I point to the boat. He looks at it for a while. "I don't know. It looks like a –,"

"I know it's a boat, but what is it doing here. We must be a hundred feet above the sea?"

"I don't know," he waves dismissively, and appears to be more interested in looking at the open view toward the ocean.

I persist, "Well, Gary."

"Well what?"

"You are the fish guy."

"Yes", he says, "I'm not a sailor."

"Let us ask her." Tim says, pointing to the waitress, and Gary does. "Oh that", she says with a wave of her hand, "It's been there since I started work three years back. They say it happened during the earthquake." She leaves to go get our food. "What is she talking about?" Tim asks. That bemused expression has returned to his face.

"The earthquake," I tell him.

Tim asks, "Wasn't that back in the sixties"?

"Yes, 1964. The great Alaska earthquake. It happened ten years ago."

Gary keeps staring at the boat, "Come to think of it, there were quite a few tidal waves," I say.

"What kind of waves?" Tim asks.

"Tidal", I reply slowly, "Tsunami and seiches. The waves were experienced all over south and southeast Alaska, although the earthquake was in the middle of Gulf of Alaska." I look back. Tim and Gary are not listening to me, they are both looking out to the ocean, and Gary is pointing to a tugboat pulling a barge.

An old timer sitting on the next table has been working on a crossword puzzle, and now turns to me, "You are right. We had a tidal wave an hour after the earthquake and it came right up, pushed many small and large boat on to streets. They hauled most of them back to the water, but this one is wedged in too tight. They didn't want to take a chance on damaging the boat and the two buildings."

I thank him as the waitress arrives with our food, "You guys still talking about the boat? This old timer was here ten years ago." I had learnt about the Great Alaska Earthquake in school, but seeing the boat right outside the restaurant window nearly a hundred feet above the sea clarifies everything.

"You suppose these people are pulling our leg, and this boat was constructed right here?" Gary asks, and Tim chimes in, "Like those people who build toy ships inside a bottle?" I protest, "No, no, they're right, I've seen pictures of scenes like this, maybe even this boat. It's true what they're saying."

COFFEE WITH CHICORY

Through the meal I keep looking at the boat, which has made the Great Alaska earthquake come alive for me. Just like the difference between holding a live salmon in contrast to chunks of deep fried fish.

We pay our bill, take a last look out the window, and walk out into the small town of Kodiak. We climb up in the pickup truck to head down to the port named Kodiak. All this while we are on the island also called Kodiak, and no one seems confused by any of it.

Six-Way Thrusters

THE PORT of Kodiak has only one berth where a sizable ship can dock, and that is where our vessel, Caldrill I, is tied up. Gary parks the vehicle right on the dock, and goes looking for the expediter to return the truck keys. I notice Curly walking down the gangway that connects the ship to the dock.

"Curly, what time are we leaving?"

For a moment he is not sure where the voice is coming from, and looks back to the ship. Then he spots me standing on the dock near the bow, and waves. Curly is a man of about fifty with thick brown curly hair, a strong and burly frame, all wrapped up in an easygoing manner. His gaze is always down, as if searching for something. When at work he displays a tenacity I have rarely seen. As his feet hit the dock Curly walks toward us, and says, "By eight tonight". Tim stands on the dock with hands in his trouser pockets, a bemused expression on his face, and asks, "Are we on schedule?"

"We better be," says Curly, "a big container ship is coming in at midnight, and I want to be out of here."

The container ship company owns the dock, and I've heard stories of boats having to leave the dock and moor in the harbor until the container ship is done, and then return to complete their business. As we stand on the dock talking to Curly, a truck with last minute supplies including vegetables and milk drives up on to the dock, right next to where we are standing, and starts unloading. The ship's cook, Simon, is directing the unloading. Curly notices him and says, "Most of the crew was in town sightseeing, and he's been here all day, re-stocking the dry goods."

Tony climbs up the gangway and goes onboard, probably to his cabin. I stay on the dock checking on things with Curly. "What about the drilling mud and bentonite?" "Yep, all on board." "Is the pipe all stacked up in the racks?" "Yep." Knowing his thoroughness, I don't ask for further details, and feel confident that we are prepared to leave soon. Curly's nominal title on the ship is Superintendent, but in reality he runs all operations, and even the ship's captain looks up to him. The boat is set up as a full-service sampling boat for hire, with its own drill rig and drilling crew. I only have to deal with Curly, who then directs the ship's captain, the drilling crew, and the other boat operations.

I climb aboard, go to my cabin, and read for a while. Like all workboats, Caldrill I has a little library; a collection of paperbacks left behind by the earlier crews and workers. There is a nearly complete collection of Kurt Vonnegut's books, including his latest, Ice 9, the 1975 edition that just came out. I have been devouring them at the rate of one every two or three days.

Six-Way Thrusters

I look up from my book, it is past nine. Curly and the captain had assured me that we are leaving at eight. Here it is an hour over the departure time and we're sill moored. We have several hours of travel ahead of us, and I don't want to lose any more time in Kodiak. I walk down to the bridge. Both Curly and the captain are there.

"What's up, guys, why haven't we left the dock yet?"

"The bloody cook," Curly says.

"What is wrong with the cook?"

"Nothing, we just can't find him. I've sent two guys to look for him."

"Wasn't he here earlier?"

"Yes," the captain says, "While others were sightseeing, he was busy all day working and restocking food. So at six he leaves to go get a drink before we sail."

"But that was over three hours ago, Curly?" I'm getting impatient. "So what are you planning to do?"

Curly is furious, "I'd like to fire the son of a bitch, but where am I going to find another cook at this time of night in this godforsaken place?"

The captain stands there and nods. He is letting Curly deal with the situation. I go back to the cabin. There are a lot of bars in this small town, so I hope they find him soon. Another hour later, about ten, I finally hear the hum of the engines, a sign that we are about to get underway. I decide I'll get the details the next day and go to bed.

My alarm clock is ringing. It's time to get up, get ready, and get a good breakfast for the full day of work

COFFEE WITH CHICORY

ahead. I head down to the galley, walking on an exterior gangway. I approach the galley and hear laughter, loud conversation, and the sound of dishes. It seems like a festive meal is underway. This is strange. The first breakfast after leaving the dock is usually a somber meal. Some of the roughnecks are hung over, while others are struggling to get into the mood for work. As I enter the galley, a cheery voice welcomes me loudly. It is Simon, our cook.

"Yes sir, Mr. engineer, what is your dining pleasure this morning?" I do a double take. Is this our cook? I don't remember hearing his voice during the last ten days that I've been onboard. Yes, it's him, but in costume. He is wearing a chef's tall white hat, and a long white apron that reaches to his toes. An array of pots and pans is scattered about him. Before I can answer him, he turns around, and with a spatula in his hand, scoops up a pancake, flips it high in the air, and catches it on the plate he has picked up. The drilling crew breaks into applause. I notice they all have sizable breakfast portions in front of them. "Yes Sir, Mr. Curly, here is your pancake, just perfecto, with scrumptious blueberries." He turns around, folds an omelet, sprinkles it with some herbs, and gives to Curly.

I find an empty chair and sit down next to Curly, who has a grin on his face. I look at him quizzically, and whisper, "What is going on here Curly, I thought you had lost the cook." "He was lost for a while," Curly says with a smile. "We sent out three parties to search all the bars, and kept getting reports from half a dozen bars that he had been there. Finally we found him, and this is the way he's been."

"Has he slept?"

"No, he's been up all night, cleaning and scrubbing the galley, and last couple of hours he has been getting ready for the breakfast, cutting and chopping."

"Don't you find this a little strange?"

"That is fine with me", Curly says, "I'll take him any way he comes."

I ask for two eggs over easy with toast, and receive it on the cleanest plate I have seen in the last ten days. Soon the drillers finish eating, and start getting up to go to the work deck. The boat has come to a stop; we must be at our destination. Curly also gets up, "I better go and set up the positioning system."

Ah yes, the positioning system with its six-way thrusters. Most workboats are shaped like big tubs, tied to four heavy anchors in order to hold their position at the seabed sampling location. Not so with Caldrill I, which is a WW II Navy surplus patrol vessel, and different in two ways. First, for running alongside destroyers and gunship, it has a sleek and narrow profile like the old clipper ships; great for slicing through rough seas, but not very stable when treading water and trying to stay in one place. Second, its long, narrow deck does not have room for heavy anchors. To stay in one place this ship is outfitted with a dynamic positioning system consisting of six-way thrusters – small propellers attached to the hull around the boat at 60-degree intervals. The six thrusters are constantly turning on and off and adjusting their thrust trying to hold the ship in one place above the intended sampling location. The six thrusters are supposed to work in concert, and are controlled by a computer of 1950's vintage. When I first saw the control panel it reminded me of the bridge of the spaceship Enterprise in the TV series Star Trek, half a dozen amber dials with needles that swing about, a dozen multicolored lights that blink incessantly, and ten large black knobs that require frequent turning. Curly is the only one onboard who has any idea how the computer is supposed to work. Sometimes in the middle of a work shift the computer re-sets itself, forcing Curly to re-adjust every control.

About one-half hour has gone by, and as I pour my third cup of coffee. I can sense that the dynamic positioning system has now taken over the ship's controls. The boat's propeller is off, and the engine is idling with a low hum. The six thrusters whirr and buzz in varying combinations, like large insects tied to the ship's hull. The ship's motion has changed. Rather than a sleek and steady forward motion, the ship now moves like a gymnast trying to balance himself on high wire, or a surfer trying to stay upright while riding over rough waves. Some people find this stationary dance very disconcerting, while others don't even notice it.

The cook and I are the only two people left in the galley. I have finished the eggs, but decide to have one more piece of toast with jam to go with my third cup of coffee. The cook looks around, and says, "Well, now my greatest creation for myself." I watch him assemble a large omelet and pile up a tall stack of pancakes. He arranges a place setting with forks and spoons, and pours a large cup of coffee. The boat's motion is now reaching its nexus with the waves and currents. The six-way jabbing of the thrusters, the phased cycling of the waves, and the pull of the currents are overlapping in an unnerving combination. The cook is standing near the dining table next to his place setting. I notice that his complexion is losing its color, and he looks pale. His smile is gone, the glint in his eye has dimmed, and he seems to be a little unsteady. The evening of bar hopping is finally catching up with him.

"Are you OK," I ask.

"Yes," he says, not very convincingly. "Once I eat my breakfast," he says, "I'll feel much better," and seats himself in front of the large omelet that must be a foot across. Next to that is the stack of dozen pancakes, two kinds of syrup, an open jar of honey, a large cup of coffee, and a tall glass of milk. As he looks at the food, his paleness deepens, and he turns almost green. He picks up a fork in his left hand, and a knife in his right, and raises his arms as if about to attack his meal. While his hands are up in the air, a pained expression comes over his face. I turn away to refill my empty cup, and hear a

COFFEE WITH CHICORY

loud gurgling noise. I turn around, and it takes me a couple of moments to comprehend the scene. Simon has thrown up over the omelet, the pancakes, the syrup, the milk, and much of the table. Everything is covered with green vomit. His mouth is open, but his eyes are closed, and he doubles over, with his face going straight into the plateful of omelet and green vomit. His knife, fork and elbows crash to the table. I shake his shoulder but he's passed out, sprawled over his elaborate, colorful breakfast and the green vomit.

"Curly," I scream.

Just then, Curly walks in and says, "We are ready to go to work." "Fine", I tell him, "I am on my way," and point to the table, "You take care of this,"

For the next three days we don't see the cook. He is too ill to get up. And each day, every meal consists of cold sandwiches.

The Fishing Life

It's early afternoon when I take off from Anchorage airport, heading to the small town of Yakutat in southeast Alaska. This is 1975, so a *stewardess* wearing a dress brings the refreshments, and the plane is soon filled with cigarette smoke. We start flying over water, and I can see small fishing boats plying the Gulf of Alaska. Soon we are over woods drenched in the early afternoon sun. A few vehicles are moving on a winding road along the forest's edge. The small propeller plane flies low, and I can see individual tree tops, some bare ground between the trees and brush, and winding trails. I see a bear walking along one trail. The size is difficult to judge from two thousand feet up in the air, but he looks large, and has a brown coat shimmering in the sun. His strong hindquarters give it a distinct shuffle that is propelling it forward. He could be a grizzly.

It's difficult to gauge the time of day by looking at the sun's angle, but I'm far enough south of the Arctic Circle that the sun will definitely set, at least for a few hours. After landing in Yakutat I climb down the few steps, go around to the back of the plane, and pick up my blue duffel bag from the pile of luggage that has just been unloaded. With my briefcase in the other hand, I come out of the small terminal building on to the open road. I see Jimmy sitting in his pickup truck. He is our shore man who has been stationed here in Yakutat for the summer. He spots me, grins, but keeps sitting in the truck and starts the engine. I fling my duffel bag and the brief case in to the back of his pickup, noticing the two large drill bits I had called him about already sitting on the truck bed.

"How are you Jimmy?"

"Great, great," he answers while maintaining his grin. As soon as I enter the passenger side, he lets go of the clutch and we take off. The pavement near the airport is new, but soon we're driving on a rough road. Most homes and businesses in town appear to be prefabricated, and many are oriented at odd angles to the road. The structures have their sides or backs facing the road, and none are quite square to the roadway that is their main access.

Up ahead I see the first building that has any air of permanence. It is not a large structure, but so far the most prominent in town, perhaps newly built, and the beige color gives it the appearance of an institutional building. As we drive by I notice the large lettered sign across the top of the building. – 'Alcoholism Treatment Center, Yakutat, Alaska". I had heard that alcoholism is a big problem in some parts of Alaska, just did not know it was big enough that one of the town's most prominent buildings is devoted to it.

It has taken us less than ten minutes to drive across town, and we are now heading towards the ocean, leaving the hills behind us. As we turn right, I see the shimmering Gulf of Alaska and the Yakutat Bay in front of us. Driving past the tall trees, I am also able to see the dock. We stop near the harbormaster's office, which is in a large shack adjacent to the dock, and check the departure time. Yes, he tells us, the crew boat that will transport me to my destination is ready to steam any time.

We walk around the harbormaster's shack and see three guys standing on the dock. I spot James and wave to him. A faint smile crosses his lips, and he nods. I walk up and shake his rough, calloused hand.

"How is California?" James asks, not really wanting to hear any details about the state of which he holds a low opinion, all fluffy and imaginary, not solid and real like Texas. James is in his early forties, but looks older due to his outdoors work, and his mature manner. His ambition is to save enough money to buy a farm in Texas, and, secretly, I think, to be a gentleman farmer. I don't think he finished high school, but he chooses his words carefully, and is trying to improve his vocabulary. He's a quiet man, so doesn't really need many words. He introduces me to his helper, "This is Jim-Bob," who thrusts his hand out, "Jim-Bob Ki-i-ing," inserting two long vowels between the consonants at both ends of his last name. Soon the third man, who has a small beard, and was smoking at the other edge of the dock smoking, joins us. He has a small beard, and a Texas cowboy felt hat at a rakish angle that gives his face an odd skew. As he comes closer I recognize him, it's Andy. As a technician, he's capable of reading instruments, identifying trends in the data, and is the most literate of the crew. He may even have attended some junior college. He has always been very aloof with me, overly friendly with the crew, but both behaviors seem contrived, and it's unclear what his real feelings are. He takes the cigarette out of his mouth and examines the ash, providing himself an excuse to not shake hands with me.

Being around an all-Texan crew for days and weeks on end, I'm beginning to recognize regional dialects. The north Texas speech pattern is rather clipped, while the south Texas consonants are almost muffled. The west Texans seem to stretch the syllables out beyond any recognizable length.

I get my duffel bag and briefcase from the truck, and we walk toward the crew boat that is essentially a heavy-duty water taxi. It's about 50 feet long, and constructed as if it's a very large ocean-going pickup truck – the front half covered with a low roof and the rear half with an open deck. The metal roof over the front portion is covered partly with rust and the rest with oily grime. An overweight man in his mid forties steps out the front door of the covered cabin, wearing a blue coverall with grease spots on the bib. As I walk closer I notice he hasn't shaved in a couple of days. Looking at his unkempt appearance, and the grungy condition of the boat, he must be the captain and perhaps even the owner of this boat. The support vessels in the oil patch are typically hired on short-term contracts, generally run by people who cannot find full-time work, and this boat and its captain seem to fit the bill. I cringe at the thought of riding in this boat, but mercifully the ride will last only a couple of hours.

The large covered cabin over the front half of the boat is fitted with one bucket seat forward for the captain facing the bow, and two long bench seats arranged along the starboard and port sides of the boat for passengers. On the open deck in the rear is where we all drop our luggage and the two large drill bits. A couple of us go in and the others remain standing on the deck. The captain sits down in his bucket seat and revs up the engine, and suddenly it is too loud to hear any conversation. "I am Jim-Bob King", I repeat under my breath, trying to sound out the last name to rhyme with 'skiing'.

The boat takes off, and it gets very cold on the deck, so passengers enter the cabin and settle down on the bench seats. The cabin is reeking of diesel, partly due to the use of lubricants and oils, and partly because some of the exhaust fumes are coming up from the engine. The captain keeps his left hand on the helm, and controls the radio communication with the microphone in his right hand. Everyone else other than the captain – whose two hands are busy – lights up a cigarette, and the cabin is engulfed in the repulsive mix of diesel exhaust fumes and cigarette smoke that I recall from so many other rides aboard crew boats.

I sit at the very rear of the cabin by the open door, trying to stay away from the diesel smoke and catch some fresh air. Instead, I catch more of the diesel exhaust blowing back in through the open door along with the cold air. To keep my nausea down I focus my eyes on the horizon far away, avoiding the swaying deck and the undulating water rushing by. Jim-Bob points to the back, and I turn around and see a dozen dolphins jump out of the water in unison, execute a perfect arc dive and disappear under the waves. Jim-Bob has a nervous smile on his face, and is clutching the railing along the bench seat. The rushing water, the swooshing wind and the radio chatter in the boat are all too loud to have a conversation, although essential messages can be exchanged by shouting, accompanied by some hand gestures and facial expressions.

We have been steaming through the Gulf of Alaska for about two hours, and now, for the first time, we see something on the horizon in front of us. It appears as a speck at first, and then as a blob, and it takes us another half hour before we are in the vicinity of our destination, a semi-submersible drilling platform. James touches my arm. His right hand is made into a fist, with the thumb sticking up, and he is gesturing upward. He gets up, and I realize he is asking me to get up. The boat slows down, and makes an arc around the rig, as the captain tries to gauge the direction of currents and tides, and the winds next to the massive rig. He is constantly talking on the radio with someone on the huge rig towering over us, while we slowly buzz like a fly around a giant.

Our boat cuts the throttle down to the point where we are just holding our position against the wind and waves. Finally, conversation is possible in the cabin. "OK, guys; get ready for your ride in the sky," the skipper says, but his meaning is unclear to me, until we all walk out on to our boat's deck and I look up to see a tall woven basket cage being lowered by a huge crane from the rig looming several stories above us. The wind makes the cage swing on the crane's cable back and forth, while the waves are making our boat bob around on the surface of the sea. The large basket dangling by the steel cable touches the boat's deck and the cable goes slack. One of the roughnecks loads up our duffel bags into the basket, and then stands on the base of the basket and clings to the outside. The crane operator reels in the cable, lifting the basket that swings through the air in wide arcs criss-crossing the air above our boat. The roughneck is clinging to the outside for dear life as the basket rises several stories up to the main deck of the semi-submersible rig. After a couple of minutes the empty basket is lowered to our boat's deck again. One by one we grab on and cling to the outside of the cage and are transported up to the deck of the semi-submersible.

COFFEE WITH CHICORY

The main deck of the semi-submersible rig is several stories above the ocean's surface, and has a very slight back and forth sway reflecting the dampened forces of the waves hitting its eight legs. I soon learn that the top authority on the rig is the tool pusher, Red, who is in charge of the drilling operation while the rig is holding its position. As new arrivals, we are ushered into his office.

"What is this sorry bunch. Don't bring them in here." I look at James with raised eyebrows, and he nods toward a sign on the wall, 'I am the law on this rig.' We are assigned bunks in three different cabins, drop our luggage, and check to see if our equipment has arrived yet. I walk out on to the deck, which is as big as half a football field. There is a loud crackle in the air and the PA system fires up. Red's voice comes through, God-like, "Give this man a hard-hat." The rig's bridge where Red is sitting is three stories above me, and the sun is in my eyes. I immediately duck back into the lower deck quarters, and wind my way through the hallways to my cabin to locate my hardhat, before venturing out onto the open deck again.

The next ten days are a blur, as we work long hours, eat, and catch whatever little sleep we can get. After ten days when we are done, we catch a boat ride back to shore, and the little plane from Yakutat to Anchorage. After reaching Anchorage I stay back for two days to check with the Minerals Management Service about the sand waves in the Cook Inlet, as James and the rest of the crew travel to Seward to begin our next assignment. It takes me two days to complete my meetings, and then I travel again to Yakutat. The plane is late, but when I land at Yakutat airport Jimmy is waiting for me and we hurriedly drive out to the small dock. He ducks into the harbormaster's shack and comes out with the news that the crew boat has already left.

"The crew boat has left?" I look at Jimmy.

"Don't worry," he says, we have a fishing boat also on contract, let me call them." He goes back into the harbormaster's shack and raises the fishing boat on the radio. I wait outside, taking in the scenery, and looking at the wildflowers growing between the concrete sidewalk and the wooden dock. These look like Texas bluebonnets, but are taller than any I have ever seen in south Texas. Plants, birds, insects, and perhaps even animals, show an urgency to grow in the short Alaska summer with long daylight hours. The flowers in Texas where the sunshine is available year round do not seem to feel any urgency to grow quickly. Jimmy comes out of the shack, "They should be here in five minutes," so I unload my duffel bag and the briefcase from the pick up truck and put them on the dock.

A wooden boat is heading toward us, about 80 feet long, and unlike any crew boat that I've ever seen. This boat looks sleek and maneuverable, and is finished in a light wood stain and has the mermaid-like bust of a mythical sea goddess affixed to its bow. The boat comes

COFFEE WITH CHICORY

alongside the dock, and a tall young man in his early twenties jumps on to the dock with a rope, and ties it up. He then comes over to Jimmy, and they start talking, but my attention is affixed on the blond girl standing on the boat's deck. She comes to the edge of the boat, grabs my duffel back from my hand and swings it back onto the deck. I then climb aboard with a briefcase in one hand, and as I step on its deck, the boat hits the dock with a slight bump. I start to lose my balance, but she reaches over and grabs my arm, steadies me, and everything is OK.

The small upper deck is at the level of the wheelhouse, and I see a brunette in a tight tee shirt and bell-bottom pants. This is the 1970's so bell-bottoms and long flowing hair are not uncommon, but in this setting on this sleek wooden boat she seems to epitomize the appropriateness of her clothes. I am taken to the wheelhouse to see the skipper, and see a muscular, broad-shouldered, blond young man of medium height. He stands up with an outstretched arm, but keeps his other hand on the helm, and says with a broad smile, "Welcome, I am Lars." I shake his hand, and grab the railing.

"I see that you already met my sister Brigit on the deck." So he did notice that the blond girl on the deck had to grab my arm to stop me from falling.

"This is Crystal," he points over his shoulder toward the brunette that is entering the wheelhouse cabin. She manages a faint smile and waves at me, but does not stop and keeps moving ever closer to Lars, until she snuggles right up to him and puts her hand on his hand resting on the large brass wheel, as if to clarify her relationship with the skipper.

The tall, young man in his early twenties with wavy dark hair is still on the dock, untying the rope that had been used to tie the boat to the dock. Brigit, the blonde girl, is on the side of the boat lifting up the round bumpers that protected the boat from impact against the dock. After throwing the rope over, the young man jumps on to the boat's deck, where Brigit is already rolling up the rope and they finish the task coiling up the rope and intertwining their arms in the process. Lars notices me looking out to the deck, and says, "That is Brigit's boy friend, Tony. He is working with us as a deck hand."

Crystal is no longer in the wheelhouse, so I look outside to see her perched halfway up the small mast, adjusting a light. Her long limbs and obvious muscle flexibility make the maneuver appear like a movement somewhere between ballet and modern dance, rather than the grunt work that it actually is. The boat is now making a wide arch while coming about, and banks to one side. The wheelhouse has only one seat, a high swivel chair on which Lars is perched, so I hang on to the shiny brass rail along one of the windows, looking out. As the boat begins steaming toward the open sea, Lars notices my tightening grip on the rail, "You may

COFFEE WITH CHICORY

want to go down to the galley and sit down." I wave at him to say it is OK. I prefer to be in the wheelhouse where I can see the panorama of mountainous coast and the open sea. Once Lars establishes the heading, and we are past the last buoy in the harbor, he settles back in the chair. As if on cue, Crystal shows up with two mugs of coffee. She hands one to me with a vague smile, as if she is uncertain about what facial expression is appropriate, and holds the other cup out toward Lars. Lars' hand on the wheel jerks, the boat swings to the left, and Crystal feigns loss of balance and ends up in Lars's lap. She lingers there as the boat steams ahead.

Stacks of rolled-up nets are piled up at the back of the deck, and I ask Lars what they are for. "We are a fishing boat," He says. "We are based in Hawaii, fishing there during the winter, and fishing up in Alaska during the summer. We arrived here just in time for the fishing season, but it has been delayed."

"Delayed? Have the fish not shown up?"

"The fish are here, but the Fisheries department is late in its count, which will tell us how many days we'll get."

"So when is the fishing season beginning?"

"Any day now, they will let us know 24 hours in advance, I am monitoring the channels, and when that happens, it's bye-bye, we'll be gone like that." He snaps his finger.

The Fishing Life

"We weren't doing anything, just sitting in port biting our nails. This gets us out on the sea."

"Do you own this boat?" "Well, our family does, my dad is out on another boat somewhere out there, but he now prefers to stay around Hawaii. These Alaskans waters can be treacherous."

Changing the subject to our current destination, I ask, "How far out are we going?" Lars has picked up a small towel and is busy wiping the gleaming brass railing. I can see Tony and Brigit on the rear deck down below, laughing, with Tony holding a mop. "About another hour", Lars says, looking out the window.

This is the shiniest, cleanest support vessel I have ever seen. The boat's light stained wood, and the bright brass railings and fittings are shining in the bright sun. The usual support vessel looks grungy and has a crew like the one that I'd just gotten off. Just out of graduate school, I am wondering how I can trade my Ph. D. for a boat like this, along with its crew, of course. I could be steaming back and forth on the open sea, running errands as a support vessel. I'm almost sad that our ride is going to last only one more hour. The support boats I usually ride are steel-hulled vessels, shaped like a tub, and laden with tools, supplies, and miscellaneous junk. They travel in a slow, lumbering fashion, and seem to always be low in the water. The sea has been calm, and we are running at a fast clip. This wooden boat is

COFFEE WITH CHICORY

skipping along the glassy surface of the sea, and I linger on the bridge taking in the view and enjoying the boat's run. If you're going to catch fish, you have to be fast and be able to maneuver quickly.

About 20 minutes into our journey we make the turn out of Yakutat Bay and head toward the center of Gulf of Alaska where the drill boat is already anchored. The sea surface begins to change, and there is a light chop on the surface that picks up as we go further out, and the boat ride becomes rather spirited. The boat's movement is no longer a simple forward glide, but includes a swaying motion and an occasional hop, as it skims off the top of one wave and lands on the next. As my head and body move with the glide, my stomach and intestines get left behind, still caught up in the sway. I think of the eggs, hash browns and toast I had for breakfast, and can't seem to recall why I wanted to finish the whole platter. I keep my eyes on the horizon, and stay calm, but Lars senses the loss of color from my face and my struggle to keep swallowing my saliva, and says, "It's only going to get worse, you may want to go down to the galley and sit down." I manage to nod, and make my way down along the stairs, holding on to the brass railing with both hands.

The galley is on the lower deck in nearly the exact center of the boat, and the sway is definitely less here. There is a stove and a sink along one wall, and a wooden table and two bench seats occupy the remainder of the small room. I sit down and immediately feel some relief from my rising nausea. I am not alone very long as Brigit and Tony walk in, nod to me, and continue to lean against each other near the stove. "Would you like some tea?" Brigit asks, and I nod in the affirmative. She takes out a bag of Tetley black tea, puts it in a mug and pours steaming hot water from the kettle into it. I sip my tea; look at a magazine sitting on the side shelf. We should soon be getting to the drill boat that is my destination.

I'm absorbed in the magazine, and after finishing my tea put the empty mug down on the table, and as I let go, it slides away. I put the magazine down and notice that the pots and pans hanging along the wall are swinging. I get up and look through the open door to see that the whitecaps on the ocean's surface have grown much more numerous, and some are big enough to produce froth on the water. The PA system in the galley crackles as Lars' voice comes on, "Tell the engineer to come out to the deck, we are approaching the drill boat." I stand up, and immediately have to grab the wall to steady myself, as the entire boat is swinging back and forth. I make my way down to the deck, and am happy to see the firmly anchored drill boat.

The waves around us are over five feet high, and the contrast between the movements of the two boats is staggering to look at. The large, grey drill boat, laden down with its equipment and supplies, and held down by its four-point mooring, moves up and down less than a foot every two to three minutes, while the smaller shiny brass and wood fishing boat with empty fishing nets aboard, and a tiny anchor is bobbing up and down about six to eight feet every ten or fifteen seconds. In order for me to transfer from one boat to the other, the two decks have to be at the same level long enough for me to jump from one to the other. I stand at the edge of the shiny wooden boat, with Tony and Brigit standing next to me, and try and gauge the exact moment when the two decks will be momentarily synchronized. Every time I look at the large, anchored boat, its deck is either five feet above my head, or five feet below my feet. If there is a split second when the two decks are at the same level, it is so fleeting and unpredictable, that I don't dare step from one to the other, especially as both decks are wet and slippery from the sea spray.

Several crew members from the drill crew are standing at the gunwales at its edge, ostensibly to help in my transfer, but obviously ogling Brigit and Crystal. Some of these red-blooded seamen and drillers have not seen a woman in some weeks, and certainly not two shapely and beautiful girls that move like ballerinas and work like roustabouts. We make half a dozen attempts at approaching the anchored ship, but are unable to achieve any kind of synchronicity between the two decks, and Lars' voice comes on the fishing boat's PA system, talking to the other skipper on the boat's radio. "Captain, we have to back off and wait for it to calm down, we don't want to crush your engineer between the two boats." I later hear that a couple of days ago a technician who was transferring fell and dislocated his shoulder during the transfer. Lars is also apprehensive about bumping against the large, steel-hulled drill ship; as such a collision would severely damage his sleek wooden boat.

Our boat backs off, and Brigit tells me to go back to the galley until the sea calms down. I make my way back up slowly, and the boat starts to make to and fro loops in the shape of an infinity symbol. I sit down on the bench seat and try to read again, but find it harder to concentrate, wondering how much longer I have to stay here. Soon Crystal walks in, takes out the frying pan, and as the smell of frying builds up in the small closed room drops of sweat start to appear on my forehead. I open the door to the deck to let in some fresh air. Without turning around, she says, "Would you like some eggs and hash browns?" That does it for me, and I rise up from the bench. Upon hearing no response, she turns around. My pained expression and her woman's intuition tell her all she needs to know.

"Bathroom is down this hallway," She's pointing to the side door.

I manage to close the door behind me and try to muffle my howling and heaving, and after a few minutes my stomach seems to settle down. I slowly make it back to the galley, paler and more distressed than before. Lars is there now, sitting down with Crystal and they are having a hearty breakfast. "Would you like some?" he asks, and sets off another rumble in my middle. I make another trip to the bathroom down the hallway, and return.

I've been seasick on workboats, but that was in front of rough and tough men who, while working hard, were on temporary holiday from the normal etiquettes and formalities of society. Working on the back deck under the open sky, it was normal for roughnecks as well as sailors to spit tobacco, blow their nose, and as luck would have it, get sick and throw up, without once asking to be excused or apologizing. These were all considered normal bodily functions, and no one was wearing any perfume. In their work clothes most of the roughnecks are covered in drilling mud, and the sailors in grease. There are no clients or inspectors or other strangers on the boat who aren't working themselves and therefore might stand around judging us. But here, on this gleaming wood and brass piece of art, in front of these two mermaids? No, this was too humiliating. I'm supposed to be heading to a drill boat full of manly drillers and roustabouts, and how could I have such a weak constitution?

"Who is handling the helm?" I ask Lars. "We work in six hour watches", he says, "Crystal and I are now off for six hours," as he caresses her thigh with one hand under the bench. He gets up as she clings to him, and seems to rise up from her seat without use of her own limbs. He looks out, "This doesn't look too good, engineer, you better get some rest. You are not leaving any time soon." "I am OK," I say weakly, and as they leave I lie down on the bench in the galley. After my three or four trips to the bathroom I am beginning to feel weak. About an hour later Brigit comes in to get some coffee for Tony, and sees me lying down on the bench seat. "Oh, you can come and rest in one of the bunks." She takes my hand to keep me steady, and leads me to one of the small cabins with one bunk inside. The bed seems unused, and as I step in she says, "See, there are four one-bunk cabins on the boat, but we only use two," she points to the bed, "This is Crystal's, but she prefers to rest in Lars' cabin."

I keep getting up every couple of hours to make trips to the bathroom to puke, although by the fifth or sixth time I am down to dry heaves. Brigit hears my heaving and brings me sliced apple. "I don't think I can eat anything", my voice is fading. She says firmly, "You must, this will settle your stomach and give you some strength." I lie down and perhaps dose off. Some time later the cabin door opens slowly and it is Crystal, offering me a cup of tea. I thank her, so six hours have passed and this is the next watch. The night progresses like this, with the girls taking turns checking up on me. By morning I do feel better. It is mid-morning now and the sea is calm enough for me to transfer over to the drill boat. Most of the all-male crew on the drill boat is lined up at the gunwales on the drill ship, though only a couple of them half-heartedly help me with my luggage,

COFFEE WITH CHICORY

also without taking their eyes off the two girls. For the next several days I get envious ribbing from the drill crew for using the rough seas as an excuse to spend the night on the Hawaiian fishing boat in the company of two beautiful girls.

I quickly improve on the rock solid deck of the much larger, firmly anchored drill ship, and by early afternoon can eat solid food. I get busy with work, and the romance of a fishing life fades in my consciousness. I even look forward to returning to land and to my desk job on firm ground. However, in my daydreams I sometimes command a fishing boat with Crystal and Brigit, and I'm never seasick.

Forty at Sea

I TRAVEL to distant oceans to investigate and test the seafloor for durations of a week to a month, then return to the office and get busy with engineering calculations and technical writing for a month or so. Then it's back to the workboat or a rig in another ocean for a week to ten days. I have had my share of travel to Straits of Magellan, Java Sea, Gulf of Alaska, and Santa Barbara Channel. But the place I return to for repeated and most frequent assignments is offshore Louisiana in the Gulf of Mexico.

December is our busiest month. Thanksgiving holiday seems to remind every client that the leftover budget has to be spent; otherwise next year's budget may be reduced.

It's the Monday after Thanksgiving. I get to the office a little after 8 AM, get a cup of coffee, and settle down for a day of work.

"Shell is on the line," Vicki, the group secretary announces in the hallway, not addressing anyone in particular. Fred, one of the two project managers, speaks up, "Vicki, I'll take the call."

I go up to Vicki's desk, "Who is the caller from Shell?"

COFFEE WITH CHICORY

"Sounds like an intern." At this time of the year, we take everyone from a major oil company seriously. I can hear Fred, "Yes, yes, we can take care of that. Is it Sabine Pass? Yes, we have a boat working in the area."

I go back to my desk, get busy with calculations and keep my head down. Anyone sent offshore now won't get back till after Christmas, and I start thinking of excuses.

Fred hangs up and walks into Jimmie Aycock's office across the hall from me, and I can just barely hear them. "Jimmie, we have a situation,"

Fred can turn on his small-town sincerity any time. "Yes, I heard the call." Jimmie is going to take this head on. "It's the 8th month for Alice". What's he talking about? Oh, yes, I remember, Jimmie's wife is pregnant again. Fred says something in a whisper and they both laugh; must be a remark on Jimmie's virility. Fred comes out into the hallway; Aycock's excuse is legitimate enough. How in the world did he arrange for a Christmas baby?

Fred goes into Mark Halpert's office on the other side.

"Mark, I have an assignment for you." Mark is prepared, "I'd love to Fred, but I'm volunteering as the deacon's assistant this year, and we have such a heavy schedule during the holidays, and you know…" "Yes, yes," Fred interrupts him. Mark knows about Fred's rooted South Texas respect for Christian traditions. If Fred himself does not undertake the church duties, at least he can earn some brownie points by allowing Mark to do so. I'm suspicious of Mark's religiosity that blossoms each time he needs an excuse. But, as Fred would say, "That's something between him and the Lord." Fred leaves Mark's office, now with a worried look on his face. This is not good. Mark has reminded him of the religious aspects of the holiday season.

As I would have guessed, Fred's next stop is Efrain's office. Efrain is a Cuban but happens to be of Jewish faith. He is also the youngest in the group, recently married, and with no children. "Hope you understand," says Fred as he leaves Efrain's office, and we are all off the hook – at least for a while. I've heard the 'understand' bit before; being Jewish, Efrain should not have to worry about being away over Christmas. Tell that to his wife, who is at the mall shopping for Christmas presents. I see Efrain leaving the office, "Heading out?" I ask. "Yeah. I have to find Angelina. We can't go to her parents' tonight."

It is the second week of December. The boat has been working offshore with Efrain on-board. He should be able to make it through the holidays. Sitting in my office, cranking out calculations and reports, I feel safe. It is mid-morning when Vicki announces in the hallway. "Radio call from offshore." The operator must have patched it in. Fred is busy, so the other assistant manager, Dwayne, takes the call.

COFFEE WITH CHICORY

"Yes Efrain, I can hear you loud and clear. Go ahead. Yes, I got it, Morgan City, tonight at 8:00 PM." Dwayne hangs up, comes out of his office, and goes in to see Warren Crabb, the group manager. Fred is already there. There is something brewing. Maybe there is a mechanical problem, and the boat is unable to finish the assignment. Well, the clients will just have to wait.

Then Dwayne walks out into the hallway, looks around, and goes into Mahesh's office. "We got a situation, Mahesh." This does not look good. Mahesh is the lone Hindu in the group, and hence another target for travel over Christmas. "But, but…" Mahesh is trying to get a word in, but Dwayne first wants to finish his appeal, "The boat is coming in to the Morgan City dock tonight, and Efrain has to get off." Mahesh is clever, and loads himself up with important office work at this time of the year. He is also a very good analyst, so the complex projects gravitate to him.

"The Exxon Research report is due by Friday," Mahesh is finally able to get a few words in, and it's a punch line. No one wants to offend Exxon Research. Dwayne walks back out into the hallway, now with a concerned look on his face. This close to Christmas, I know where he is heading next. I am the lone Muslim in the group.

He walks into my office. "Something has come up", Dwayne is trying his best to look somber, and "Efrain has a family emergency, somebody has to replace him on the boat." At this point, I'm supposed to volunteer in the spirit of the season. Being a Muslim, I shouldn't have any qualms about being away at Christmas. "Sure Dwayne, I'll go." I might as well go, before he orders me to. I don't want to tell Dwayne that my kids are at the mall getting their pictures taken with Santa Claus.

I'm beginning to suspect Efrain's family emergencies. True, he has a large extended family living in Houston, but how many of these emergencies does he need to attend to personally? No doubt he'd used up the grandmother's funeral long before I arrived here, but still has plenty of close, elderly relatives in his sprawling Cuban family.

I go home, pack a bag, leave a note for my wife, and return. The drilling crew is already in the equipment yard.

"Ready to go, partner?" James asks me. He lives in an apartment near the office so he can leave on short notice, and will be the head driller again. I nod and ask, "Still at it James?" He is over 50, which is old for the grueling offshore work. He smiles, "You just watch. I'll have my farm soon". We load up our stuff in the red van, and head out to the Louisiana coast.

I sit up front in the passenger seat, while James drives. "Don't worry, I am getting close."

"Close to what James, we just left the yard."

"The farm, my friend."

"Oh that. Just watch the Interstate please."

COFFEE WITH CHICORY

"I am watching. Two more years, and I'll have enough to buy me one." The look in his eyes tells me he may be looking at the interstate, but he's seeing rows of golden corn.

The rest of the crew is packed on the two bench seats behind us. I can hear Dusty, the technician from the heart of Texas, complaining about his wife.

"You wanna know how she welcomes me when I get home from offshore? Cold coffee and crossed legs. That is how."

"Shoot, that would send me right back out in a big hurry", says one of the two roughnecks sitting next to Dusty.

The other one nods. The two roughnecks, James told me later, have had their run-ins with the law. Petty theft for one, and drunk driving for the other. Working offshore is one way to get out of sight for a while.

It seems that everyone in the van has a reason for going offshore and putting up with the strenuous, grimy, and demanding work. James is looking forward to saving enough money so he can buy a farm where he'll settle down. And he does make good money. Working 12 hours a day, seven days a week as an hourly worker, he accumulates double and triple overtime wages, resulting in paychecks that are more than double the salary of those drillers who work on land and get to go home every night. Plus, there's no place to spend any money as long as he's on the boat. Although his wife and family probably make up for his lack of spending. But as an engineer I don't get paid overtime, so I make the same money offshore as when I work in the office. I can't think of money as a reason for going offshore. Dusty is here to avoid his marital problems. I think to myself, but what is my reason? What is it that motivates me?

The workboat is waiting for us. We get on board. "Let's make the load check, James". We go to the rear deck where the expediter from the supply company is waiting, "About time," he says.

"You got nothing better to do." James pats him on the back, "let's go see the goods." We spend the next few minutes going over tools and expendables, and then signal to the captain for departure. The boat lumbers out to the sea; overloaded with a drill rig, pipe, mud, and crew trailers. At full steam it barely makes 7 knots, and it takes us till midnight to reach our first location. The boat anchors up, the boat crew goes into their quarters, and drilling crew emerges from their bunks. We begin sampling the seabed. Hours turn into days, and every couple of days we move to a new sampling location. Soon, days become weeks. Christmas comes by and is gone.

Today is New Year's Day. It's early in the morning and I can see the sun coming up over the gleaming ocean. The boat is heading to the next sampling location. Its large diesel engines are groaning, and the deck is swaying gently under the heavy drill rig and supplies. The

COFFEE WITH CHICORY

sailor crew is very busy manning their stations, while the drilling crew is probably asleep. I go down to the galley, fill up a mug with chicory-flavored coffee and sit down. After several years of working on boats run by Cajuns, I don't need to mask the chicory flavor with condensed milk. James, the head driller, comes in through the galley door, "You also can't sleep?" I nod. He also gets some coffee and sits down. His face is covered with stubble that has gone from grizzled to white over the years, and his fifty plus years are showing.

No words are spoken for a good while, and then he says, "Your cat died?" I smile weakly, and look through the galley window out to the rear deck. "What is the matter," he says, "Spit it out."

I turn to him, "It's so pathetic, James."

"What is?"

"Damn it, I am going to be forty this year, and I am still working on boats." James doesn't say anything. I turn away and look at the deck again. He takes a long sip of coffee, with a slurp. "Let's buy a farm together," he says.

"Me?" I look at him, "A farmer?" He sees the expression on my face, tries to resist, but it's no use. We both burst out laughing.

James re-fills our mugs. "I reckon you are not here for a farm," he studies my face, "So what are you here for? How many thousands of miles from home." I didn't know James could say three sentences in a row. He is always playing the strong, silent Texan. I look at the ceiling, look outside to the rear deck, and then look back at him. His stare is fixed on my face; he wants an answer.

"I, I am, I am sort of ..."

"Yeah?" he says, "What?"

"Well, I want recognition. For my efforts, for my abilities, my achievements."

"Is that so," he says, "You ain't gonna get known sitting on a boat. Better find a way to the 7th floor."

Seventh Floor? Oh yes, the seventh floor, the top management's floor in our headquarters building. I have always considered management to be so manipulative. How should I explain this to him? He senses indecision on my face.

"You either kick ass, or take a licking yourself," his interpretation of something one learns in an MBA class.

"You think so, James?"

"Yup," he says, "Why do you think I became a head driller?"

I thank him for the management lesson, go up to my cabin, lie down, and stare at the ceiling. What James doesn't realize is, that I am a foreigner, a south Asian. I'll never get a management assignment in an old-line Texas company. All the managers are good old boys from central and south Texas. They think of El Paso as a foreign country.

By the end of the week, my replacement arrives, and I reach home only four days into the New Year.

COFFEE WITH CHICORY

"Dad, dad, look at what Santa brought me," my son comes running in his new cowboy outfit. My daughter brings out the new Barbie. "Dad, she's a nurse now". I see their pictures with Santa at the mall.

My wife is standing in the corner of the living room watching us. Soon the kids get busy with their toys. She comes over and sits down with me, "You don't seem happy to see us."

I try to smile, "It is not that."

"What then?"

"I am just tired of being sent away to the workboat in the Gulf of Mexico every Christmas."

"Don't worry, it will end soon."

"Yea, maybe."

Two weeks go by, and I go through the motions each day, at work and at home. Then one day the department secretary Vicki comes to my desk,

"Warren wants to see you."

"In his office?"

"Yes." Oh great. This must mean a trip to West Africa, the hellhole assignment for offshore work.

"Sit down please," This sounds worse than I thought, surely it is to the Niger Delta or the Gulf of Guinea. Warren has always been very gracious, but he does not need to do this, I am a grown up and I can take it. I sit down. He hands me a letter. I am having trouble reading it. It is signed by the company president. I have been selected to be an Associate Partner. I am also being promoted to Project Manager, just like Fred and Dwayne. "Congratulations," Warren says.

This must a cue, because both Fred and Dwayne come into his office. "Great work," Fred says. "Make us proud," says Dwayne. Warren shakes my hand, then Fred, and then Dwayne. I stumble back to my desk. My mind is on fast forward. I'll be given my own office, my own secretary, and my own project group. It is still the same year. My fortieth birthday is still a few months away. I've been recognized. There is recognition of talent after all, regardless of the color of my skin, my name, or my religion. None of it matters. America *is* the land of opportunity. All those immigrants are right in trying to push their way in across our borders.

Françoise Sagan is Dead

Françoise Sagan is dead. I notice a brief mention in *Time*, close the magazine and sit down. A few minutes later I open the magazine again; the news appears to be genuine enough. It includes a brief bio. "Françoise Sagan was 17 when she wrote her first book, *'Bonjour Tristesse'*, or, 'Welcome, Sadness'. The book became a national bestseller in France".

I remember the book, and my thoughts take me back 40 years into the past. I can recall when Sajir first told me about it. It was our junior year in engineering school. I was waiting for him before outside the lecture room, expecting to see him show up with a large drawing of the structural project we had been working on. Class was about to begin when he appeared, but where was the drawing; all he was holding was a book.

"Where is the drawing?" I ask.

"Oh yes, the drawing, we'll talk about that later. I have to tell you about this book I read."

"What book, Sajir? There was no book assignment this week."

COFFEE WITH CHICORY

"No, no, not for class, it's fiction, no wait, it's kind of a memoir. Actually it's quite autobiographical."

"Sajir, be serious, the drawing is due this afternoon."

The lecture was starting, and we went in. It was two more hours before I could vent my anger at his tardiness, but all he wanted to talk about was his discovery, "This girl is just 17, and she has such insight into life." A girl? OK, so I was interested, "What girl are you talking about, is she mentioned in the book?"

"No, no. She wrote it, she actually wrote the book, her first book, in French, just translated into English."

He produced a small, skinny book, not much compared to the large and complex engineering texts I was used to carrying around.

"That's it?"

"It is really very good. You must read it."

"OK, OK, give it to me, now what about the drawing?"

I snap out of the reverie, and read the magazine again. There is a photograph of a young woman included with the obituary. I don't think I have ever seen her picture before. The face is not familiar. She is quite ordinary looking. I keep staring at the photograph, and again drift back four decades into the past.

I am walking on a red sandstone terrace, along a low railing with short, carved sandstone posts. It's late evening, and the sky is dark. I can't see very far beyond the dim lights, but I can hear the surf. Someone is walking along, and even without turning my head I know it's Sajir. He is talking about Françoise Sagan, "She is remarkable. She has such great insight into life, into relationships, and the meaning of existence." The terrace is about a mile long, and although it's crowded until sunset, after dark it's quite deserted, adding to the sense of mystery induced by pounding of the Indian Ocean on the nearby beach.

We keep walking back and forth, well into the deepening darkness that is peppered by the few dim lights along the terrace, eagerly talking about the book and its author, as the evening closes in around us, around our conversation, and our thoughts.

"Do you think she is telling the truth?"

"Who knows, it's France, so anything is possible."

We speak on end for several hours. The simplicity and the power of her prose; her take on men; her reaction to women. The night air by the beach is damp and cold by the time we leave.

But here I am, in California, forty some years later, looking back, and the past is rushing toward me, as if through the wrong end of a telescope, close enough to reach over and touch, yet so fuzzy, and very unclear around the edges. For four years in engineering school, I lived in the dormitory, and Sajir was a day scholar, commuting from home, but at school we were always together. I haven't spoken to Sajir in four decades. I don't know what has gone on with him, and I'm wondering if he has heard about Sagan's death, or if he even remembers who she was. Does he even remember who I am?

I look through my address book, the database in the computer, and my Rolodex, but no, there's no entry for him. I log into Google and type in Sajir's name along with the country and city, in various combinations, but no luck. From the depths of memory, a word surfaces, M-e-r-i-d-i-a-n. Meridian. Yes, Meridian, Along with his name I add Meridian to the keywords in Google search, and hit return. The very first entry has his name, address and phone number, listing him as president of Meridian Engineering. Blood rushes to my head. This was the business name we had dreamed up in college. So he did go through with the plans we had made, and opened a firm with the same name. Maybe he still remembers Françoise Sagan and her book.

It's early Saturday morning on the other side of the globe. Do they still work on Saturdays? I dial the number from the Google screen. It rings.

"Hello, Meridian Engineering," a male voice answers, reminding me that the receptionist's job is a male position in some parts of the world.

"Is Mr. Sajir in?" I use the south Asian custom of attaching a formal title to the first name. There is no immediate answer. I hear a conversation in the background. "No, sir, Mr. Sajir is not in today," comes the answer now, "He'll be in on Monday." The receptionist is reluctant to give his boss's home number to a stranger, so I thank him and hang up.

My thoughts again take me back to the same red sandstone terrace by the beach. The terrace was built to commemorate some important occasion, perhaps Queen Victoria's Golden Jubilee, celebrating 50 years of her reign. It was a grand structure almost a mile long that used to stretch into the ocean, but over the years the coastline had receded, and now the structure was surrounded by sand and native shrubs. The surf was hidden from view, but could be heard through the still night air. Only during rare storm surges seawater would come around the terrace for a few hours.

It was during one of our walks here that we had discussed our future careers. I remember how we planned various details of our future business. What kinds of clients we will have, what technical areas we needed to master, what graduate schools we should go to?

"I want to learn more about buildings and structures." Sajir was first to make up his mind. Soon afterward, I announced my intention to learn about tunnels, dams and highways. Together we would make a great team.

In the here and now, I am eager to read Sagan's book. I drive to Barnes & Noble, pick up a copy, and finish it by Sunday evening. When it is Monday morning on the other side of the globe, I make the international call again, and this time Sajir is in his office. I identify myself. There is a pause on the other side. He repeats my name slowly.

COFFEE WITH CHICORY

"Where are you?"

"I am in California, in Los Angeles, actually near Los Angeles, in Orange County."

"Orange County? Yes, yes, I know where that is."

He is homing in, as if in a gradually tightening spiral. We chat for a couple of minutes about innocuous topics. Now I'm certain he knows who I am. "Sajir, do you remember who Françoise Sagan is?" I can picture him, early on this Monday morning, getting a call from half way around the world, from someone he knew 40 years ago, and being asked about a French-sounding name of an uncertain gender.

"No, who is that?"

"An author, a woman, she wrote a book many years ago, *Bonjour Tristesse*, do you remember the book?"

"I am not sure. Maybe, vaguely."

This is not going well, perhaps I expected too much. I tell him about his eagerness when he read the book the first time. I describe my own excitement. I bring up the hours of conversation we had about the book, about the author and about life. Then I mention that she died last week, I saw the obituary, thought of the shared excitement we had felt. No, nothing rings a bell; he has nothing to contribute about this Sagan or her book.

"Are you planning to visit any time soon?" he asks.

"Sometime next year, how about you?"

"Well, actually, I am coming to the States next month to visit my daughter who lives in Houston."

"How about coming to California also?"

"No, it is too short a visit, I'll barely get over jet lag." We exchange some niceties, the phone call ends, and I adjust my schedule to fit in a weekend trip to Houston. Over the next three weeks we exchange several e-mails and phone calls. He will keep one evening free in Houston so we can get together and have dinner along with our wives.

It is three weeks later. My wife and I land at Houston's Bush Senior Airport on a Friday afternoon. I turn the cell phone on to find a message waiting from Sajir, reminding me about our appointment the next day. We drive to the hotel, check in, have dinner and go to sleep.

The next day I call his number. He answers, we chat for a while and discuss the dinner plans.

"Why don't you select a restaurant", I suggest, "Your daughter must know some good ones. He agrees and puts his daughter on the phone, "Uncle, where will you be coming from?" she addresses me in the south Asian custom. "I am staying in a hotel near Loop 8 and the Southwest Freeway."

"Oh yes, I know where that is, you are not very far from our house," and she proceeds to tell me which exit to take, which street to turn into, and that her house is at the end of the third cul-de-sac on the left.

It is evening, and my wife and I leave the hotel. I estimate about 45 minutes for my drive, including

COFFEE WITH CHICORY

10 minutes for missing the exit and backtracking. I'm glad to be picking him up from his daughter's house rather than meeting in a crowded restaurant, perhaps being unable to recognize each other. People do change over 40 years. I wonder if he's bald, as I am. My youthful broad forehead changed to a receding hairline in middle age, ending in near baldness that I am now comfortably settled in. Well, perhaps, not so comfortably.

I pull up to the house, but before I have a chance to get out of the car and ring the door bell, the front door opens and a kid pops his head out, followed by a slim man in his sixties, standing at a peculiar angle, leaning noticeably to the right, as if he is about to lose his balance, except that he does not. His pose looks odd, and also oddly familiar, but I cannot place it. His hair is grey; so OK, he has more hair than I do.

He waves to me in recognition, goes back in, and a moment later, emerges with his wife. I get out of the car to open the rear door for them. We shake hands, exchange a brief greeting, and then we're off.

"Where to?" I ask.

"The Aquarium," he says, "I hope you like seafood."

"Yes, we do", my wife and I answer in unison.

Sajir's wife adds, "Our daughter took us to this restaurant last year. It has a beautiful aquarium." We're approaching the freeway ramps.

"Tell me, should I go north or south?"

"North, definitely north, and straight on the Southwest Freeway," he always was certain about the little things, "And keep going till you cross Highway 10. I think it's what you call an Interstate."

"Yes, 10 is definitely an Interstate, it goes all the way to Los Angeles." I'm looking for things we can quickly agree on.

We're focused on the directions to our destination. We comment on the neighborhoods, read exit signs, and keep talking, as if to get used to each other's voices. I'm meeting a close friend after forty years, and all I can recall from his past, our past, are the mundane and superficial. What were the really meaningful things?

We get to the restaurant.

"Please wait, we have a seating delay," the hostess informs us. So we stand in the restaurant entryway, right next to a tall aquarium, almost three stories high. "Look at the striped fish, so translucent," my wife is pointing up. Sajir is running his fingers on the surface of the aquarium, "I wonder if it is made of glass or acrylic, and what its wall thickness is?" Sajir and I start calculating the hydrostatic pressure.

His wife senses we are drifting into engineering jargon, and immediately says, "How many kids do you have?"

"Oh, two," I answer, interrupting my arithmetic, "A boy and a girl." We talk about our kids for a while. They have three, two girls and one boy.

We have been standing in the restaurant entryway for a while, and I notice Sajir begins to lean to one side.

COFFEE WITH CHICORY

Slowly, I recall an incident from 40 years ago. We were lined up for the class graduation picture. The photographer emerged from behind the hooded tripod, and singled out Sajir, "Over there, third from the left in the back row. Please stand up straight, this is not the time to be jaunty." Everyone laughed. Sajir straightened up, and the photo session went forward. Yes, I remember that stance now. Sajir never stood straight. But we were young. His slight lean to the right was a stylish, slightly roguish expression of confidence. But now, it appears as another frailty in someone who is no longer young.

We are finally seated, in full view of the huge aquarium; the waiter takes our orders, and departs. I am dying to talk about Françoise Sagan, and try to bring her up a couple of times, but realize that a conversation between four people has its own flow, its peculiar rhythm, and not as easy to control as when two of us used to talk. But I press forward, and interject, "You know that Francoise Sagan, when she was only seventeen…." The conversation stops, and they all look at me as if I had knocked my drink over. Our wives have not read the book, and Sajir does not remember anything about it. I look around; a couple of fish have stopped swimming and are staring at me. "What I wanted to say was, has anyone noticed the hidden lights in the aquarium that create this glow." The fish swim away, and the conversation resumes.

So I won't talk about Sagan or her book, but I still desperately want to get into a conversation that is insightful, and pithy, and about the inner meaning of things. But how do I do that, when I don't even remember whether my close friend prefers Coke or Seven Up. Or was it lemonade?

Soon our food arrives, and we sit there like normal people and talk about normal ordinary things, our kids, the movies we have seen, the weather last Thursday, and the décor in the restaurant. I feel awkward biting into seafood in full view of the colorful tropical fish swimming by. It seems inhumane; perhaps also cruel and unusual. I decide this is an insightful topic, and speak up "I think to eat fish in front of other fish is not in good taste?" They all laugh. I opened with a boring topic, skipped the meaningful, and have now slipped into comedy.

I don't want to talk about the war, or about global warming, or about the hunger in the world, while having a five-course meal. So I shut up, and eat. Sajir's wife is speaking, "Our second daughter, Shazia, lives in New York, and is still not married. She has such high criteria. I keep telling her to be realistic." Sajir interjects, "She is an architect, designing high-rise buildings, so her head is always in the clouds." My wife adds, "Give her a chance, creative people take longer to mature. Our daughter graduated from Art Center College of Design in Pasadena, but still behaves like a teenager."

The kids, the weather, the colorful fish, the mundane, and the ordinary, are our props, and gradually, right before my eyes, or rather, right within my hearing, the conversation is evolving into something meaningful. I keep listening, and give up my hurried and harried approach, and tell myself that I am trying to reach across a 40-year chasm and now both Sajir and I have become connected to many other things and many other people. Women we have exchanged vows with. Children we brought into this world, and share our genes with. We are no longer surrounded by college friends we could always ignore.

Things are coming along, and this may yet prove to be the start of another great friendship, but it is not the old friendship. And it requires time, and patience and requires the tacit approval and understanding of others who depend on us, and in turn, upon whom we depend.

A Different kind of Dentist

THE VAGUE discomfort in my left upper jaw is becoming a throbbing pain. I look through the medicine cabinet in the bathroom and find a small bottle promising toothache relief, pour it into my mouth, and wait for fifteen minutes. Nothing happens. I brush my teeth, slowly, gently, hoping to catch up on some past neglect, but there is no improvement, except that my breath smells fresher. It is late on a Sunday evening, so I take a couple of aspirins and go to bed.

I fall asleep thinking of a story I once heard about alchemists in a quest for immortality. They devised a brew that was going to provide them the answer. They stirred it, and added esoteric ingredients at critical moments. After many days and sleepless nights they were exhausted. The brew was coming to a final moment of culmination and had to be watched over very carefully. One by one the alchemists were dozing off from exhaustion. One had a severe toothache, and could not sleep. He was left to watch over the cauldron on this final night so the others could rest.

COFFEE WITH CHICORY

The lone alchemist sat there stoking the fire, holding his throbbing, painful jaw in one hand, and stirring the cauldron with the other. It was well after midnight when the boiling stopped, and the whole pot began to glow. There was a flash of lightning, a bird materialized, fluttered around, and then spoke, "What do you want to know?"

The alchemist's instructions were to ask, "What is the secret of immortality?" But what came out of this mouth was, "Whet is the cure for toothache?" The bird stopped fluttering, and shrieked, "Pliers." There was another flash of lightning, and the bird disappeared.

Next morning I get to the office thinking of the unfortunate alchemist. By now my speech is limited, so I seek my secretary's help in locating a dentist who can see me right away. She looks through the yellow pages and starts calling dentists one by one. It takes her almost an hour, but she does find one who can see me.

The sign on the door says, "Dr. Smythe, Family Dentistry". The waiting room décor reminds me of the pre-school our son attended. The walls are decorated with characters out of nursery rhymes and fairy tales. There are some very small chairs around, in addition to the larger adult chairs. There are toys, comic books, and illustrated storybooks. Two families are waiting in the room, and judging by the patients' ages, Dr. Smythe's practice appears to be limited to children's teeth.

A smiling receptionist appears at the inner door, asks my name, tells me to sit down, and chats with a couple of the kids with the easy confidence of a kindergarten teacher. A few minutes later I am led inside and seated in a dental chair. There are cardboard mobiles hanging from the ceiling. The wallpaper has pictures of clouds and the undersides of hot air balloons, giving the feeling of being outdoors. A smiling, kind-looking dental assistant comes in and talks to me as if she is telling a bedtime story, and then Dr. Smythe joins us. He is mild-mannered like a community college teacher, and seems pleased to have an adult patient to talk to about grown-up subjects, but starts telling me jokes from some children's humor magazine. All this time I am sitting in the dental chair clutching my jaw.

Another smiling attendant comes into the room with a tray full of instruments. The doctor begins to tap on my teeth, and I give a muffled yell when he hits the right one. An x-ray is taken and confirms his prognosis that the tooth has to be taken out. I am in no condition to resist his suggestion.

The doctor leaves the room, and a couple of minutes later shows up wearing a large apron that covers his whole front side. The two assistants are also covered up in half-face masks and gloves. He injects a local anesthetic and the whole crew gathers around me. The doctor picks up a pair of pliers from the instrument tray, attaches it to the tooth and pulls hard. Nothing happens. He goes to the other side, and pulls sideways. Still nothing. Then he tries to pull it downward, almost squatting down, and though my head receives several jolts, the tooth stays. He tries to twist it out by circling around me. He, the dental chair, and I are all tangled up in a big twist, while I stare at pictures of hot air balloons on the ceiling.

After a few more attempts the doctor steps back, takes off his gloves and wipes his forehead. The dental assistants look distressed as they see the look of defeat on the doctor's face, and their smiles are gone. They leave the room, and I can hear them whispering in the hallway. A couple of minutes later the doctor comes back, but he is not wearing his apron. "You have to go to an oral surgeon". "A surgeon?" "Well, he is another kind of dentist. We have made an appointment for you with Dr. Muller." The assistants come in to wipe my face, remove the bib, help me get out of the chair, give me a map to Dr. Muller's office, and seem to be wishing me luck.

A half hour later I am entering Dr. Muller's waiting room. This is a different kind of dental office. The waiting room is devoid of anything that might make the place look weak or soft. There is an image of a soaring eagle on one wall. The eagle is about to swoop down on some poor bird. The receptionist sitting by the window looks like a bureaucrat from an eastern European socialist country. After confirming my name, she wants a full payment for the upcoming procedure. This seems rather unusual, but I go along, and hand her the money.

After paying the full fee I am shown into Dr. Muller's office. He has a handlebar mustache, is built like a wrestler, and wants me to sign a waiver of liability with a lot of fine print. I don't even try to read and just sign.

The doctor takes the papers from my hand, "My assistant Max will show you to the room". I turn around to see a muscular man in his thirties towering over me. He leads me to a room that is unlike any dentist's office I have seen. It does not have a dental chair, but has a surgery table. I look up at the bright circular light.

Max has the build of a mixed martial arts instructor, and stands in the door of the surgery room with his arms folded across his chest. "I am a veteran of Desert Storm", he says as a way of introducing himself, and starts telling me about the intricacies of desert warfare, while blocking my only escape route. Soon Dr. Muller arrives, and asks me to lie down on the surgery table. I close my eyes against the glare. Max covers my chest and most of the face with what looks like a large bib. Dr. Muller injects a local anesthetic. About one minute later, both the doctor and his assistant pounce on me in a surprise attack that lasts only a few seconds. I cannot tell who is pulling and who is pushing, because it is all over so fast. "Well, we are done," Dr. Muller, says, and I realize that I have not felt any sensation in my mouth at all. The offending tooth is gone, and my mouth is stuffed with a wad of gauze. Max checks my blood pressure, and about five minutes later I am shown out the back door with a prescription for painkillers in my hand. I leave with the distinct feeling that Dr. Muller is a different kind of dentist.

The Visible Moon

Each day I get up at dawn to eat an early meal, and then refrain from food or drink until sunset. I have followed this routine for nearly a month. In a couple of days, Ramadan, the month of fasting, comes to an end. Muslims living in Orange County have been talking about a countywide prayer gathering this year.

Realizing that only a couple of more days are left, I call up Reza, our program chair.

"Reza, have you finalized the arrangements yet?" There is a pause at the other end, "Well, I have reserved the banquet hall at the Marriott, but there is still some confusion. Why don't you come over tomorrow afternoon and give me a hand."

Confusion? What confusion could there be? Then I remember the Ramadan confusion we used to have in the small town where I grew up near the Afghan border. After breaking the fast at sunset on the 29th day, everyone was in the streets, looking for the new moon. Rumors were rampant; the moon had been seen on Jinnah Road, or in the Hazara district, or perhaps near the railway station. Some years each neighborhood was on its own in deciding when to celebrate.

COFFEE WITH CHICORY

Then the town administration set up a moon sighting committee of prominent scholars and imams in town. On the evening of the 29th day of fasting, just before sunset, the committee would board an airplane, take off, and circle the city, while searching the horizon for any sign of the new moon. An hour or so later, the plane would land, and the mullahs would make their pronouncement, having just descended from heaven.

One year the atmosphere in the city was too hazy to view the moon, both on the ground, and from up in the air. The moon sighting committee met in the Grand Mosque and announced that we had one more day of fasting, and the festival would be held the day after tomorrow. About an hour after the official announcement, two villagers showed up at the Grand Mosque, claiming that the weather was quite clear up in the mountains, and that they had seen the new moon. The committee was hastily re-assembled.

When I arrived five bearded men were seated in the center of the mosque in a circle, and over a hundred people were gathered around them, all straining forward to hear what was going on. The two villagers had been brought in, and they looked bewildered. The older villager was in his fifties, and the younger in his twenties. One of the committee members asked the older man.

"What is your name?"
"Murad"
"Well, Murad, where do you live?"

"In Baleli, behind the Dead-Man Mountain."

"How old are you?"

"Forty."

"What day is it today?"

"Tuesday."

Another committee member raised his hand up. "How many fingers do you see?"

"Five."

A third committee member asked, "You see that billboard across the street," Murad nodded, "What does it say?"

Murad stared at the billboard, but did not say anything. Someone from the back shouted, "He is blind." Murad shook his head, leaned over to one of the committee members and whispered something. The committee members turned around, "He says he can't read or write."

The proceedings went on and on. The village Imam and the night watchman were called in to vouch that the two villagers were reliable individuals. Finally, near midnight, the committee reversed the earlier decision, declared that the Eid festival was to be held the next day, and allowed Murad and his young companion to return home. Town criers were sent out with drums to make announcements in the streets. It was past midnight, but stores started opening so people could buy new clothes, new shoes and groceries for the big feast. I don't think anyone in town got much sleep that night. But that was fifty years ago in a small town in the Hindu

COFFEE WITH CHICORY

Kush Mountains. But now, in the 21st century, in this age of instant communication, surely there can't be any confusion.

The next day I arrive at Reza's place in Fullerton to see charts, faxes, and e-mails scattered all over his living room. He is talking on two cell phones, and peering at the computer screen. The house phone rings. I pick it up, walk over to Reza, and try to draw his attention.

"The manager from Marriott Hotel is on the line."

Reza removes one cell phone from his ear, "Tell him I don't have the answer, I need another half an hour."

I inform the manager, there is a pause, "Tell Reza this is the final half-hour extension, I'll not be able to hold the banquet hall any longer."

I wait for Reza to get off his cell phones. "What is all this about? Haven't you confirmed the banquet Hall yet? Reza, you were supposed to do this two weeks ago."

"I know, I know, but I have not been able to confirm the moon sighting," he sighs. "Tomorrow is only the biggest Muslim holiday of the year, and I still don't know whether it is actually going to happen."

I stare at him for a full minute, "Reza, you know what this sounds like. Imagine this is December 24, and we are trying to decide whether to celebrate Christmas on the 25th or 26th." Reza does not look at me, "The Marriott guy already used this example; please don't repeat it."

I keep quiet and let Reza gain his composure, any more teasing and he will never volunteer again. He finally looks up.

"I have been trying to get a consensus, why don't you check with the Tustin Group."

I call up Muhsin, the physics professor.

"Have you guys decided about the joint prayer gathering?"

"What is there to decide," he answers, "It is purely a scientific decision."

"So what are you saying?"

"I am saying there is no need to be staring at the heavens to see the new moon, we should look up the almanac. It tells us when the new moon will appear, and celebrate accordingly."

It sounds reasonable to me; I hang up, turn to Reza, and tell him.

He wipes his forehead, "I just spoke with the Costa Mesa representative."

"You mean one of the Wahabis?"

He nods, "They think it is almost heretical to look up the almanac on our own."

"Well, what are they suggesting?"

"We should follow Mecca, and observe our festivals exactly on the same date as the City of Mecca".

"Reza, you know that some of the groups simply won't follow anything dictated by the Saudis."

COFFEE WITH CHICORY

"Well, the Costa Mesa community is adamant." Reza looks helpless. "They think that if we all followed the Saudi calendar, things would be lot more harmonious."

I call up Dr. Mateen. He knows many of the Indians and Pakistanis. "Don't worry about us. We are ready to celebrate with the very first group." Next I call up one of the Abu Malik brothers to check what the Syrian families want to do. "I am on a long-distance call with Damascus, waiting for their decision."

I hang up and look at the clock; we have barely ten more minutes left before the Marriott deadline. Reza is again looking at his Mac.

"Are you searching for guidance from that screen? You have to make a decision in the next ten minutes."

He looks up, "I am looking at this web site called 'visible_moon.com'. It's being run by two astrophysicists from Caltech. They take the astronomical calendar, which tells us when the new moon will be above the horizon. Then they look at the weather bureau forecast, which tells us about the atmospheric conditions such as cloud cover, and make a prediction of whether it is physically possible to see the moon. They have just posted their final statement for tonight."

"Spare me the theory Reza, and tell me what they say."

Reza turns back to his Mac, "In plain words, it is physically impossible to view the new moon tonight, anywhere in North America." Calm has returned to

Reza's face, "The Eid holiday cannot happen tomorrow. We will celebrate it the day after tomorrow."

Reza picks up the phone, calls up Marriott Hotel, cancels the reservation, and turns off his computer. "One more day of fasting, and then we'll have the prayer gathering and the feast," his voice trails off as he sinks into the sofa.

The doorbell rings. Reza does not move a muscle, so I open the door. It is Selim, Orange County's resident Muslim scholar from the Laguna Hills mosque. We exchange greetings and I inform him that we have checked the web site, and the Eid festival will not be held tomorrow. Reza has sunk so far back into the sofa to be almost invisible. Selim stands in the middle of the room, scratching his beard, as I describe to him how we arrived at the decision, how we canceled the banquet hall, and how we are making plans for day after tomorrow. He keeps staring straight ahead.

"That is why we cannot leave decision-making to hacks like you and Reza," he says.

There is movement in the upholstery, and Reza sticks his neck out of the sofa, "What are you saying?"

Selim looks at him. "Just that you have not used the only authentic method recommended by our noble prophet, peace be upon him; you two are not following the example of the scholars."

Reza again disappears into the sofa.

COFFEE WITH CHICORY

Well, at one time everyone in the world followed the moon." Selim begins in a scholarly tone. "The lunar year is approximately 355 days long, but the earth takes 365 days to complete its orbit around the sun. So every three or four years they had to add one month to keep summer in June and winter in December."

I don't get his point, "Are we Muslims the only ones left who follow the lunar calendar?"

"No, but the others use it in a limited way."

Selim looks me in the eye, "Do you know how the date for Easter is decided?"

"I know it is never outside March or April." I hazard a guess. "I think it is the first Sunday following the first full moon that occurs after the spring equinox."

"You are close, but once again, wrong." Selim finally sits down. "It is not the actual full moon, but the ecclesiastical full moon, and the spring equinox is fixed at March 21. This method is based on calculations done in the third and sixth centuries, so it is remarkable that the ecclesiastical date is only two or three days off from the actual full moon."

Reza rises from the sofa, "And what about the Jewish calendar? Hanukkah and Rosh Hashanah are always shifting around by a few days."

Selim's tone is softer, "Well, actually, the Jews are the closest to us Muslims, because they follow the lunar calendar for all their holidays and festivals. Each day in the Jewish calendar is one spin of the earth on its axis, beginning at sunset, just like ours. Each month in their calendar is one full rotation of the moon around the Earth, just like in the Muslim calendar."

I jump to a conclusion, "Then their festivals should rotate around the entire year, but Hanukkah is never in July, is it."

Selim speaks one word at a time, "Because you did not let me finish. Their year is one rotation of the earth around the sun. So a year in the Jewish calendar is either 12 or 13 months so everything fits within the Gregorian calendar."

"It is simple then", Reza looks hopeful. "We Muslims should follow their example."

Selim stands up erect, "No, we Muslims must actually view the moon, that is our tradition." Selim looks at both of us "Have you two tried to go out and actually look at the horizon today."

Reza and I look at each other, "No."

Selim looks at his watch, "Well it is too late to do that now, but I can call some people in Anaheim Hills who were on their way up to Santiago Peak with a telescope. Their observations must by complete by now." Selim takes out his cell phone and starts pressing the keys very deliberately, one by one.

"Hello, Faisal, are you guys still up there? You are packing up the telescope? What did you say? You actually saw the moon? And do you have two witnesses? Who are they, put them on the phone." As Selim talks to the two witnesses, his voice is rising, and Reza's shoulders begin to droop. Finally, Selim hangs up. "Allah be praised. The moon has been sighted, right here, in Orange County. The Eid prayer will be held tomorrow morning." "But, but..." Reza moans.

"No ifs or buts, if this method was good enough for the prophet of God, peace be upon him, then it is good enough for me." I tell Selim about the computer calculations done by the Caltech astrophysicists. It is physically impossible to see the new moon tonight anywhere in North America "Well, they are human, aren't they, their pronouncement is not the word of God, is it?"

The argument ends with this word of God. Reza picks up the phone, and sheepishly dials the number for Marriott. I think I hear hysterical laughter at the other end; Reza is on the phone for several minutes, pleading. Finally he hangs up, and turns to us, "The banquet hall has been given away, but the breakfast area is still available. As for the prayer congregation, well, the best they can do is give us the rear parking lot"

The next morning I arrive at the Marriott in Irvine at 7 AM to find the back parking lot covered with white sheets. Men, women and children are arranging themselves in rows. There is still some fog, and it is quite chilly. Everyone expected to pray in the banquet hall, and most people are lightly dressed. I detect some shivers in the crowd, and though there are a few sneezes, no one complains. As soon as the Imam completes his prescribed sermon, the congregation rises. Hugs and greetings are exchanged, and everyone heads to the breakfast buffet. A small crowd has gathered around the hot coffee and tea dispensers, and the piping hot scrambled eggs are a big hit. I look around the room, searching for familiar faces. At the far end of the buffet line, two faces look familiar. I think I have spotted Murad, the villager from Baleli, and his young companion. It cannot be, these two are in business suits. I shake my head and look away, and when I look back, they are gone. I get my own breakfast and join some friends.

III

The Moorish Arabesque

I pick up my phone and dial the string of digits one by one.

"Ola," a male voice answers.

"Is this Senor Viega?"

"Si, Si."

"Senor Jose Viega?"

"Yes, yes."

Assured of his identity, I introduce myself. He gasps, "How long has it been my friend? Ten years?"

"Almost."

He laughs his signature belly laugh, removing any doubts about his identity.

"After so long, it cannot be a mere social call. Tell me what you are calling about."

I explain the purpose of my call. There is silence at the other end. "Viega?" I say, "Are you still there?"

"Yes, yes, I am here."

After another pause, he says, "How soon can you get here?"

"I can leave tonight."

Allowing time for transatlantic travel, we set up a meeting time. "I'll call you when I get to Granada."

"Agreed."

COFFEE WITH CHICORY

We chat for a few minutes and then end the phone call.

I make the travel arrangements, pack, and show up at the airport at dusk. I have kept my travel plans to myself, hoping to avoid any unpleasant encounters. I had impressed the need for confidentiality on Jose Viega, and I'm hoping that he will keep his word. Holding on to the briefcase, I enter the business class cabin of Iberia airlines. The uniformed flight attendant in her blue pencil skirt and white blouse greets me in Spanish, and I reply in English, causing momentary confusion on her face. There is a slight problem having brown skin, heading to Spain, and not being able to speak any Spanish. Although I have taught myself to read and understand several languages for my academic work, fluency in vernacular speech is not my forte.

As we reach cruising altitude, Iberia staff serves a sumptuous lamb dinner, followed by an assortment of deserts. Before retiring for the night I decide to use the rest room. I have wedged my briefcase between my seat and the airplane hull, and the only way to remove it is by tilting it to the right. I look around at the nearby passengers. Across the aisle an older man with a grey goatee is already asleep. One row forward a couple is busy spreading one blanket over both their seats. Directly ahead of me a businessman-type with loosened necktie is staring on a graphic display of some sharply declining business metric on his laptop computer.

The Moorish Arabesque

I get up and walk to the forward lavatory. As I look back toward my seat I notice that in the seat directly behind mine there is a woman in a white dress. She seems engrossed in a book, and has sunk very low in her seat, making her invisible from my seat. She seems to have entered that stage of life when women are still recognizable as formerly beautiful. The stage that begins in late thirties for some, and early forties for others, and lasts up to a decade or so. My glance lingers and turns to a look, but I tear away before it becomes a stare. A few minutes later I come out of the bathroom, and scan the cabin. Everything appears to be in place, and the occupants as they were. From the corner of my eye I catch a fleeting motion in white. Either the lady in white is hurriedly getting back into her seat, or perhaps merely adjusting her position. I walk back to my seat and wonder if there is something peculiar. When I went to the rest room the briefcase was upright, but now it is tilted to the left, and wedged in even tighter. It seems someone tried to remove it by tiling it to the left. Tilting to the right would have snapped it right out of its snug position. I leave it in place, but realize I need to be vigilant for the remainder of my journey, and place my leg across the briefcase.

I think of the meeting two days earlier that prompted me to take this trip. At a posh law office in Beverly Hills, the usually articulate and very famous trial attorney began haltingly, "I am sure you are aware that perfectly innocent art collectors can sometimes end up with stolen pieces." I nodded, but did not want to say anything until I knew his drift. "I have a client," the attorney continued, "who acquired a rare piece that is the premier missing item being sought in Europe."

What came to my mind were the two highly publicized paintings that had been stolen during the last few months, the van Gogh from Amsterdam or the Picasso from Copenhagen, and I decided to clear the air right away. "But my expertise is in antiquities, what help could I possibly be in identifying a Picasso or a van Gogh?"

"Well, I should tell you some more. It is an architectural piece that was acquired by my client nearly fifty years ago, without knowing that it was a stolen item. It is only recently that it has become sought after as a missing national treasure. In short, we need your help in returning it."

My foot slips on the briefcase, bringing me back to the Iberia airlines plane. We race through dawn and early morning, and by the time the plane begins its descent at Madrid's Barajas airport, it is mid morning.

Carefully removing my briefcase from its safe spot I get up to leave the plane and notice that the lady in white has already left the cabin. Madrid airport looks dazzling compared to the rather industrial architecture of the airports that I left behind in the States. Walking past the gates and ticket counters of the passenger terminal in Madrid, I see many stores that have the appearance of abundance and complete freedom for the shoppers, yet are closely watched by young sales girls lurking behind shelves and counters.

I walk into a bookstore, and notice a man standing near the magazine racks looking in my direction. When I look at him, he disappears behind his magazine. I look away, and again catch a glimpse of him looking in my direction, as if trying to size me up. He is in his forties, casually dressed, and looks stout without being overly muscular. He is wearing a grey beret, which is partly hiding the left side of his face. As he looks away, I get a glimpse of a prominent scar that begins near his left ear, and goes part of the way down his cheek. And then I notice the magazine he is reading, it is the August issue of Architectural Digest. I wonder if he has seen page 52, showing an interview I gave, along with my picture. One question I was asked during the interview was my opinion of the three most important missing pieces from the renaissance. I stated what is commonly agreed upon in the profession, the altar piece stolen from the cathedral of Notre Dame, the missing cornice from the inner gallery at the Louvre, and of course, the crown jewel of them all, the arabesque centerpiece missing from the Alhambra palace in Granada, which went missing over one hundred years ago. My field of practice is obscure and it's rare that someone off the street is going to recognize me. As I turn to leave, a couple of customers enter the store, and my path is temporarily blocked. I back up, and nearly topple over someone. I turn around to look, and see the man with the scar bent down as if reaching for my briefcase. He quickly stands up and steals away. My spine chills. I hadn't realized that he was standing right behind me, and if I hadn't stepped back, he could have easily snatched the briefcase from my hand.

The gate for the flight to Granada is almost at the end of the passenger terminal. I present my identification and the reservation number to the agent at the gate, and receive a boarding card for the business class. Once in the plane I look around at the passengers on my side of the curtain, and my gaze stops at a woman sitting across the aisle and one row ahead of me. She looks familiar, and it takes me a few moments to realize that I am looking at the lady in white, only now she has tied a red scarf around her neck and pulled her hair up, significantly altering her appearance. I can now see the book she has been reading, Washington Irving's "Tales of the Alhambra," published in 1832. I remember the book well. The palace at Alhambra had been in a state of neglect for several centuries. Washington Irving visited the palace during the early 1800's, and found that squatters were living in the palace, and renting rooms out. He took up residence in the palace for several months, and wrote his fictional account of the last days of the palace – Irving was the last person known to have seen the entire Moorish arabesque intact. Over the years several pieces of the arabesque carvings were stolen, and the centerpiece has never been recovered. I wonder if she has paid attention to page 48, which contains a complete description of the pattern carved in the palace of Alhambra.

As we land in Granada, a staircase is brought and attached to the exit door. Passengers climb down the staircase and walk the short distance to the terminal building. In front of the terminal building is a three-lane road, and across the road a surface parking lot, which seems to be the destination for most of the people. I look around but don't see any cabs. I know I wanted to arrive in Granada unannounced and unnoticed, but this isn't what I had in mind.

I hear a voice from behind me, "You like to ride?"

I turn around and recognize the lady in white, with her red scarf around her neck. It takes me a second to be sure that she is talking to me.

"Thanks," I say, "Where are you heading?"

She smiles as she says, "To city. Where you want to go?" I fumble through my pockets and find the paper with the hotel's name and address, "Hotel Dauro II," I tell her, "near the main cathedral." "Yes, I know Dauro II," she says, "I go near there." She turns around, looking back at me expectantly, as if to say, 'are you coming or not?' I hesitate. Isn't this the woman I have been suspecting of following me? Does it seem wise to go with her willingly? I look back at my desolate surroundings, then look at her, beckoning me to hurry up. I take two reluctant steps after her. She sails into her stride, reaches for the terminal door and holds it open for me. Caution again grips me.

"But how are you going, there don't seem to be any cabs around?"

"Taxis on strike," she says, "Airport charge too much tax. I rent car."

Wow, why didn't I think of that? I throw caution to the wind and enter the terminal building. This may be my only chance to reach the city today.

"Perhaps I'll rent another car," I tell her weakly.

"All cars rented. No more cars today," she says with a chuckle, and then turns around, "I am Carmen."

I introduce myself, and we keep walking. She offers to help me by carrying the briefcase. I refuse, she shrugs, maintaining her stride through the hallway. She exits through the left side of the terminal building where there is a small parking lot with rental cars in numbered parking stalls. She seems to know where she is going, so I keep following her. We get to a car shaped something between a small van and a hatchback, and she opens the back. One suitcase is already there, presumably hers. I lift my suitcase into the trunk, but keep the briefcase with me, and get into the front passenger seat. She gets in on the driver's side, looks toward me to make sure I am buckled in.

"I'm really grateful," I say.

She nods, and starts the car, "I see you wait for taxi. I know there is no taxi." We go in a wide arc through the parking lot, and as we are about to exit, I notice that another car is starting up, and the driver is wearing a grey beret. As we leave the parking lot and head on to the pavement outside, I look back to see that the other car is also coming out of the parking lot, right behind us.

I look back a couple of times trying to recall the car that left the parking lot right after us, and Carmen asks, "What you look for?"

"I thought someone was following us."

She looks in the rear view mirror for a few moments, and then speeds up to get on to the highway.

"Do you know who may be following us?"

"I don't know", she says. I can sense concern in her face, and she begins driving somewhat erratically. At first I think she's nervous, but then I realize that she's attempting evasive action. By now we've entered the city proper, and there is more traffic around us, making it difficult to put some distance between us and the other car. At one point the adjacent lane slows down as a large truck changes lanes, and we pull up along the other car. I get a glimpse of the driver in the grey beret, but before I can see his face, he pulls away, and is able to position himself behind us to the left. Realizing that the highway is too heavily traveled, Carmen suddenly takes an exit from the second driving lane, cutting across the path of several cars.

The maneuver works, and as we exit, I can see the other car with the driver in a grey beret speeding down the highway, trapped between two large vans. I see a

COFFEE WITH CHICORY

smile on Carmen's face as we see the other driver shake his fist in anger, and several of the drivers whose path we crossed cursing us. She seems to be deriving pleasure from doing something naughty and exciting, as well as putting a bad guy in his place.

We find the hotel and she drops me by the door. I thank her and offer to pay for a portion of the car rental, but she waves me off, as if she was merely doing her job. In keeping with the urban setting of the hotel, the lobby is tiny, though elegant, and newly re-modeled. There are no overstuffed sofas so typical of hotels in the States, but rather dainty wood furniture that looks quite comfortable. I look around for a registration desk, and finally locate a small counter that looks more like a built-in shelf with a lone clerk standing behind it. She also looks spare with a drawn face and wide-frame glasses that make her look like a youthful librarian.

She processes my reservation and hands me a computer-coded piece of plastic that passes for a hotel room key these days. The lobby is not very spacious, but has the look of ample roominess because of the high ceiling and the harmonious wall décor. The upper portion of the wall is dark wood paneling, and under indirect lighting, gives the lobby a depth that it may not possess if measured with a tape. The lower half of each wall is white, and covered with a geometrical pattern in faux carving resembling stone. The sameness of the décor around all four walls, and the lighting intended to make the space appear large, also make it difficult to discern openings such as the exit door or the elevator entrance. As I scan the lobby walls I become engrossed in the pattern of the faux carvings, which looks vaguely familiar, especially in Granada. Millions of people visit each year to see the Alhambra famous for its carvings and engravings in abstract geometric patterns derived from the shapes of plants and flowers. What better design for the faux engraving in the lobby than a copy of the Alhambra patterns so well recognized in the art world?

I find the elevator, but before getting in I stand to one side and study the white walls. The interior decorator has taken bits and pieces of patterns from various buildings within the Alhambra palace complex and juxtaposed them together so that one cannot follow any individual pattern for very long. If one tries to follow the pattern across two or three panels the eye loses track of the continuity because of the visual complexity. I enter the elevator and go up to my room.

I enter my hotel room and find it to be unexpectedly small, but very well laid out. There is just enough room for my suitcase in the closet, which already has a combination safe sitting in it, courtesy of the hotel. There are designer touches in everything from the beddings to the bathroom fixtures. I unpack, freshen up and rest for a while, then call Mr. Viega. I want to avoid being seen with him in public until I have completed my assignment, so he has a plan worked out. "Come in on the 11:30 tour tomorrow."

COFFEE WITH CHICORY

I put my wallet and passport in the safe and lock it, then slide the briefcase under my bed. It does not take very long before the day's exhaustion overtakes me.

The ringing phone wakes me up, and a look at the windows makes me realize the night is over and it's my wake-up call. I get up, and check to make sure my door is still locked from the inside, and then go to the bathroom. My appetite is also awake, so I dress and go down looking for breakfast with my briefcase in one hand.

I am beginning to feel anxious about exactly how to deliver the missing architectural piece back to its rightful place. After all, I am carrying contraband, possession of which carries huge penalties. I have transported missing and stolen rare objects to the museums in the past, but nothing with the notoriety and national passion attached to the missing piece from the Alhambra.

After breakfast I come out into the lobby to wait for the hotel van to take me to the Alhambra for the 11:30 tour. In the lobby area I'm again fascinated by the white faux carvings on the walls that present a fascinating visual puzzle. I'm familiar enough with the real carvings in the Alhambra, which are abstract geometric patterns based on the shapes of leaves and flowers. I know that in the Alhambra Palace it is fascinating to follow a pattern from the doorway up toward the center of the ceiling and study its increasing complexity. In this lobby the faux carvings are portions of designs reproduced from different parts of the palace, and arranged in panels juxtaposed next to each other, so it is nearly impossible to follow the progression. I stare at one of the panels intently, first at the middle, then at its edge where it connects with the next one. I get up and examine a couple of the panel boundaries closely, and yes, I am satisfied. This is the perfect place for hiding the panel with the real pattern.

Just then the tour bus shows up, the clerk at the front desk motions to me, and I head out of the hotel entry and get in the bus.

I reach Alhambra about 11:00 o'clock and find the location where the tour groups are being assembled. The guides divide us up by making announcements in different languages. The Germans gather together very promptly into a group with men rather uniformly dressed in light colored shorts, sports shirts, and good quality walking shoes. The French take a little time but eventually gather. The English language group can best be described as 'all others', and includes some native English speakers from Britain and the States, and an assortment of Japanese, Italians, and anyone else from an under-represented language group who speaks at least some broken English.

The entry into the palace proper is strictly at controlled times. The guide explains that portions of the palace are undergoing renovation and repair, limiting the area available for visitors. As we complete the tour of the fort and the battlements, we linger in the terraced gardens, waiting for our turn. I stand at the edge

COFFEE WITH CHICORY

of the high terrace, looking over the garden wall at a row of cypress trees and the old Moorish quarter of ancient Granada.

"Beautiful cypress trees, aren't they?" I look back at the young man. "Yes, and the water fountain's so intricate", I say, repeating the verbal clue Jose Viega and I had established during our phone call. Apparently my reply is accurate enough and the young man says, "Please follow me." Several of the members of our group have wandered off in different directions, so it is not particularly noticeable that the young man and I take off on a walkway behind the cypress trees. As we turn the corner he slows down to let me catch up.

"My name is Pede," he says, shaking my hand, "I am Senor Viega's assistant."

We keep walking as I ask, "Where is he?"

"As you heard from the guide, a portion of the Moorish palace is under repair and restoration. He's waiting in that section." Then Pede points to the briefcase, "Is this the real object"?

"Well, I also want to know if this is truly the genuine piece," I tell him "and that is why I am here."

"This is so exciting," Pede says, "I have been working on the restoration for five years, and so much effort has been focused on re-creating the center piece."

"How have you been approaching it?" I ask him.

"Well, as you know, the Moorish carvings in Spain include no graven images of humans or animals, and

The Moorish Arabesque

the designs are based on shapes derived from plants and flowers."

"Yes, I know. Hence the name arabesque for these intricate abstract patterns."

"Exactly." Pede says.

We leave the garden and enter the main palace through a rear door. The interior of the palace in this section looks like a construction zone, bustling with scaffolding, construction tools, building materials, and workmen. Pede leads me through this maze to a side room where Jose Viega is waiting. "It has been a long time, my friend," he says, and we hug.

"Would you like a cup of coffee first?"

"No, no. Let us proceed."

Jose Viega laughs in his usual hearty manner, "My Americanized friend," he says, "all work and no play."

Lead by the assistant, we walk through a corridor and then enter a dark cavernous room. Pede fumbles around, finds a switchboard, and one by one turns on several flood lamps, all pointing upward at the ceiling. The large room has a circular domed ceiling that is carved in an intricate geometric design, except for a small area at its zenith, where it is conspicuously blank.

Pede points to a bucket filled with a smooth, white paste, "Everyone initially thought that the Alhambra palace designs in the interior were carved out of white stone, just as on the exterior surfaces of buildings."

Viega interjects, "The patterns were actually cast in white stucco." I look closely at one completed wall,

COFFEE WITH CHICORY

but it does not look like any stucco that I've ever seen. Viega continues, "Identifying the exact composition took several more years to discover, worked out through collaboration between experienced local masons and the chemists from the University." "I am impressed with your work," I say, "this is the hardest, smoothest stucco I've ever seen."

"That was a trifle," Viega says, "Compared to the puzzle we are still working on."

Pede points to the blank area above us, right at the center of the domed surface, "You will notice that the ceiling is divided into four quadrants, each with a distinct geometric pattern based on a local plant or flower." I look up, trying to distinguish the four patterns, and Pede continues, "The design begins very simply at the base of the domed ceiling in each quadrant, and then becomes progressively complex as it moves upwards."

"And what was this room used for in the palace?" I ask.

"I forgot to mention," Pede says, "This is the famed Hall of the Ambassadors."

"Yes, indeed," says Viega, "Emissaries came from all over the world to the Moorish court, and this is where they had to come each day and wait. The wait took days, sometimes weeks. When finally admitted into the throne room, a representative of even the mightiest kingdom would have been reduced to a common suppliant with all the waiting."

"What about the missing centerpiece?" I ask.

The Moorish Arabesque

"Oh, yes," Jose Viega says, "at the very center, all four distinct patterns must be reconciled in an exact mathematical and artistic union. However, this piece was stolen along with portions of many other carvings about one hundred fifty years ago."

"Stolen?" I ask, "How?"

"Simply chiseled out and taken away, sold and resold, and never found." Pede looks up, "We have had artists, designers, and even a couple of mathematicians working on the puzzle, trying to morph the designs of the local flora, but no one has come up with a satisfactory solution."

"Do they have any suggestions?"

"We have two finalists, one is a quadrangle derived from the palm leaves, and the other an octagon based on the leaves of Moroccan mint."

I look up at the gap on the ceiling, and study the design intently for several moments. "No", I say, "either design would be a forced fit, not a natural extension of the four quadrants, and neither would enhance the beauty of the room".

Viega stiffens his posture, "Well, do you have a better solution?"

"Better?" I say, "I have the perfect solution, the only one that truly belongs in this space."

Pede looks at me, "And what would that be?"

"Look at the four quadrants, Pede", I say as we all look up, and Pede re-adjusts one more floodlight toward the center of the ceiling, "As each of the four sections approaches the center of the zenith, it begins to curve in a gentle arc, so a straight-sided pattern such as a quadrangle or an octagon would not fit in."

We keep looking up, "What would fit in most naturally is a double parabola based on the manzanita flower."

Pede keeps looking up, but Jose Viega and I look at each other, and he says, "Yes, that would be simple yet elegant, and provide a fitting and focal climax for the four quadrangles," and then he says what I have been anticipating all along, "But how can you be sure?"

"Because, Mr. Viega," I point with my left hand to the briefcase on the floor beside me, "I have the solution right here."

Just then I hear footsteps approaching from behind and feel two strong hands grab my wrists. I try to turn around and see a uniformed officer and two policemen with handcuffs, "You are under arrest for the theft of a national treasure," the officer says, as he grabs the briefcase while one policeman puts handcuffs on me.

"Jose, what is this, you gave me your word?" Jose Viega is staring at the floor, and looks up, "I am sorry", he says, "I have been forced to participate in this."

I turn to the uniformed officer, "But what treasure are you talking about?"

"Oh, don't act so innocent," he says, "Our agents have been following you all along." He takes a red scarf from his pocket, waves it in the air like a banner and stuffs it back.

"So you mean, she...?" I stammer.

He dismisses me with his other hand and holds up the briefcase, "What more proof do I need?" he says, "I heard your confession that you have the missing Moorish arabesque right here. You know the theft of this piece has been declared a criminal matter for over twenty years, and you had the nerve to walk into Spain with the briefcase in your hand." The policemen start to lead me away. I turn to my left, "Pede, please get the key from my left pocket, and help the officer open the briefcase."

The policemen stop, and Pede eagerly puts his hand in my left jacket pocket, takes the key out, and approaches the officer, who holds up the briefcase with a triumphant look on his face. Jose Viega moves closer with his eyes wide open. Pede unlocks the briefcase and shouts, "It is empty."

"What," the officer says, "You just said the answer to the missing puzzle was right here, in the briefcase."

"You are mistaken," I say, "You misunderstood my gesture because you were looking at my left hand, while you should have been watching my right hand," I tell the officer, "The solution was up here," and I hold up my right index finger to my temple, "I was simply pointing to my head."

The officer looks at Viega, and then at me, "I don't believe you," he says, "I have very reliable sources, and next time you will not be so lucky."

The policemen stand around while the officer asks questions of Jose and Pede, writes up some notes, and the three of them leave, without actually ever apologizing to me, taking my briefcase as evidence.

Viega has a resigned look on his face. "I was under duress," he says, "and had no choice but to cooperate with the police." Pede is still stunned by the whole episode, and somewhat embarrassed at the treatment of a guest, and asks to be excused, professing further workload. I suspect he is heading to his computer to try to check the solution based on a parabola. Viega and I are the only two left in the large cavernous room. He starts to turn the flood lights off one by one, as he reaches for the last switch he pauses, looks at me and asks sheepishly, "Do you have any dinner plans?"

"Do you?"

"No," he says, turns the last flood light off, and we step outside, "I know this small restaurant in Albaisin."

"Are you referring to the old Moorish quarter?" I ask, and he nods.

We walk out of the Alhambra palace using a back door that is being used as a construction entrance, climb up the hill across from it into a maze of narrow alleys, and half-way up the hill come upon this small restaurant with outside tables and a view of the old palace. They seem to know Viega, "I have been coming here while overseeing the renovation," and that is the last reference either of us makes to today's events.

All through the leisurely dinner that lasts well into darkness, we talk about many things, graduate school, the conference on Roman antiquities in Anatolia, the

The Moorish Arabesque

heroic deeds performed by one of our fellow students at the Kabul museum in preserving priceless pieces, and the paths each of us has taken during the twenty years since graduate school. After dinner he gives me a ride to my hotel, and I crash into bed. The next morning I'm leaving on the first flight, so I get up early and sit in the lobby waiting for the hotel van, and admiring the Moorish arabesque center piece wedged in above the doorway on the lobby wall.

It is now time to unload my burden. I send a text message to Jose Viega's cell phone, "You must come to the Hotel Dauro II, look at the wall pattern above the gift shop door, and look very closely." I climb into the hotel van and leave for the airport.

The flight back to Madrid is brief, and as we land I take out my cell phone and switch it back on. There are already two messages from Viega, and both say about the same thing, "Call me immediately, urgent," in a very excited voice. Jose Viega, ever the passionate Spaniard, just as I remember him from the graduate school days twenty years ago.

I dial his number, "Viega, what is so urgent."

I hear a choking sound, he is excited, "Thank you, thank you, our work is now complete."

"I don't know what you are taking about," I say.

"That was brilliant, that was daring," I keep listening, "I went to your hotel, but you were already on the flight to Madrid."

COFFEE WITH CHICORY

"Well, you wouldn't want me to miss it, do you?"

"No, no. So I look at the lobby walls, and the decor is a good reproduction, and the juxtaposition of the panels is like a mathematical puzzle,"

"Yes," I say, "quite complex."

"Anyway", he says, "Then I look at the wall above the gift shop entrance." "Jose", I say, "take a deep breath, you are going to pass out", "Yes, yes," he says, I am too excited. But anyway, at first I don't see anything, just another panel, like the rest of the lobby. So I sit down."

"Good", I say, "You should learn to be more calm", but he is continuing with his story, "And then I see it. Right above the gift shop entrance, the pattern is different, it is more complex, and it is more beautiful. And then I realize what I am looking at, and I nearly faint."

"Jose, Jose," I say, "Calm down, you are going to faint again."

"No, no," he says, "I am OK now, but let me just drink this water." I look up at the departure schedule display. My flight is the next, so I get up, holding my cell phone to my ear, and walk toward the gate.

"I am back", Jose says, "And then, sitting in that lobby, I realize what I am looking at, there is an extra panel that someone has placed over the door jamb, and it is the missing Moorish Arabesque."

"No kidding," I know I am still on Spanish soil, and still under surveillance, "You are starting to make things up now. Anyway, good bye, my flight is leaving." I am not about to admit any part in returning the rare, stolen piece back to Spain.

"Thank you, and thank you again," Viega says, choking up.

"You are not crying, are you Jose?"

I hear laughter at the other end, "No, I am overjoyed, you have returned a national treasure. Spain is grateful to you."

"I don't know what you are talking about, but you are welcome anyway," I need to keep this pretense until my plane takes off, "I'll see you next year at the European congress in Vienna. And then we'll talk more," I hang up and board the airplane.

Flyboy

1

CLAUDIO HAS started his senior year at the San Gabriel high school, and asks his dad one day, "Dad, I am thinking about college", for several minutes his dad does not answer, and then says, very weakly, "That might be difficult, son", confirming Claudio's fear that his education is going to end with high school. At home things have become stressful. His younger brother, actually his stepbrother, is starting high school, and the stepmother is constantly worried about her son's upcoming college expenses. Every penny has come under scrutiny. "That good-for-nothing son of yours," Claudio overheard her talking to his dad, "If it wasn't for him, the college fund would be a lot bigger." And she repeats something she says when she is particularly frustrated, "He looks like a Japanese to me."

It has become impossible for Claudio to get the basic necessities, let alone any pocket money for a snack after school or a movie with other kids. He has had to increase his hours as a stock boy at the Safeway to buy some of his school supplies, and he has never been able to join in any of the extra-curricular activates that require extra money. It's ironic how college is being discussed so seriously for his stepbrother, but has never been a topic for him. As far as his stepmother is concerned, his education can end any time. He has to do his best not to run away from home.

It's career day for the senior class, and several recruiters are set up in the gym. Entering the gym, Claudio can almost taste his freedom from school, from home, and from dependence on others. He pauses near the gym door, keeping his eyes open for a company name that does not immediately evoke manual labor and industrial operations. He's beginning to lose hope as he gets close to the back wall. He recalls what his counselor had told him, "Claudio, companies with high-end positions have stopped coming to the high school job fairs."
"Why is that?"
"They go to the colleges, and may be to the junior colleges, but no longer to the high schools."
Claudio can see it with his own eyes as he walks down the gym floor looking at the row of industrial outfits, construction companies, and representatives of the military services.

As he gets to the back wall, he comes across a table with no waiting. The sign says, 'Sears', and a man in a crisp suit and a bright necktie is sitting behind the table. He looks like a pleasant man, and smiles when Jamie makes eye contact. What the heck, he thinks, I have to start somewhere, and so he stops. The Sears representative stands up, his handshake is strong yet friendly, and he points to the chair across the table. Claudio sits down, but doesn't say anything. First he wants to hear what the man has to say.

"Welcome to the Sears table. We're here to offer careers, not mere jobs."

Claudio isn't sure what the difference is, but he nods, a career must be better than a job.

"Have you visited some of our stores?" Claudio nods again.

"And what do you think?" the man asks, "Well, my mother likes them." He doesn't want to explain that actually it's his stepmother. His real mother, living in the Philippines, has probably never seen a Sears store. "That is good," the man says, "So you come from a Sears family."

Claudio realizes he may have encouraged the recruiter too much, "What kind of jobs do you have?"

The man smiles again. Claudio isn't sure why the man keeps smiling.

"Well, we have a whole range of positions." He looks at some notes on a pad of paper in front of him, "We have openings all the way from stock associates and cashiers to floor supervisors, and even some management track positions." Claudio isn't sure what he just heard, did the man say management? Sears just went up in his esteem. He has been wrong. Obviously, he has been biased against the store because of his dislike of his stepmother, but in reality they are an enlightened company, one that hires high school graduates and then promotes them all the way to managers. "How do I join the – is it management track?" he asks the man. He knows about his dad's longing to move up to the management level.

2

Several days later at the Sears office, he checks the box for 'management track'. Kevin, another senior from his high school, doesn't want to do that, surprising Claudio.

"I just don't want the responsibility."

"Responsibility for what?" Claudio asks.

"For pushing others around," he says.

Claudio is sure Kevin doesn't quite understand what it means to be a manager. "But Kevin, what about the status?" he asks.

"No thanks, I want to do my work and go home. If I have to lose sleep to get the status, I don't want it."

Claudio attends a one-day orientation session, and is then assigned to the same store where Kevin will be working. As a management trainee he has to help the assistant manager open the store, and often has to stay late to help with the inventory. He works longer hours than the other associates, but is not allowed to enter any overtime on his time sheet.

One day the assistant manager calls him to his office, "Claudio, you're doing a great job." Claudio maintains an appropriately eager and earnest expression on his face. "The company appreciates it, and we know we can trust you." Claudio is wondering if he's about to get a raise. The assistant manager leans forward and lowers his voice. Almost involuntarily, Claudio also leans forward.

"I'd like you to keep an eye on Kevin and Delia," the assistant manager says. Claudio nods, but feels queasy. Kevin is from the same high school, and they joined at the same time. Delia is from out of state, and has just joined Sears.

"What do you want me to do?" He wants to be sure of what he is getting into.

"Well, just keep an eye on them. See if they get back to work on time from their breaks, and do they stand around chatting or are actually productive."

"OK." Claudio has been so busy that he never pays attention to others, but this sounds harmless enough.

"And another thing," the assistant manger says, "Try and see if they are taking any merchandise home". What, does this guy think Kevin and Delia are stealing?

"How do you mean?"

"Well, Kevin is your friend, isn't he, so maybe you can just ask him. And Delia, she sometimes leaves her bag in the break room, and you might be able to take a quick look."

Claudio's stomach tightens up; this man is asking him to spy on a friend and a colleague. "I'll watch their break times, but I don't feel good about looking into somebody's bag," he says weakly.

"Well Claudio, you have to keep your eye on the ball. Just remember, you are on the management track." He nods, but his palms are sweaty. He begins keeping an eye on Kevin's break times, and finds that, yes, there are days when he gets back to work late, but nothing too extreme. Delia is very erratic in her schedule. There are days when she does not take any breaks, but on other days she stays out twice as long. He casually brings up the subject with her.

"What's that to you?" she says, "You're not my boss." He isn't prepared for her defensive response. Had somebody warned her? Does she know he is spying on her? "Well I am asking only because sometimes Kevin and I have to fill in the gap."

Kevin, on the other hand takes his advice constructively, and becomes more regular about his breaks. They are out having lunch one day when Claudio decides to probe.

"Have you heard shoplifting is up these days?"

"No, I hadn't heard."

"Yeah, man, we should keep an eye on thieves."

"Definitely," is all Kevin offers, and Claudio can't really figure out if Kevin himself is taking anything.

The assistant manager calls him to his office the following Friday, asks him about his progress on monitoring other associates, and expresses mild disappointment at his not having checked Delia's bag. He reminds him about the management track, "Here is another opportunity for you," he says, "I'm supposed to work this weekend, but I have some unexpected family stuff. Can you cover for me? Of course you will be the acting assistant manger." Confusion shows in Claudio's face. He's supposed to have this weekend off, and has already made plans to see a movie with a girl he knows from high school. On the other hand, this might just be the ticket to the manager's office, so, with a heavy heart but a smile on his face, he agrees.

All weekend long he has to face one aggravation after another. There's a faulty fire alarm that refuses to shut off, and then a couple of the people call in sick, so he has to stay late both nights and do the inventory himself. He's worn out by the time Monday morning comes, when his own workweek begins, and a little envious when Kevin tells him about all the fun he had.

On Monday afternoon he turns in his time sheet. A few minutes later he's called in see the assistant manager, "What does this mean, Claudio?" He is checking the time sheets and he is in a foul mood.

"Is there a problem?"

"You bet there is a problem. Your schedule shows you were off, how come you have put down hours for the weekend."

Is this guy serious, Claudio thinks, doesn't he remember that I worked my butt off this weekend. "But, ..."

"But what, Claudio? I gave you an opportunity this weekend, and this is how you re-pay me?"

COFFEE WITH CHICORY

He picks up his time sheet, puts the weekend work down as training time, and has his first doubts about the management track.

Claudio has been working at Sears for over two years. He has not been given a raise, and still can't afford to move out. One evening he gets home late. His dad is almost done with his newspaper.

"Dad, I want to ask your opinion about this Sears job".

"Yes?" His dad turns the page, but keeps the paper in front of his face.

"It has been almost two years. I work far more than the others, get paid the same, and no sign of a promotion."

His dad turns another page, then says, "And?" Either his dad is not really listening, or he wants him to come out and clearly say what he was thinking.

"I wonder if they do really have any openings for managers. Rumors are that the company is in financial trouble."

"You never know," is all his dad offers.

His dad is not his usual vehement supporter of management track, and indeed has not lately mentioned how close he himself is to becoming a manager. He is too stubborn to ever admit to his son that he has been passed over for a promotion, but his silence does mean something.

Claudio has spent the last two weekends working without pay. On Monday afternoon the assistant manager calls him to again demand that he obtain some information from a new employee in confidence, and report it back. That evening on his way home Claudio stops at a 7/11 store. As he approaches the counter a young man in uniform turns around to walk out and yells, "Claudio?"

It takes him a moment, "Is that you, Robbie?"

Chatting over drinks later, he finds out that Robbie joined the Navy. He hears about the egalitarian spirit in the service, and how initiative and hard work are rewarded. All that week Claudio's heartaches for the egalitarian life where all are equal, and no one is trying to get ahead by stepping on others. One week later he turns in his resignation. He's not surprised that his dad doesn't disapprove. The look on the assistant manger's face alone was worth the resignation.

3

The air force recruiter notices Claudio's glance and says, "Now, let's get on with the important questions. I hope you know that even though you'll be in the air force, with just a high school diploma, you're not going to be flying airplanes?" Claudio looks around the room. Every poster shows a fighter jet with a pilot sitting in one or standing next to it. "Well, at least I'll be sitting in one." The recruiter pauses, then looks at the posters, "Well, you'll sit in airplanes, but not in one of these. You'll ride in the transport planes, you know, to get from one place to another." He keeps looking at the posters, admiring the dangerous yet beautiful machines, and says, "So I'll be working on them?" This time his tone is somewhat tentative. The recruiter purses his lips, looks at Claudio to make sure his expectations are getting close to reality. "Yes, yes, that is a possibility," he says, "If you get attached to one of the squadrons. Of course that way, you just stay in one place."

Claudio is beginning to look bored. "What I can promise you is that if you sign up for ground operations, you'll get to see the world. I hope you want to see the world." The recruiter wants to keep the process moving. "Let me do this," he says, "Here's a list of the ten places where we need airmen in ground operations, you pick four out of these, and we'll try to get you to one of those spots." Claudio completes the paperwork and selects four locations, Colorado, North Carolina, Arizona, and Northern California, in that order. "And one more thing," the recruiter says, looking at Claudio's paperwork, "Let's put your name down as Claude."

"Why? My name is Claudio."

"Where did you say you were from?"

"Philippines."

"Oh, right." He glances at Claudio, "You know you could pass for Japanese." Claudio looks warily at him.

"Anyway," the recruiter continues, "You don't know these flyboys as well as I do. Don't make life any harder for yourself, and write down Claude."

Claudio starts basic training as Claude, and is too busy too wonder if the name really makes any difference. During basic training the picture of 'ground operations' that keeps swirling in his head is from a war movie he saw as a kid. The movie didn't even have anything to do with the Air Force, but was about the navy, with fighter jets aboard an aircraft carrier. The image that repeats in his head has fighter jets taking off and landing on the deck of the aircraft carrier, with guys who orchestrate and handle everything on the deck. They give the pilot the signal for commencing the take off, and then secure the deck after the plane has cleared the ship. They tell the pilot when to land – at least Claude thinks they do, since they seem to be waving and signaling vehemently to the pilot. True, most of them don't have any responsibilities with respect to how the plane is flown, but they are crucial to the overall mission, and nothing can be accomplished without them. He realizes he's not in the navy, and he's not going to be working on an aircraft carrier. However, he imagines the ground operations to be that kind of immediate and tactile relationship with the mission and the plane.

Basic training is over, and everyone is heading to a different place. Claude learns that he's been assigned to his fourth and last choice, Northern California. Having lived in the smog belt near Los Angeles for most of his adolescence, he's excited at the prospect of leaving the San Gabriel Valley and going north.

The day comes, and he reports for duty at the Hamilton Air Force Base. He feels anxious and tries to compose himself. At the main gate he is told to go to Building 22. He enters the building and salutes the first uniform he sees. The uniform salutes him back. It's not clear which one of them is more nervous. It turns out he's saluted another new recruit reporting for duty. Sheepishly they look each other over, and try to hide their nervous smiles. A few minutes later both are standing at attention across the desk from a sergeant.

"Is that clear, men?"

"Yes sir," they exclaim in unison. Sarge, as everyone seems to call him, is in his late forties or early fifties, with a squat build and an almost non-existent neck. "OK then, go see the quartermaster for your supplies, and the base clerk for your dorm assignments. Report here at 0700 tomorrow morning." They both salute, and as they exit, finally exhale.

"So you're Claude?"

"Yes, and you're Billie."

"Yes, from Victoria, Texas."

"And I'm from San Gabriel, near LA."

Billie is a gangly young man of about 19, with high cheekbones and short-cropped blond hair.

Claude reports to Sarge the following day at 0700. "Base operations, traffic group." Sarge is looking at a paper on his table, "Go and see Senior Airman Santiago in Building 12." Sarge hands him the paper, Claude salutes, and walks out. Traffic group, so his wish has come true, just what he had imagined he will be doing, directing the planes, telling the flyboys when to take off and when to land.

Leaving the administration building, he instinctively starts to walk toward the sound of airplane engines. After about 50 steps he stops. Now which way is Building 12? He realizes he is going in the wrong direction. Building 12 is located nowhere near the runways and taxiways. In fact, it is very close to the front gate. He is puzzled. Why is Senior Airman Santiago directing traffic sitting so far away from the airplanes?

He reaches building 12, and finds Santiago, about 5 years older than him, with an easy air about him. Claude salutes him, and Santiago waves dismissively. "You don't need to do that." He takes the paper from Claude's hand, and says, "Oh good, I have been waiting for this. The annual base parade is only three weeks away, and there is a lot to be done." Watching Santiago's pleasant face, Claude feels comfortable. He's pleased and a smile best expresses his happiness. Santiago points to the chair, and starts looking for something in a file cabinet. Claude sits down, looks around. Finally he asks, "So what kind of planes are in the parade?" Santiago looks up at Claude with a blank face, then looks down again at the paper Claude has delivered to him, pauses, and asks, "What did you just say, airman?" Claude hesitates, "Sir," he says, "I was told I am being assigned to

COFFEE WITH CHICORY

the traffic group, so I am wondering what kind of planes are we dealing with, fighters or transports." Santiago's blank expression changes to amusement and then to laughter, "Airman, Airman", he says when he regains his composure. "You are assigned to base operations. The traffic you and I deal with is not airplanes, it's motor vehicles." Claude sinks low in the chair. Santiago chuckles, "And by the way, you are looking at the traffic group, it's just you and me." He takes a map from the drawer and spreads it out on the desk, "The parade is taking a different route this year, so we have to decide the routes for the regular base traffic." Claude is still slumped in his chair. He feels beads of sweat on his forehead. It must be the brisk walk he took on the way to building 12. Santiago is talking, but all Claude can hear is the roar of airplanes taking off.

Every few weeks Claude's assignment changes, two weeks ago he was doing inventory of vehicles, this week he's checking the sewer manholes, and next month he'll be checking the asphalt on the roads and counting potholes. It's now one year into his assignment. He's again working with senior airman Santiago. He has also getting to know Billie, the airman he met on his first day.

At the end of his first year as an airman at Hamilton Air Force base near Vacaville, Claude puts in a request for transfer to another base and dreams of where he will be assigned next. Perhaps he'll go to the jagged, snow-capped Rocky Mountains in Colorado, or to the painted deserts of New Mexico. Italy will also be nice some day. After about five years of living in the barracks, he moves into an apartment near the base. He keeps rearranging his wish list, and keeps renewing his request year-after-year, but the orders never come. All he sees is the soggy, marshy, landscape around the base. 'I was right', he thinks, 'See the world' belongs to the Navy. He's made his own recruiting slogan, 'Join me and see the delta'. He never gets to go anywhere, or see the world. He's forgotten by the air force in Vacaville, in the delta of the San Joaquin and the Sacramento Rivers.

Ten years have gone by and he's never left Vacaville. Base operations has turned out not to have anything to do with the airplanes at all. This month he is assigned to the base facilities group, and is kept busy checking the buildings. He has never stepped inside a fighter plane. Ten years after that conversation with the recruiter in Pasadena, Claude puts in a request for discharge. He has decided to leave the air force to try his fortunes elsewhere.

On Claude's last day Billie invites him out for a Chinese dinner, "My uncle Darrel is visiting from Dallas." Claude knows the Chinese buffet near the base where some of the airmen eat sometimes. Cousin Darrel is at the base to sign a supply contract. With the signed contract in his briefcase, he comes to pick them up and they head out of the base, driving toward the freeway. Claude realizes that they have left the Chinese buffet

COFFEE WITH CHICORY

behind, but keeps quiet, while Billie and Darrel are busy with family conversation. Darrel is expecting a bonus when he gets back, and tells Billie, "The least I could do is treat my cousin and his airman friend to dinner."

They drive to Walnut Creek, and locate P. F. Chang. Leaving the car with a valet they enter the restaurant. It's Friday night, and even with reservations they have to wait before being seated. The restaurant is filled with upscale customers. The large dining room is engulfed in animated conversation, hearty laughter, and the tinkling of silverware and china. Young professional women in black evening dresses, sipping wine in expensive looking crystal are sprinkled throughout the dining room, some with young men, and others with older ones. Both Billy and Claude can't stop looking around, and the waiter has to make an effort to catch their attention.

Darrel leans forward, "How do you boys like this Chinese?"

"It's great," Billy says, without taking his eyes off a young blonde. Claude's eyes wander around the room and Darrel says, "These babes are almost as good-looking as back in Dallas." Billie nods, and Darrel says, "Only skinnier."

Waiting for their order, Claude notices that everyone is eating what vaguely looks like Asian food, yet presented in unfamiliar arrangements on the plates.

"What are you thinking Claude," Billie asks, "about the future?"

"No. I am thinking this sure is different-looking Chinese food."

Darrell looks at the surrounding tables, and says, "Food fusion."

Billie says, "Gotta be Chinese, this is supposed to be a Chinese restaurant."

The only two fragrances Claude can detect are expensive perfume and good wine. The food is being prepared right in front of his eyes in a kitchen that is half open to the dining area, but he detects no obvious aroma. Soon their order arrives. The dish is arranged to delight the eye, is tasty enough to satisfy the palette, and flavorful in his mouth, but does not emit any odors beyond the edge of the plate.

After the meal Darrel drives them back to the base, and then wants to get going, "Claude," he says, "Now that you are leaving the air force, remember to soar high up in the sky." Claude nods, as Darrell's hand glides upward. They shake hands and Darrel drive off. Claude feels a choking in his throat. What soaring has he ever done in the air force, he wonders. He drives to his apartment in Vacaville. Lying in bed he starts thinking about the last ten years, but the good meal in his stomach soon takes over and he falls asleep.

4

The next day Claude goes to the base, and after completing the paperwork, he drives through the guard gates and is now outside the base, out in the wide world. He doesn't want to go to the loneliness of his apartment, at least not yet, not right away. He keeps driving, and finds himself taking an unaccustomed detour through the tiny downtown of Vacaville. He drives slowly, passing a couple of boarded up storefronts, then some antique shops. There is an old diner, which looks empty and dark. The crosswalk has been recently redone in red brickwork, and the newly installed streetlights evoke gas lamps of a bygone era. It seems downtown Vacaville is struggling along a convoluted path from dilapidation to urban renewal.

Claude is thinking about lunch, but doesn't want to go to the gloomy diner. He parks his car, and as he starts walking, the fragrance of stir-fry enters his nostrils. He realizes he's quite hungry, and notices the half-open door of a storefront restaurant. The sign says, 'Pad Thai'. Not very original, but the aroma draws him in. The décor is downscale Asian, with a well-worn vinyl floor, fluorescent lights, faded Formica tables, stackable plastic chairs, and an assemblage of small plastic jars on each table, containing soy sauce, vinegar, tooth picks, and probably hot sauce.

His sense of smell is under an intense yet delightful assault by the fragrances and odors emanating from the kitchen. A couple of the tables are occupied. He stands by the small counter near the front and looks around. In addition to the jars of soy sauce and condiments, each table also has a couple of menus stuck in a plastic stand. He takes that to mean that it's open seating, picks a table in a corner and sits down.

His mind is still occupied with the last ten years. Perhaps he should leave and resume his walk. Maybe he should go back to the base and ask for his job back. "You want food?" The melodic voice of a young woman brings him back into the restaurant. He looks up, and keeps looking. She waits for him to say something, but he doesn't respond, so she repeats, only louder, "You want food?" He's startled.

"What? Yes, I want food." The girl is tall, slim, well proportioned, and has sharp, almost chiseled features. Looking serious, stern and very attractive, she reaches down and slides the menu toward him.

"What food?" Claude is still lost, "Hunh?" And keeps looking at her. His usual friendly grin is beginning to look idiotic. Watching him, she is amused, and the hint of a smile escapes from the corner of her mouth, dissolving her stern expression into a naughty one. Another customer sitting a couple of tables away is waiting for his bill, so she prompts Claude.

"You want special?"

"Yes, the special". "You know what is special?" Claude doesn't answer. He is looking at the small nameplate on her lapel, 'Helen'. The customer from the next table waves, and she walks away. Claude's eyes keep following her. 'Helen', he is thinking. This is a Thai restaurant, so perhaps, 'Helen of Bangkok.' She gives the bill to the waiting customer, and goes into the kitchen, leaving him wondering what is it that he just ordered.

COFFEE WITH CHICORY

A few minutes later Helen returns with the food. Seeing her again, he doesn't care what exactly the special is. He can see the noodles, and he can identify some forms of sea life, but is unable to recognize some of the other ingredients. In his confusion he doesn't want to tackle the chop sticks, and uses the fork to eat. The food is fresh. It also seems to be food in which the cook has achieved a delicate balance between the spices, the herbs, the pasta, the vegetables, and the meat. He's always considered himself quite familiar with Asian food, but now realizes that what he's been eating for the last two decades was Americanized Asian food. He thinks of the odorless, decorated dishes at PF Chang last night, and he feels this may be the first time he is tasting authentic Thai food. He looks around. He wants to talk more to Helen, but decides to take it slow, and after paying his bill, leaves.

5

It's late at night, and sitting in his apartment in Vacaville, Claude looks through the want ads for job openings. A display ad catches his eye, 'Traffic Technician, City of Vacaville.' He tears it out of the paper and puts it on the kitchen counter. Still thinking about Helen, he falls asleep.

The next morning he gets up early, and drives to the Vacaville city hall. He shows the Traffic Technician ad to one of the administrative workers, and gets directed to the public works building in the next block. With the experience acquired in base operations he can be a productive worker for the city right away, an he gets hired as a temporary employee.

By the time he finishes all the paperwork for employment, it's early afternoon. He leaves the city hall with a list of things to do before starting work the next morning. However, his growling stomach reminds him of food, and the buoyancy in his mood at having so quickly secured a position reminds him of Helen. He drives to Pad Thai, locks the car and goes into the restaurant. It is well past lunchtime, and there are no customers. He takes the same corner table as the day before, and sits down. There is no one in the restaurant at all. He waits at the table for about five minutes, and then gets up to leave, perhaps they're already closed and just forgot to lock the door. He sees that the sign in the front window that says, 'Closed', which means it must read 'Open' from the street. Just then he hears the sound of women's laughter coming from the kitchen door in the back of the restaurant.

He walks back to investigate. The door is ajar, and he can hear the sounds of a conversation. He slowly pushes the door into the kitchen, and sticks his head. Before his eyes can grasp any details a commotion erupts in the kitchen, a chair turns over, a plate drops from the table and shatters, and someone trips over a low stool, nearly falling over and spraying a red drink, perhaps a juice of some kind, all over the kitchen, including some

COFFEE WITH CHICORY

on Claude's face and clothes. What follows happens so fast that Claude is only able to grasp it in bits and pieces. There is one high-pitched female shriek that is immediately choked and brought under control. A towel in an uncertain condition of cleanliness is rubbed on his hands and face with a gentle yet vigorous effort, and then a string of apologies uttered in broken English blended with Thai or Vietnamese, he can't tell. He takes a couple of steps to the side to take it all in. He's standing inside a small, crowded kitchen, and is amazed that he hasn't put his foot into something. Buckets, baskets and pans are strewn all over the floor. He sees the two startled women. One is scurrying around the kitchen straightening things out, gathering and collecting stray pots and pans. She is in her early forties, a little on the heavy side, with a scarf covering her hair, tending to the kitchen cleanup at some kind of supersonic speed, and determined to avoid eye contact with Claude.

The other woman is standing in an embarrassed posture, slightly hunched over, with her hands folded in front of her. It's Helen, with a sheepish grin on her face that seems ready to break into a naughty smile at any time. "So sorry, I'm so sorry," she is repeating like a mantra under her breath. And says it louder once they make eye contact, "I'm so sorry." Claude waves his hand in the air. "Don't worry. But I am hungry. Can I have the special again?" Helen keeps standing, as if in a trance, so he says, "Please?" breaking the spell. She snaps out of her apologetic stance, and into action as the restaurant hostess she is, "Yes, sure. Please sit down" – as she points towards the dining area.

He goes and sits down while the frenzied sounds of cooking and cleaning continue in the kitchen, mixed in with some muffled giggles. After some sizzling and pot stirring, and whiffs of seasonings and spices and flavors the food is brought out. Helen glides out of the kitchen, balancing a platter heaped to the point of overflowing in one hand, and a glass of water in the other. She puts the water down first, brings the platter to the edge of the table, holds it with both hands, and slowly slides it across the table, as if making an offering. Claude senses the subtle gesture implied in the act, and thinks it would be sacrilegious to actually eat such an exquisite gift, presented so delicately by someone so good-looking. His stomach growls and he starts to wolf down the special. While eating he can picture what his Airman friend Billie would say, "She won't last very long, partner. You better move fast."

One third of the way through his meal, partly sated, Claude realizes he's not likely to finish this huge platter, at least not in one sitting. He's been noticing Helen, glancing at him every couple of minutes from behind the half-closed kitchen door. The next time her face protrudes beyond the doorjamb, he raises a hand, and her face continues to emerge, followed by her neck and the rest of her body. She walks over to his table, conscious that he's watching her walk across the room.

COFFEE WITH CHICORY

"Have a seat," Claude says. Helen stands behind a chair holding its back firmly with both hands, and leans forward attentively. Claude points to the chair, but she keeps standing. "Sit down," he says. Perhaps he sounded authoritative, or seemed to be pleading, but it works. She sits at the very edge of the chair with a tentative look on her face, and steals a glance at his stained shirt.

"Tell me your name," he says. With a look of surprise in her eyes, she points to the small plastic nametag pinned to her blouse.

"My name is Claude," he says, and extends his hand. She lifts both her hands from her lap, and holds them up together in a gesture of greeting, "Hello, Claude." He keeps holding his hand out, as if he still wants a handshake, and as she reluctantly unfolds her hands from in front of her. He holds both hands up together, copying her way of greeting. They literally reverse their positions. Now he says, "Hello, Helen." She bows her head down slightly to acknowledge his greeting and his salutation. Her hands are back in her lap, and he says, "Is Helen your Thai name?" She starts to laugh but then controls herself, and shakes her head, "Nooo, Helen my American name."

He has an expectant look on his face, waiting for her to say some more, but she starts to straighten the little jars on the table, as if getting ready to clear the table. "And—?" he says.

She looks up at him, "And what?"

"And what is your Thai name?" he says finally. She draws back, using the entire seat of her chair, and leaning into the backrest. She speaks with a mix of reserve and curiosity, "Why you ask?"

Claude is thinking fast, why indeed, "Well, for one thing," he says, "So we can be better acquainted," and looks at her face to realize that she didn't quite understand him. "So we can be friends."

Her face relaxes, "Be friend with American name," she says with a coy smile, "Be friend with Helen."

Claude decides he is not going to be dealt out so easily, "I want to be friends with the real you, not just the American you."

"Oooh—" she says with a naughty smile, "You don't want to be friend with Helen?"

This was a misstep, "Yes," he corrects himself, "I want to be friends with American Helen, and with the Thai Helen." She does not say anything, just keeps looking at him with amusement, enjoying watching him beseech her for something so earnestly. He's getting impatient with this old-world pace of introduction, and says with a hint of annoyance, "Why do you want to hide your real name from me?"

She waves her hand to sweep away his unpleasantness, and says, "I tell you. Ready?"

He leans forward, "Yes, what is it."

She smiles, and says almost under her breath, "Su-Chi".

COFFEE WITH CHICORY

He can barely hear it, and says, "Su-Ki?" She smiles again and seems flattered that he is so interested in her name, "No," she says, "Su-Chi."

"That is a beautiful Thai name." He repeats it, and then says, "I like it."

She shakes her head, "It is not a Thai name."

"No?" he says, "So what kind of name is it?"

"Name from Burma."

"Why do you have a Burmese name?"

"I am born in Burma."

"So how come you work in a Thai restaurant?"

"I go to Thailand ten year old."

"So you were born in Burma, moved to Thailand when you were ten years old."

She nods.

"Helen," Claude says, "I got a new job today, and I want to celebrate. Would you like to go out to dinner?"

"Go out eat dinner? We got dinner right here." She says, barely concealing her smile. The irony of inviting her out to dinner dawns on Claude, he smiles, begins to laugh, and she joins in. The dining area resonates with laughter and the cook comes out of the kitchen with concern on her face. Helen notices her standing in the doorway, and waves to her to go back in. The cook withdraws, shaking her head.

"Well, how about a movie?"

She shakes her head and says, "Too busy."

"A walk in the park?"

She shakes her head again and says, "Same."

"Which day does the restaurant close"?
"Never."
"Never?"
"Well, Sunday morning only," she concedes.
"OK, then, what are you doing Sunday morning?"
"Go for service. To church."

Aren't all Thais Buddhists? He wonders, "Christian Church?"

"Yes, Christian church, on 7th street. You come?" she asks.

He does not respond right away, so she says, "With me," which is all that is on his mind, never mind the destination. "Yes," he says. "What time"?

She thinks for a moment, "Eight o'clock."

"Can I pick you up on Sunday morning, and we go together?"

"No, you meet there."

He picks up the box of leftovers and says bye to Helen.

Driving to his apartment he is thinking of the last time he went to church in his childhood in the Philippines. He accompanied his mother every Sunday morning, and some Wednesday evenings, to a Catholic church. He remembers the formal, structured ceremony of the Catholic mass, but not much of the dogma or the catechism that he was taught. He also remembers listening to a lot of Latin, and to some English and Tagalog, but not understanding much. He fondly remembers being a part of the boys choir, and singing his heart out in Church, whether the joy he felt, whether it resulted from the presence of God, as the priest told them, or the joy one feels in good music. His mother always made sure that he prayed regularly, but he was a child, and the main purpose of praying to God seemed to him to be to ask for things. Some of his prayers were fulfilled right away, and in precisely the manner in which he had dreamed they would, and some others were also fulfilled, but with such odd timing that he wondered why he had prayed for such a thing, without being more specific about the manner in which his wish was to be fulfilled. And then there were a great many that never got fulfilled, or at least they hadn't been so far.

As he grew up, left Philippines, and finally started living on his own, he found organized religion to be irrelevant to his life as a young man, and rarely attended church. He did, however, retain the spirituality he learnt from his mother.

On Sunday morning the alarm wakes him up on time. What happened to his day of rest? He takes out his laundered clothes, and eats a good breakfast, another childhood reminder from his mother. After putting the clothes on he drives out, taking Munroe Street so he can enter 7th street at its very start. Driving along 7th street, he doesn't get a good view of buildings located in low areas, and before he knows it the street comes to an end.

He turns the car around and goes slower this time, looking at both sides, and spots a sign, "Community Church," on a building that looks like a barn.

In the parking lot there is an assortment of vehicles. Most look like the vehicles of newly arrived immigrants of meager means, the 8 to 10-year old small Japanese and medium sized domestic cars, but sprinkled among them are examples of what he considers red-neck transportation: pick-up trucks with large wheels, SUV's with cattle grilles and 4-wheel drive trucks with hunting lights and pulley winches. The parking lot is quite full. A couple of Asian women in their Sunday best scurry across the parking toward the rear entrance.

He watches a young Caucasian couple arrive in a four-wheel-drive pick-up truck and get out. The woman is blonde, and is wearing a white dress that does justice to her form. The man also has light hair, cropped very short, and looks stout without looking bulky. They stride across the parking lot, leaving Claude wondering about the composition of the congregation. He examines his car in the parking lot one more time with satisfaction, admiring his own parking skill at having placed it exactly between lines, and starts walking toward the rear entrance of the church. A hymn strikes up inside the church. The tune seems vaguely familiar, but he can't make out the words. He concentrates, but to no avail. He opens the rear door of the building, hears the words, and realizes it is not English. He goes in and finds a seat in the back. It appears to be an evangelical service, and the congregation is a mix of Southeast Asian immigrants, and working class Whites. Claude looks around for Helen.

6

One year has gone by since that day when Claude started working for the City, and first saw Helen. He is now a permanent employee and settled in his job as the traffic technician at the City. He is also married to Helen.

In the evenings he helps out at the restaurant, seating the customers and cleaning the tables. He has been surprised by the size of the community that Helen and the cook, Imong, belong to – a mixture of Burmese and Laotians, all of whom lived in Thailand before arriving in America. He is touched by their meager and often difficult circumstances, and impressed by the help the church provides them. His fluency in English, his American citizenship, and his marriage to Helen have made him an informal liaison between the community and the church. He strums along on his guitar when they practice their hymns. He also helps them with their visa applications, and the paperwork for government assistance.

He doesn't much think about soaring in the sky any more, but has achieved the peace of mind and the satisfaction that eluded him before. Perhaps it is Helen, or perhaps it is the maturity that comes with age. The work at the city, the time at the restaurant and his community outreach leave little time for contemplative reflection. Each day and each week is full of activities that provide him with a balance between productive labor, religious spirituality, artistic expression, empathic dialog, and physical intimacy – all the essential ingredients of a satisfied and satisfactory life.

Made in the USA
San Bernardino, CA
23 January 2013